PRAISE FOR *AMERICAN ARCADIA*

A gorgeous riff of a New York City novel. Mina, Chry, Dare, and Nyro are unforgettable characters in a potent, beautifully composed, pitch perfect drama.

–Wayne Johnson, Multiple Pulitzer Prize-nominated author of *The Red Canoe, Don't Think Twice,* and *Six Crooked Highways*

Gorgeous and lyrical. *American Arcadia* is a haunting lullaby of yearning set in 1980s New York. A foundling left in a baptismal font—to drown or be saved, she'd like to know—envies the privileged life of her best friend, who envies her right back. The lesson of this riveting and distinctly American story may be that, in the end, we are each improvising our life.

–Mary Kay Zuravleff, author of *Man Alive!* and *The Bowl is Already Broken: A Novel*

American Arcadia by Laura Scalzo is both a compelling portrait of a bygone era that glittered with possibility and a profoundly personal novel. It traverses the territory surrounding desire, love, grief, and friendship, while acknowledging the walls, locked gates, and distances that make accessing the heart of any of them so difficult. Every paradise must have a border. And yet Scalzo's masterpiece is compassionate to the seekers lost in that fringe of scrub—and generous. There are revelations to be found in the tough but gloriously surviving weeds, and Scalzo allows her characters to discover them, as well as themselves. She lets her characters grow. I loved *American Arcadia.* At once sweeping and searingly intimate, it's a stunning achievement.

–Melissa Ostrom, author of *Unleaving* and *The Beloved Wild*

American Arcadia is many things—a love letter to New York City, a coming-of-age tale, a paean to lost innocence, a lens on the early years of the AIDS epidemic, an exploration of friendship and family. Laura Scalzo's writing has a kinetic quality, perfect for her characters in freefall. Her prose is sharp and snappy, and yet there is a note of bittersweetness running through it all that gives this novel a deep emotional resonance. American Arcadia is a beautiful work about what, ultimately, is worth having in life, and how we serve—and betray—those we love.

–Molly McCloskey, author of *Straying* and *Circles Around the Sun: In Search of a Lost Brother*

American Arcadia evokes a moment in time when the world was shifting—awakening to the confusion and suffering of AIDS —when secrets could no longer be hidden, and mysteries of sex, love and life must be revealed. Like a great jazz song, the novel weaves stories together, builds to a crescendo and ultimately creates a haunting melody that lingers after the last page is turned.

–Maria Rodale, author of *Love Nature Magic*

Gorgeously written, this poignant story of four young New Yorkers in the heady 80s will stay with you long after you close the book. Laura Scalzo has created vivid and unforgettable characters whose lives weave and intersect in breathless, unexpected ways. Most of all, Scalzo's expansive imaginative powers are stamped on every page—just when you think you know what to expect, she opens a door to a new thought, a new idea, or a new way of seeing the world we thought we knew. This novel is a gem.

–Alexandra Zapruder, author of *Twenty-Six Seconds: A Personal History of the Zapruder Film* and *Salvaged Pages: Young Writers' Diaries of the Holocaust*

Some people are beautiful writers, some are meticulous researchers, and some are great storytellers. Laura Scalzo is all three. I've read American Arcadia multiple times and, each time I do, I love it even more. It perfectly captures the hope, despair, exhilaration, and malaise of the immediate post-college years.

–J. Hunter Bennett, author of *The Prodigal Rogerson: The Tragic, Hilarious, and Possibly Apocryphal Story of Circle Jerks Bassist Roger Rogerson in the Golden Age of LA Punk 1979-1996*

American Arcadia is a force! Scalzo's voice is stunning and authoritative as an interrogation of the American Dream in the 1980's with all its trappings. The novel unravels the truth behind our careful, cultural facades to reveal the hope and failings of our shared humanity. With dreamlike, lyrical prose, Scalzo considers class, memory, and redemption. *American Arcadia* left me with an ache for the pain we inflict on ourselves and others but also with renewed faith in the human spirit's ability to endure and to triumph.

–Melissa Scholes Young, author of *The Hive* and *Flood*

Laura Scalzo has worked her magic yet again in a beautifully written book that wrapped me up in a fresh, exquisite story of friendship, family, and modern love. Her characters are compelling, whether from Wall Street, the US Capitol, or a working-class Hudson River town. Scalzo is a master of the subtly unfolding narrative, including narrator Mina's encounters with the worlds around her and the discovery of the secret of her birth. Scalzo skillfully weaves in the mesmerizing legend of Sirena Fuggitiva, and leit motifs that come together in surprising, significant ways: Queen Anne's lace, for example, and three wooden boxes, each with a carved rose compass, turning up in an Arcadian world. The language is fresh, unassuming, just right and weaves together seamlessly the visual, aural, and olfactory. A must read.

–Carol Shiner Wilson, author, editor, academic dean emerita, Muhlenberg College

AMERICAN ARCADIA

Laura Scalzo

Regal House Publishing

Published by
Regal House Publishing, LLC
Raleigh, NC 27605
All rights reserved

ISBN -13 (paperback): 9781646033614
ISBN -13 (epub): 9781646033621
Library of Congress Control Number: 2022942690

Cover design by © C. B. Royal
Cover image by guigaamartins/Shutterstock
Author photo by Erik Kvalsvik

Regal House Publishing, LLC
https://regalhousepublishing.com

The following is a work of fiction created by the author. All names,
individuals, characters, places, items, brands, events, etc. were either the
product of the author or were used fictitiously. Any name, place, event,
person, brand, or item, current or past, is entirely coincidental.

Printed in the United States of America

for Chris

Another flower which possesses the same remarkable power of bursting open all doors and locks is chicory, provided always that you cut the flower with a piece of gold at noon or midnight on St. James's Day, the twenty-fifth of July. But in cutting it you must be perfectly silent; if you utter a sound, it is all up with you.

—James George Frazer, *The Golden Bough*

WINTER

1

The walls are whispering but I don't understand. I'm on the lower level of Grand Central Station, outside the Oyster Bar, waiting. Upstairs, train times whir and click on the big board while travelers come and go. They crisscross the main room, check their watches, rush or wait, kiss hello and goodbye, all under the signs of the zodiac spread wide across the blue starry ceiling.

I left Chry at a party on the Upper East Side. She was supposed to be here, but I came in her place, trading her excuses for my own chance to celebrate with Congressman and Mrs. Risk.

Back on Lexington Avenue, it's Truth or Dare and Chry chooses Dare, which is an answer to a party game but also the name of the boy who has given her a reason to shed, yet again, a family obligation and rush into something reckless.

So, in the first hour of the new year, while the walls in Grand Central Station are whispering to me, Chry is preparing to be lowered into the East River. She doesn't care that it might kill her, she wants Dare to notice her.

He does. "Crazy. Crazy girl," he says low and sweet and puts his arms out for her shoes and coat.

Nyro finishes untangling the climbing rope, harness, and pulleys, and hooks Chry into the gear. A light January rain is falling and by the time Chry climbs up on the railing, she's soaked and shivering in her sleeveless silk party blouse.

As Nyro lowers Chry into the river, Dare watches him for signs of cruelty. They've known each other for a while now.

Chry shouts as her body hits the water. The combined ecstasies of Nyro's expensive champagne and falling for Dare are wrecked by the river, cold as razor blades. Regret takes hold of her as she realizes this punishment is by her own hand. She's not ready to die. Now she knows.

Chry closes her mouth and holds her breath. The river, the rope, something solid grazing and possibly slicing into her side, Nyro's will, her own panic—any or all of these things could kill her. Chry focuses on the panic, the one thing she might be able to control. She concentrates on the immutable truths of her life. She is a soul and a body, and each is a child of these waters. She grew up on Sandy Hook, a curve of beach at New Jersey's northern edge, not fifteen miles from here. She is amphibious, a sea creature. Her toddler years are a memory loop of sand and sky, of emptying and filling her pail with the salty sea water, part of the tidal estuary whose grip she is currently in. She knows wind and weather, tables and tides. She's logged a thousand hours in these waves on her surfboard with the New York City skyline over her right shoulder, freighters entering the harbor over her left.

Chry had not expected this Manhattan baptism, a drop into the East River, to be different from her days at Sandy Hook. She had expected it to feel like home, but it does not. It's foreign and frightening.

She moves her arms and legs to stay afloat and physically fight back the panic. She employs her mind to do the same, speaking to herself inside her head with all her strength, *I am the sea, I am the sea, I am the sea.* Over and over, a tidal rhythm.

Becoming a lost soul at sea was never her concern. *Someday* she'd depart the earth to the air through the ocean, she'd long felt this to be true, but that day was a long way away. Not now, not this day. Not in the East River. No. She stretches her neck and lifts her chin to keep the foul, polluted water from seeping into her nose and mouth.

Dare shouts to Nyro, "Enough, pull her up," loud enough for Chry to hear. Some of the others who'd come to see if she'd really do it are saying the same thing. "Come on, Danny, pull her up."

Chry's face and arms shimmer blue as two girls in tight jeans and high heels help her back over the railing. Dare is there but he's out of reach. She's confused and shaking violently, and very, very tired. She wants to lie down right there on the walkway, but she remains standing as Nyro unhooks the gear. He wants her to collapse in his arms. Chry can feel it but she will not succumb, and she surprises herself, keeping upright with a last scrap of strength. Thin rushes of air from passing cars on the FDR threaten her resolve but she stays standing.

"Cool," says Nyro as he unwraps a tangle of rope from around her leg, acknowledging, finally, that she's made it out of the river alive.

"Come on, Danny, hurry up," says Dare and the girls who'd helped her over the rail chime in.

"Mina?" Chry tries to say my name but she can't. Neither of the high-heeled girls is me. I'm the one who knows Dare. Dare's the one who knows Danny Nyro. Chry doesn't know anyone. Did I leave? Did I say goodbye? Chry can't remember.

Dare sees that Chry's black taffeta coat is built for looks not warmth so instead of handing it back he takes off his own puffy down jacket and wraps it around her, zipping it up to her chin. "You'll be warmer if you take off that wet shirt," he says.

Chry doesn't answer but she squeezes one then the other elbow in through the sleeve holes of her blouse. Dare unzips the coat back down to her clavicle and gently pulls the shirt over her head.

She had not known she would care about dying so much and it pinches her, makes her feel less free.

Dare pulls the zipper back up to her chin, then hugs her tightly to transfer some of his own body heat. She smells like diesel fuel, salt, and sewage.

"I'm going to pick you up," he says.

Chry is confused, but when he lifts her over his shoulder into a fireman's carry, she understands he meant he'd actually be picking her up.

Dare carries her all the way back to the party and just outside the apartment door places her unsteadily on her feet. She lets herself lean into him.

The party is still going full tilt. There are shouts and cheers for Chry, but she doesn't respond. She's aching with cold and still not certain she's going to live. She wonders if she's in shock. Inside Dare's big coat, she grips herself, arms crossed over her chest, hands holding opposite shoulders. She can't see ever ungripping herself, imagines being lowered into the grave this way.

Dare takes an empty sleeve of the coat and holds it where her hand should be. He walks her through the crowded living room and then through an enormous formal dining room. Someone's moved all the chairs away from the long table and a guy with a short mohawk is playing a makeshift game of Ping-Pong with a preppy version of himself. Twins? They're downtown, uptown renditions of the same person or…Chry's not sure. Everything is through the wrong end of a telescope. Dare leads her down a long hallway and into an elaborate kitchen still holding the coat sleeve.

He situates her on a high stool and scoots it to the counter, then moves to the other side where he rummages through a long row of cabinets ultimately producing a box of Hershey's cocoa, a cannister of sugar, a saucepan. From the refrigerator, he pulls out a carton of milk, smells it to make sure it's not spoiled, then sets to work making hot cocoa. While it's on the stove heating, he takes another pass at the cabinets and returns to Chry with two mugs. Holding one in each hand, he reads their slogan: VOTE FOR CUOMO, NOT THE HOMO. He flips both wrists out to show Chry. She moves her mouth to ask *who lives here* but can only manage to shape her lips into the kiss of the first sound.

Dare understands the question and says, "It's Danny's aunt's place but she's hardly here. She travels a lot, hiking, exploring, saving people in remote parts of the world. I don't know, something like that." Dare smiles to let her know he's not impressed but not unimpressed either. He looks down at the mugs. "It's from a few years back. Koch ran against Cuomo in the primary for governor."

Chry looks up; her eyes are the only thing working in her frozen face. Her mouth is still trapped in a kiss.

"It's a pretty fucked up slogan, don't you think?"

Chry tries to nod though she's not sure her head moves. *Yes*, she wants to say, *extremely*, but she can't make the words.

Dare holds up a finger for her to wait right there and then disappears.

She waits.

He returns with a bottle of Meyer's Dark Rum, unscrews the cap and glug glugs it into the cocoa.

"I'll bring you back to life," he says.

Chry's face begins to thaw. She wraps her hands around her cup to warm them as she takes small sips of the cocoa and raises her eyes from time to time to look at Dare. She remembers what happened to me.

Her parents were expecting her at the Oyster Bar in Grand Central Station by midnight, but when it was time to go, Chry had just met Dare and didn't want to leave. "Mina, Mina, Mina," she'd said with a begging face, "Mina, Jamie and Marg would rather see you than me anyway, pleeeeaaaase tell them something."

"How about I tell them you met someone who wants to give you a real job, take you out of the temp racket, keep you and your bass out of all those clubs nobody's ever heard of."

"Yes, perfect. Mina, my beautiful, brilliant, successful friend. You'll make them so happy. You'll make me so happy."

Who am I to deny these people their happiness? I don't mind being Chry's stand-in; her parents love me like a second daughter. They like the way I think inside the box, they like my influence on Chry, who doesn't want to be in any box, and even if she did it wouldn't be their box. I'll ring the new year in with the Risks and a pack of their fancy friends at the Oyster Bar in Grand Central Station, sure.

I'd said, "See you next year," to Chry like a kid in elementary school. She'd said it back and kissed me on the forehead, her face full of gratitude.

And I don't see her until next year, except it wasn't just the other side of midnight like the joke implied, but nearly a whole day later when I finally heard her keys in the locks on the door to our apartment. By then I'd picked up and put down the phone receiver a hundred times, knowing a call to her parents would set a high-level search in motion for which Chry would never forgive me. I spend the long hours of the next day, New Year's Day, my maybe birthday, watching the sky turn shades of gray, lavender, indigo, and finally black, telling myself the chances were high that she was fine.

2

What was even the question?"

Chry hears Dare's voice but she doesn't know where she is, what time it is, what day it is. She wills herself awake, shedding a dream she's had before. It's a music dream where she's doing the thing she wants to do more than anything—she's playing harmonics on the bass, she's playing harmonics like Jaco Pastorius. Outside the bass-playing dream is a rhythmic thrum, a lub dub of a drum or a heart. The room itself is warm and beating.

She can feel the honeycomb-patterned tiles pressing into the side of her face, thighs, and stomach. It doesn't bother her. The floor is as warm as the air. She's covered in something soft and heavy. A bathmat, she guesses. Correct. A laundry room, she guesses again. Also correct.

Chry begins to understand the question about the question wasn't in the dream. There's another body in here with her. She feels it breathing and smells its party-soaked skin and Head and Shoulders shampoo. She opens her eyes but it's too dark to see. The small movement of lifting her lids is excruciating. Her pupils dilating in the darkness is excruciating. Everything hurts.

The body is Dare. He's sitting with his back to the dryer, which thrums on, lub dub, lub dub, lub dub.

He whispers again, "What was even the question?"

"What's the question?" Chry croaks low, her throat too dry to fully speak.

"Why the river? Why not just tell the truth?" he says.

"Oh," Chry says. Then, "I have to pee."

"Umm"

"Like emergency pee."

"So, it's almost another night." Dare says, still whispering. He checks his watch. "It's after five. People are here. They're getting ready for a dinner party or something. I'm not sure, but I think Nyro's aunt is back."

Chry, comprehending more and more, absorbs his words and her own mind confirms them with the sound of busy footsteps up and down the hall. "So, like what? We're trapped in here?"

"I don't know what Nyro's deal is. He left this morning, I said I'd wait until you woke up."

Chry sits up now, slowly, every moving part a rusted hinge. She pulls the bulky mat around her, but it doesn't quite cover. The laundry room is too small to fit them both without touching. Yes, now she remembers them coming in here, taking off their wet clothes.

"I've been running the dryer all night to keep you warm. It was this or the ER. Your face was so white, even your lips. I was afraid for you."

"Pee." Chry stands up. She's glad to see she's still in her underwear. The bathmat is over one shoulder and she awkwardly and painfully gathers the ends at the opposite hip, reminding herself of the sheepskin she wore as a kid in the Nativity, a shepherd, not an angel. She tries to pull Dare up to his feet, so he won't be eye level with her crotch, but he's heavier than he looks. Still, the crisis of having to pee doesn't overrun her senses which are absorbing the handsome feeling of handling his body. He frees himself from his own dead weight and together they stand him up.

"The bathroom?" Her voice is a hoarse pleading whisper.

Dare nods, moves to the door, and unlocks it. He puts his ear to it and waits. Chry prays out of fear and longing and maybe love. Please. Please. Please, she prays, please let the bathroom be nearby.

Dare turns the knob slowly, peers into the hall, and motions to Chry. "One door over," he says, as she squeezes by him and through the partially opened door. "To the right." The shepherd's cloak bathmat doesn't make it through. Chry scrambles to the bathroom in her underwear, but unseen.

Dare keeps the door ajar and a watch on the hallway. When Chry peers her head out of the bathroom, he says, "Go," and Chry makes it to him in two long leaps. He intercepts her, pulls her in to him and shuts the laundry room door all in one movement. Their bodies can't override momentum and gravity and they go down together. Dare navigates falling in the narrow space like the high school quarterback he was. He manages to break Chry's fall while keeping from hitting his own head. They are face to face, body to body on the floor. Chry makes a laughing attempt to unravel the knot. Dare uses his arm strength to gently move her off him and gets back to his feet. The lace of her bra grazes his bare chest as they stand. He tries to turn away, but they tangle and bump.

Ultimately, the room is long enough to hold them side-by-side so when they retrieve their clothes from the dryer, they're able to dress without touching. Chry's jeans and shirt smell like the East River and so do Dare's by their all-night association tumbling in Nyro's aunt's dryer.

"How do we get out of here?" she says. The escapade to the bathroom was one thing but she doesn't want to encounter the aunt.

"Let's just go." Dare feels for her hand and takes it. This time the real thing, not the empty sleeve. He puts his ear to the door and his other hand on the doorknob as he had before, and when he hears the footsteps subside, he squeezes Chry's hand and they walk out into the apartment.

The hallway shows no signs of last night's reveling, nor does the dining room show any indication of the twin-on-twin Ping-Pong match. It's pristine, the table now set with china, silver, and crystal for twelve, tall elaborate vases of flowers and two ornate candelabras. The living room is in transition. Chry and Dare step around a man on his knees with a broom and dustpan tending to a pile of broken glass. The rest of the cleaning army is in full motion, vacuuming, scrubbing, polishing. None look up from their work. Nor does the doorman take notice of them as they exit the building.

Outside on Lexington Avenue the evening is mild and moist, and the dusky-colored sky is bleeding the days last light.

"Where to?" he says.

"Other side of the park."

"Okay, I'm on this side. I'll get you a cab, how's that?"

Chry doesn't answer.

They walk uptown toward Seventy-Ninth Street where there's a stream of yellow cabs heading west. "You never said." Dare's direct question impresses more than unnerves Chry, but her psyche is in a wobble and she can't reciprocate his honesty.

"Said what?"

"You know."

She does know. Chry likes the truth but she doesn't know how to tell it here. She doesn't want him to know she risked the East River just to get his attention. "The question was 'Who do you love?' I said Dare."

Dare stops. He turns to her and pulls her in, speaks into her hair. "You don't even know me," he pleads.

"I was messing around. I don't know, I thought it might be fun." Chry forces a laugh, trying to undo this new thing which has thrown Dare. She doesn't believe in love at first sight, but he thinks she does and she's letting him because why? The truth is abundantly more foolish.

Dare, in his new urgency to part company, turns and starts walking backward, arm raised for a cab.

"You have work tomorrow?" says Chry, trying to keep up and to keep it light, maybe start this thing fresh. A goodbye is looming.

Dare nods.

"Where's that?"

"Wall Street."

Chry doesn't answer. She quickens her step. "It's hard to explain," she says, now almost breathless from the pace Dare's set them on, "but I really didn't think it was going to be a big deal, the river." Chry is rambling. She can't shut it down. "I grew up right over there." She points in the direction of Sandy Hook. "Across the bay."

Again, he doesn't answer. And now she's indignant because he isn't comprehending this important thing about her. Her idyllic girlhood surfing New Jersey's northern hook of beach, the Manhattan skyline tipped with the Twin Towers in the distance, her connection to the winds and tides. At Seventy-Ninth Street, they cross over. When they had started up Lex, she'd imagined a chivalrous show of Dare hailing a cab, opening the door for her and giving the driver a twenty. She'd tell him her address and he'd repeat it to the driver and to himself, to remember, but something's been wrecked. He's dense. From some landlocked state, she imagines, now here, working on "Wall Street" which could mean anything and she's pretty sure if you have a big money job, you say something like munis or junk bonds or Kidder Peabody, you don't say "Wall Street." She's pretty sure about that. She puts her middle fingers together in a V and brings them to her mouth, sending a sharp whistle out to the cab that's coming their way.

"Thanks for bringing me back to life," she says.

Dare's smile is genuine. "Happy New Year."

"Same," says Chry, matching his sincerity. She smiles too, catching his eye and acknowledging their story, its beginning, middle, and now end. They've lived some version of a lifetime and it's still the first day of the year. Here we go 1985, she thinks as she slams the cab door and tells the driver West Seventy-First Street, please.

3

Icy air seeps through the deteriorating French doors of our apartment's sleeping alcove. Night shadows from the tangle of the garden shift and sway, on the wall, on me, on Chry. We're in our regular spots. She's cross-legged on the top bunk practicing finger positioning on her bass and telling me her life in technicolor detail. I'm stretched out on the bottom bunk, not sleeping, listening to her life through the low thrum of her unplugged bass, asking questions if I think she's missed something. Tonight, it's the river and Dare.

"My Dare?" I say.

"How is he your Dare?"

"I mean the Dare I work with? How many can there be?"

"Wait, is that how we know him?" Chry quits thrumming her bass.

"Yeah, that's how we know him. He's the one who told me about the party."

I pull the comforter and the two extra blankets on top of it up to my chin against the freezing river water in her story and the freezing air seeping through the doors.

The apartment is a miracle, really, a sublet in a rent-controlled brownstone a half block from Central Park. It's a big room on the ground floor with one set of drafty French doors in the alcove and another in the main room. The alcove's only large enough for the bunks, my books, and Chry's two basses, but the other room has space for a sofa, a couple of chairs, a wardrobe and two dressers. There's an old stone fireplace that takes up almost a whole wall and that we've been instructed not to use under any circumstances and a kitchen separated by a bar with some high stools. The bathroom is black and white tile with fixtures from the early part of the century, identical in form and space to nearly every New York City bathroom I've seen.

Because we're on the ground floor our entrance is an iron gate underneath the big set of stairs out front that lead up to glass double doors through which the upstairs tenants come and go. It is in the alcove of this rent-controlled sublet where Chry talks me to sleep every night. There's a moment between wake and sleep, a dazzling moment where we are released from the visceral into the ethereal and the gift of the unconscious relieves us from the day. There are times for me when this moment is as it should be and there are times when something goes very, very wrong. My head explodes with gunshots and thunderclaps, knives falling into piles, bombs, and hail rattling windowpanes. Instead of wandering off into the sweet life of dreams, I startle back awake, drenched and shaking. Not always, sometimes, but enough times so the very act of laying my head down has hotwired my neurology. I'm afraid to fall asleep. I need Chry to tell me her stories.

The apartment came through Chry. And if that throws the balance of our friendship off, well the balance has always been off. My scrimping student scholarship status at college to her endless supply of money and powerful parents threatened to shipwreck us, but we sailed on. Chry thinks only I have this equilibrium problem. In her heart of hearts, she doesn't know what I am talking about when I try to bring it up. I can't make her understand and that's fine. Besides, I have a lot to offer, and she'd be the first to acknowledge it, if she ever understood what I was trying to say.

Chry's uncle used to do the overnight shift on the pop radio station here in New York. Now he's in LA doing afternoons and that's why we have this apartment. He says he's not coming back which means we can live here, theoretically, forever.

We're a pair, Chry and me. She: Chrysanthi Risk. *Chrysanthi* for the retsina her parents drank the nights they spent in Santorini. Her name is as seductive as a postcard from a Greek island. *Risk* for the daughter of Congressman and Mrs. (Marg with a hard G to her friends) Risk, the distinguished couple from New Jersey. Me: Mina Berg. *Mina* from the pastor's wife who found me on the altar of the Dutch Reformed Church, two hours up the Hudson River, and *Berg* for Rebecca Berg, the ER nurse who received me and eventually adopted me after I'd been brought to the Hudson Valley Hospital by, as she says, "an Auspicious Parade of a firetruck, an ambulance, and a police car."

Scandalized from the start, I may or may not have been Hudson Valley Hospital's first baby born in 1963. I arrived at the ER New Year's Day, but who could prove I wasn't from that tired old year of 1962? There was a baby goody basket filled with coupons and supplies including a voucher for a year's worth of diapers on the line. There was my mother's reputation as an honest and hardworking nurse on the line. She gave my crown to baby boy Boogman whose arrival on the maternity ward at some point during my Auspicious Parade was documented by several witnessing parties. Baby boy Boogman got a full spread in the Sunday paper, the diapers, the basket, and a fifty-dollar savings bond. He also got a lifetime of torturing rights since we went to school together, torturing rights specifically for me. His upbringing was so ragged, his legitimacy against my well-known nonlegitimacy was all he had to go on. He's the one who told me one sunny afternoon on the playground what the rest of the town said about me. There wasn't a single other person within a hundred miles who had sea water green eyes and hair the color of an old penny. I was the child of a traveler, someone passing through, a monster maybe, a monster who crawled up the banks of the Hudson River and left her child on God's doorstep. What kind of mother leaves her baby to die? A monster mother. He told me if the monster ever came back to town, she'd pay for her crime, he'd see to it. When he sensed my rejection of this valiant offer to be my self-appointed protector, he turned on me.

Boogman and his merry band of torturers were relentless throughout elementary school. The abuse waned in middle school, but the story was, by then, written on the walls of our minds. By high school, no one even mentioned it, too much of a part of things to be worth repeating. The sky is blue. The river is wide. Mina is a monster's spawn.

I suppose I should thank Boogman for getting the ball rolling all those years ago. His torture was enough to propel me from a young age through long nights of homework at the kitchen table when my mom was still at her shift. I was determined to go to some place the Booger could not follow. I hoped his version of who I was and where I came from wouldn't either. As far as anyone knows, January 1 is my birthday, but Chry was missing all day. I watched the Rose Bowl Parade. One of the floats had Miss America, all the American Beauty Roses in the world, and the Statue of Liberty's honest-to-God torch. She's under construction—the Statue of Liberty not Miss America—getting a new torch among other structural upgrades. Anyway, there it was, the old torch, floating down the road on a rose-covered truck in Pasadena. It's a wild, wild world.

Chry's been telling me the details of her life since our freshman year in college, but in the few short months we've lived on West Seventy-First Street, the stories have gotten longer. Maybe there's more to tell, maybe my fear of falling asleep has gotten worse. Chry's good at recounting the details of her life, but not good at remembering the details of mine. Like my birthday, which is maybe today. I don't take it too hard. She has a pure heart and a distracted mind; all she wants is to play the bass like Jaco.

She has two Fender Jazz Basses, one with frets and one without. The one with frets is the one she had the day we met and the one she can play. The one without came along later. She'd bought it secondhand from some place in Staten Island. It has a three-color sunburst design, same as Jaco's, and she removed the frets, same as Jaco. She pried them off with a dinner knife—though Jaco had used a butter knife, she felt it was close enough—then filled in the grooves with plastic wood, sanded it, then added several coats of Pettit Poly Poxy. When it was dry and strung, she said, "Nothing left to do but practice."

But there was one more thing left to do—see him play. There were rumors he was in New York. No one she knew had seen him, but everyone had heard he was here. Rumors were he was showing up for late night sets on MacDougal Street, or at the basketball courts on West Fourth Street, or playing for change in Washington Square Park. Still, there were no reported firsthand sightings. Could be all wishing and myth. Chry wants to believe.

Chry will not be tamed by her congressman father or her society mother. I only want to be tamed, tamed with manicures and box seats at Yankee Stadium, subscriptions to the Met, reservations at Le Bernadin, tamed with Hermès scarves and Ferragamo shoes.

Chry doesn't mind the life I want, but she refuses to pay even the smallest price for it. By day, she's an office temp; she spends week after golden week not having to answer to any one person. At night, she plays her bass in bars you never heard of with a band that's going nowhere. Her parents want her to move to DC, where they spend half their time, so she can drink from the waterfall of opportunities and connections. Chry does not want waterfall opportunities, she wants to have some fun and to play the bass like Jaco Pastorius. And now, something else. She wants Dare. She starts by telling me the story has a beginning, middle, and end, but before she finishes, she says, "I take back the end part."

I nod, though she can't see me from her bunk above, and think about Dare, with his sandy hair hanging in his eyes and the easy way he holds and moves his body, how he refuses to acknowledge my sliver of seniority but doesn't hold it against me that I want it, how after taking shit from the brokers all morning we have lunch together in the conference room while we check their deals, how he eats liverwurst sandwiches with yellow mustard on rye.

"I mean it, Mina," says Chry.

"Okay, next time we all go out, you come," I say, hiding a sorrow I didn't know was there.

"Shit," says Chry and the low thrumming bass goes quiet, "the Risks."

I turn on my side, keeping tight under my blankets. Maybe if you don't have a birthday you don't miss it as much. There was a card from my mom, Snoopy and Woodstock, with twenty dollars and a note: *It was an Auspicious Parade. Treat Yourself. Love, Mom.* I'm tired enough to be almost sleepy. I'll forgive Chry tomorrow. It had been an auspicious parade, The Statue of Liberty's real live torch on a bed of American Beauties. I don't answer Chry, let her wonder.

"Were they upset?" she asks, her voice only tinged with worry.

I pull my legs up in close, a tight bundle like a baby, like the day I might have been born twenty-two years ago. "They were pleased."

"Because I didn't show?"

"That you were making contacts, remember?"

"Oh yeah, Mina..." Chry trails off.

"I'm supposed to kiss you Happy New Year for them. Kiss." I pucker my lips and blow their love up to her.

Chry makes a kissing noise back. "Happy New Year, Congressman and Mrs.; Happy New Year, Mina."

Chry reaches over the end of her bunk and gently lowers the bass to the floor. "How was it?"

"Really nice, eventually. Champagne and oysters all night. Confetti, balloons, paper crowns, a Kennedy, the Risks."

"What do you mean eventually?" Chry doesn't care there was a Kennedy. She doesn't even ask if it was John Jr. It wasn't—a cousin I never heard of—but who doesn't want to know if it was John Jr.?

"They were late, and I couldn't get in without an invitation."

"*Mina.*" Chry is offended for me. "Where did you wait? Down in that hallway? Was it deserted? Were you scared?" The Oyster Bar at Grand Central Station is downstairs, underneath the big main room with the clock and the zodiac constellations on the ceiling.

"No. I was right out in front of the restaurant, in that stone foyer with the vaulted ceilings. It was actually really crowded." What I don't tell Chry is her parents were past midnight late. What I don't say is, as I waited in the far corner of the vaulted space outside the Oyster Bar at Grand Central Station, the room whispered to me. *Sirena Fuggitiva.* That's what it said, in all different voices. *Sirena Fuggitiva*. Over and over again. *Sirena Fuggitiva*. *Sirena Fuggitiva*.

I don't tell her how when they did arrive, they hugged me tight, thanked me, ate the lie about Chry networking at a party uptown. I don't tell her how it felt to be with those men in tuxedos, her handsome dad in particular, and with those women in expensive black New Year's Eve dresses and tasteful diamonds, how when Mrs. Risk says she's a Jersey Girl, she doesn't mean the poor, overworked, tired, and uninspired ones you hear about in a Bruce Springsteen song. She means she lives in a million dollar house with water views; she means her husband is a congressman; she means private jet flights out of Teterboro; she means she owns New Jersey. I don't tell her their names alone, Jamie and Marg, Jamie for James presumably and Marg for Margaret, Marg with a hard G, not Marge or Maggie, their names alone qualify them for something better. I don't say any of that.

4

You are done. You are so fucking done, mate. I'm writing the ticket!" Ian's shouting up at Jay with a telephone pressed to each ear, mouthpieces tilted up over his head, fists squeezing the mute buttons on the handsets, eyes furious. The room's standard hum goes dead with interest, the possibility of money falling down a well, but more than that, interest in how this plays out. Whose status will rise, whose will drop. The result will be short-term, but it will add up in the long run.

Jay, two rows up, is also holding a handset to each of his ears, also clicking the mute buttons so the person on the other end can't hear the commotion, just his voice, friendly, informative, and calm. His eyes peer over his console—a bank of direct lines to the customers, bankers from around the world who've come to New York to trade Eurodollars—and he continues his simultaneous conversations while ignoring the brawl he's inciting. Jay signs off each call with a bang, bang, of the heavy phones on the release buttons on the console.

He doesn't stand up, a posturing that often happens when a fight breaks out on the trading floor, preferring to have this confrontation from the comfort of his chair. An inexperienced broker might stand and shout obscenities to make his point, but Jay knows he's already won. "I called that price off ten minutes ago. In other news, Queen Victoria is dead."

Not only has the Eurodollar section of the trading floor gotten quiet but the forward currency desks—marks, sterling, francs, yen—look up from their own commotions to see if this is going to be something worth watching or just an everyday squabble.

Ian doesn't sit down. "Well, what the living fuck is it still doing on the board?" he says, defeated. Then, to salvage some kind of face, he turns to Dare, the closest person he can find who's lower on the food chain, and says "Oy, what the fuck?"

Dare rushes to the three-month column on the massive white board that runs the length of the Eurodollar section and swipes the price with the side of his fist.

"Oy," Ian says again. "That doesn't bloody help me now. What the fuck are you doing here if you don't want to pay attention?"

He's only a few feet from where Dare and I are standing but Bobby is between them and talking on the link to our London office. "Yeah, yeah. How 'bout you take him back? Ian's got us stuffed in threes and he's blaming it on the board boy."

"What you mean blaming it on the board boy? It's his fucking fault, in't it?" says Ian.

"The market's moved a sixteenth. Why are you the only person in the whole room who doesn't know that price is long gone?" says Bobby.

Now Ian sits, defeated by something he's known all along; he's underwater on this by the collective respect Bobby garners in the New York, London, and Toronto offices, having commanded the link that connects them for nearly three years. "Well, I'm fucked," he says.

Bobby turns back to Dare. "Listen, if you see a price hanging out like that, where everything around it's been hit, call it back to the broker. Saves time and aggravation." He throws his head in Ian's direction, but his eyes sparkle with kindness.

Dare nods.

"And you," Bobby calls over to me. "You've been doing the board for months. He's new up here, help him."

I nod to Bobby but don't acknowledge Dare. We're both trainees. We're supposed to help each other, but we're also competing for a seat on one of the desks. Some desks are better than others so, fuck him. Nah, not really, he's okay but fuck him too. Let him make his own way.

My first day here they asked me, "Do you know what a Eurodollar is?" I said no. Turns out that's the right answer. No one ever knows what a Eurodollar is until they start trading or brokering them, and no one wants to work with a liar. Lies cost money. The truth costs money too. That's the next thing I learned. I watched the brokers bend lies into truth—force a reality from the possibility of a reality.

So, Dare. The boys in the room have taken to him and why not, with his easy smile and the relaxed way he moves under pressure. They sense his willingness to work hard but refusal to bow and scrape to the moneymakers, the ones with the say. The girls have taken to him too, what few of us there are.

Fine. We'll be friends, but I'm not here to pave his way. He got ripped a new asshole for not paying attention. Not my problem. Chry wanting something from him through me is a problem. We'll see. We'll see.

Noon. Lunch in New York, quitting time in London. The brokers who are going out to lunch get up and put their suit jackets on. They won't be back until almost five to make sure the morning deals have all gone through, then they'll catch a train home or go back out to drink some more, depending.

Dare and I have the sandwiches we'd ordered that morning from the company kitchen while we check deals. I have turkey, mayo, wheat. Dare has his liverwurst with lettuce and mustard on rye. There are other options but come to find out we are both creatures of habit.

"I don't know how you can eat liverwurst every day," I say.

He raises his eyebrows and gives me a closed mouth smile as if to say, *my secret.* If his recent reaming is bothering him, he shows no signs of it. I admire this. He can take it. Already two trainees have come and gone. Both of them, with their expensive ties and college-graduation-gift briefcases, coming in on the PATH from New Jersey. They'll get their Wall Street job some other way, some quiet office analyst way. A trading floor, big as a city block, filled with moving money and emotion was not what they bargained for. Dare and me? Yes.

5

Chry is walking down Fulton Street on her way to the *New York Post*. The FDR now high over her head instead of rushing by as she waits to be lowered into the East River. The morning is cold and bright. The salty air coming off the river she'd so recently been dipped into blows her hair and bites her face. Passing the Fulton Fish Market, she breathes in the powerful waft of the living sea.

It's eight in the morning, and New York City is either at work or on its way, but the Fish Market is closing for the day. There's a guy hosing down the sidewalk in front of one of the stalls. He shuts down the nozzle as Chry nears so she can pass without getting caught in the spray. Chry smiles and nods, acknowledging the courtesy. "Thank you," she says.

"First day?" He keeps his clock this time of the morning by the regulars on their way to work. She's new.

Chry is past him now but she turns to answer. "Yeah, but just for a couple days." She knows she doesn't have to explain herself, but nothing about him suggests the stalker-rapist fiends her mother insists on reminding her are everywhere, not even the enormous steel hook with a fat wooden handle draped around his neck. He's wearing jeans and work boots, a thermal shirt under a dirty down vest. He has friendly dark eyes and dark brown shoulder length hair.

The guy points his hose, the stream still shut down, to the market behind him. "Long-term thing, son of a son of a son of a son," he says with grin, "all da way back."

Chry smiles too. "See you tomorrow then," she says, now half a block away.

"Vinnie! Vincent! Vin!" he calls.

She holds her hand up in a wave of acknowledgment but doesn't turn around, doesn't call her name back to him.

Glassy office towers transition to blocks of antique brick buildings and faded warehouses as Chry moves farther away from the bankers, brokers, secretaries, and other assorted downtown workers that had jostled with her up out of the Fulton Street Subway Station, and closer to her destination. She pulls a scrap of paper from her pocket to recheck the address, 210 South Street. Here it is, a paint-peeled fortress, THE NEW YORK POST emblazoned in letters big enough for passing ships to see.

These temp gigs can go either way. She's towered over the city on the upper floors of pristine midtown offices with Persian rugs and silver tea services. She's worked at every kind of business—accounting firms, cellular phone installers, advertising, the reception desk at a publishing house. She's filed, typed letters, answered phones. Some places she's done nothing, sat by a phone *in case* it rang. Chry's agency loves her. Her want for nothing material gives her a relaxed fearlessness that makes her magnetic. More than that, Chry's work wardrobe is a product of her mother's wishful thinking. Her suits are minimal and sophisticated, her shoes and purses understated and expensive. Her hair is long, straight, and brown, adding to a pared-down elegance that's in sharp contrast to the high-haired bridge-and-tunnel girls with their enormous shoulder pads and wide pleather belts who can type circles around her.

Chry's first day at the *New York Post* is challenging. There's a table stacked nearly to the ceiling with the Wednesday business section. Chry is to fold the tabloid's pullout section in half and stuff it into eight and a half by eleven envelopes. The paper's unpleasant texture and loosely attached ink is a sensory experience of the worst kind. She washes her hands again and again as the morning of paper stuffing drags on. Afraid she won't finish the task by day's end, she gives up and lets the ink penetrate her hands.

Late in the afternoon, when it looks like the pile of papers and hours left in the day are compatible, Chry washes her hands and asks for permission to call me.

"MINA, someone named Chry!" a broker shouts, annoyed.

He holds up one of his handsets with a shake. "Main number."
The afternoon markets are quiet today. The room is idle, so this
minor disturbance of the general half-doze attracts attention.

Dare and I are rewriting the prices on the board as part of
our afternoon chores. His marker squeaks to a stop mid-price.
He watches me sit in an empty chair and take the call.

"Chry?" I whisper, hoping the room will go back to minding
its own business and Dare will stop looking at me and go back
to writing prices.

"Hi. I'm covered in the *New York Post* business section," she
whispers back.

"The *Post* has a business section?"

"Yeah, and the ink they use doesn't stay on the page. I'm
dying here. Are you going out later? I'm downtown. I'll meet
you." She doesn't mention Dare. She's not the kind of person
who asks things twice.

In fact, I am, we all are. There's a training session and there's
cost-effective drinking after. Meaning free.

Every single thing about this job is trial by fire—the brokers
screaming at you; the way they encourage us to compete with
each other; the way if we don't stick together, we're fucked; the
scary fact that the slightest inattention could lead to multiple
million dollar losses for the company and a single job loss for
the perpetrator. The drinking is also trial by fire. Drink. Lose
your mind. Don't pass out on the floor. Have fun. Don't spill secrets—your own or the company's. Keep your body to yourself.

I tell Chry where to meet us. An upstairs place at the Seaport, out on Pier 17.

"Who was that?" asks Dare when I get back up to the board.

"My roommate, Chry."

"I know her."

"Yeah?"

"Yeah, from New Year's, at Nyro's. She swam in the river."

"I was there, remember? I left before the river thing."

"Did she mention me?"

"No, why would she?"

"No reason."

6

Chry's at the bar with clean hands. She's scrubbed the *New York Post* off them with ladies' room soap and hot water. Her winter-white wool suit, streaked and smudged, was not remedied so easily. Her forehead has a faint remnant of four blurry black finger trails from her eyebrows to her hairline like she tried to scrub it as clean as her hands then stopped caring.

There are six of us from work. We move through the crowd and set up shop at the opposite end to where she's standing. I give her a quiet come-over wave. Not sure I'm allowed a friend. Tommy, the broker who's in charge of us tonight, throws down a credit card and gestures to us to go ahead, order what you want. Do what you want. Drink what you want. Stay out as late as you want. Take what you want. Just don't be late for work. This is the lesson we're practicing. When we start drinking with bankers, not just each other, the next day if we're late for work, we could miss the payback.

"Who's this?" says Tommy. Chry's made her way through the crowd to our side of the bar.

"Tommy McGinley, this is Chry Risk, my roommate."

"Chry, like boo hoo?"

"Like short for Chrysanthi," Chry says.

Tommy draws down the corners of his mouth, nods his head up and down. He doesn't understand but all right, all right. "Whatcha do for a living?" he says, referring to her ink-smudged suit.

"Absolutely nothing," says Chry. "Who knew you could get so dirty doing jack shit?"

Tommy throws his head back and laughs, less for the joke and more for her fearlessness.

In fairness to me, Dare, Bryan, Hal, and Steve, from seven

to five it's nothing *but* fear. Chry either doesn't know enough or doesn't care enough to be afraid of Tommy. And where's Dare anyway? I forget for a moment that he and Chry spent the night in a laundry room not too long ago.

"Josie, seven shots of Cuervo," Tommy barks at the bartender. She's working a cocktail shaker, nodding and making mental notes as the throng of twenty-somethings in suits call out their liquor wishes.

"Gold," he shouts.

Soon enough she hustles over, sets a row of shot glasses on the bar and expertly turns the bottle upside down, filling them one at a time, jerking the bottle from one glass to the next until the last one is filled to the rim.

"Hands out," Tommy barks to us. Scanning the group, he adds, "Where in the fuck is Fiore? Training is not over."

"Gimme that," he says to Josie, and she hands him a salt-shaker. "Lick," he commands. He licks the back of his hand to show us how it's done. We lick the back of our hands. Tommy directs three hard shakes to the wet spot on his hand and passes the shaker to me. I do the same and pass it on. "Where is Fiore?" he shouts and when Dare doesn't materialize, he says, "Fine. Josie, two more. The rest of you, limes ready."

He holds his shot glass in a toast. "Up yours," he says, licks the salt, shoots the shot, bites the lime.

"Up yours!" we say in a unified shout.

I squint in pain from the salt then tequila then lime combo. As Chry puts her hand to her nose against the burning, she sees something behind me and her eyes flash.

"Fiore!" Tommy is bellowing now. "There's a fine for skipping out before class is over." He points to the three shots of tequila left on the bar.

Dare squeezes through our group to where Tommy has his little line of shots set up. He lifts his shoulders and his chest in the form of a deep breath and fires the shots, one, two, three. No salt, no lime, no nothing. He gives a sharp nod of his head to Tommy and a smile to me, his training class best pal, and a look of recognition to Chry.

"Josie," Tommy shouts down the bar, "you got scissors back there? Josie. Josie. *Josie.*"

She looks up from the bottles of beer she's uncapping. "What!"

"Scissors?"

"Yeah, yeah, one sec."

"Fiore!" Tommy shouts when he finally gets the scissors. "One last bit of advice. Come 'ere."

Dare moves within reach and Tommy grabs hold of his tie. "My advice," says Tommy. "Is. Clothes. Make. The. Man." He opens Josie's scissors up wide and closes them hard on Dare's tie, up close to the knot.

Dare loosens what's left of his tie, pulls the scrap from around his neck and holds it out in front of him between his thumb and forefinger like it's a dead rat. "Tommy," he says, "I'm gonna thank you for this someday."

Tommy calls for round after round. Dare does not stand down and Chry keeps pace for solidarity. I do enough to keep in good standing but I'm already thinking about work tomorrow. I can't see Dare being much help on the board at this rate. I anticipate covering for him. I don't mind. I like him. And I'd rather be covering than being covered for.

When it's late enough for me to be credited as someone who can hang, I hold Chry's arm and stare in her eyes. "You okay if I leave?"

She answers by squeezing my cheeks between her palms turning my mouth into fish lips. "Nevah bettah," she says in her best borough accent.

"Your river," says Dare. He and Chry are side by side, outside the bar, with their elbows on the railing looking out over the water at the lights of the Brooklyn Bridge, the Manhattan Bridge beyond, Brooklyn, just across, lit up too. The late night is cold, but clear and still. They are awash in tequila. There are stars.

Dare turns. He matches his fingers to the smudge traces on

Chry's forehead. He follows their trail to her hairline and keeps going, smoothing her hair off her face. He brings the other hand to her hair, leans in and touches his lips to her smudged brow. Touches his lips to the tip of her nose. Touches his lips to hers.

Chry closes her eyes and lets go. She's leaning back over the railing but letting tequila and Dare keep her from falling into the East River, three stories down. She holds and holds and holds this feeling, this feeling of letting go.

Dare leans in, suspending them into weightlessness, then pulls her in away from the rail and kisses her. On and on, their hands in each other's hair, lights above, their reflections below. Chry is in the crossfire of wishing and real time. Perfect, for her. Dare's marble-carved resolve turns to liquid, evaporates, disappears.

Josie shouts for last call, but Chry and Dare don't hear.

7

For a girl who spends every waking hour blowing off her life, Chry is responsible. She will not be late for her second and last day at the *New York Post*. Though she sways and lurches her way through her morning routine, she, in fact, feels good, nearly excellent. Not even the urine sweat smell on the subway platform or the close wet wool air in the subway car interferes with her euphoria. Her euphoria is Dare. Her euphoria is a memory saturated with kissing him under the late-night stars and lights at the South Street Seaport. Her euphoria is she is still drunk.

Up out of the subway, the downtown skyscraper canyon crosswinds are blowing but this only adds to Chry's beautiful feeling. It's not until she's walked Fulton Street from the subway station to the river and she breathes in the overpowering air of the fish market that the previous night's one-two punch of love and Cuervo gives way to a bludgeoning hangover. Yesterday, the salty fish air smelled like home; today it's an assault. The bright sky and the cold morning sun are assaults. Chry gags on all of it. She digs through her purse for her Ray Ban's as her happy stride collapses into a swerving stumble. She finds them and puts them on. Her senses are so overloaded with the fish market's freshness and decay she wants to hold her nose, but here's Vinnie, Vincent, Vin hosing down the walk just like yesterday and she doesn't want to insult him.

"How ya doin'?" He releases his hand to shut down the spray.

Chry tries to answer, *fine*, but it won't come out. Instead, her body contorts, she doubles over and retches into the gutter.

The retching goes on, out of her control and escalating in violence.

The hose remains silent. She can feel Vinnie, Vincent, Vin

watching her and prays he won't come near and try to help or befriend her in this private act of puking her guts out. Finally, finally, Chry picks up her head, dazed and in disbelief, her sunglasses…somewhere…

Vinnie, Vincent, Vin comes toward her and for a second Chry thinks he's going to hose *her* down but instead he reaches in his back pocket and hands her a white handkerchief.

"Surrender?" she manages to say as she accepts it.

"Always." He motions for her to step aside. She does and he hoses the mess into the storm drain, paying attention to spraying her stranded Wayfarers without letting them go down with the rest of it.

Having wiped her nose and mouth with the handkerchief, Chry attempts to return it.

"Sweethaht, my gift," he says and laughs as he continues to spray down the mess.

Chry looks at the technicolor pieces of her insides in the hankie, then at him and grimaces in place of the words, *sorry* and *thank you*.

When her sunglasses are thoroughly clean, Vinnie, Vincent, Vin shuts off the spray and crouches down. He picks them up with pincer fingers, shakes off the loose water and hands them to her.

Chry puts them on to cover her makeup-smudged and ruined eyes and to keep out the light which is brighter still. "Thanks," she says and stops. She stops the perpetual motion machine of being on her way and takes him in through streaked, wet sunglasses—the stained down vest and thermal long undershirt, the softness of his eyes and hair, and the enormous and terrifying hook he wears around his neck. "Thanks," she says again. "Thank you, Vinnie, Vincent, Vin."

"You can pick one." He makes a quick squeeze of the hose into the now thoroughly clean crime scene.

"Vinnie."

"That's what they call me."

Chry nods.

"Ya betta get goin'. Yer gonna be late," he says.

A feeling of friendship washes through Chry's now full-blown gasping hangover. She's afraid to speak for fear of throwing up again so she gives him a sagging smile and heads for day two at the *New York Post*.

The second day's assignment doesn't involve stuffing envelopes but Chry is prepared in all black: skinny tux pants, an oversized black cashmere sweater, black patent leather belt, and black patent flats.

As is often the case, she's responsible for a phone that doesn't ring so she spends the day managing her wilted constitution with trips to the bathroom and small sips of water. She stares out over the FDR and the East River, disoriented and dizzy with the raw remembrance of kissing Dare and the blistering longing to stretch her body down beside him and go to sleep for a thousand years.

ॐ

It's Friday night, but Chry's too tired to go out. So am I. She's too tired even to practice Jaco's harmonics. We boil a box of noodles, add a stick of butter, pile on the salt. I sit my dish on my lap, prop my feet up on the small dining table and stare out at the indigo sky over our wasted garden. Chry fiddles with the boom box, detaching the speakers and moving them as far away as their cords allow. "Jaco?" she asks.

"Always." It's part of my unspoken deal with Chry—she picks the music. "But why not the records?"

"I'm making some mixtapes for my Walkman."

Chry presses play and the room fills with Jaco Pastorius and Pat Metheny and the rest of that band. They're playing "Bright Size Life." Chry smiles. She'd never admit to loving any one song best, but I know this is her favorite. I am spent on last night's tequila and limping through my own long day, but it makes me smile too.

The wild dead weeds in our garden rustle and the light whoosh of night air rattles the panes in the decaying French doors that separate us from the garden and other city wilds. I wonder again why we have three locks on the front door when anyone could break through the rickety back doors in two seconds.

The music plays.

After a long time, Chry gets up and takes my bowl, drops it in the sink and fills the teakettle with water. She goes into the alcove and brings out a blanket for each of us. She throws hers on the sofa and tucks mine in around me. When the kettle whistles, she makes us tea and settles into the sofa with her blanket and steaming cup to tell me the details of kissing Dare until past last call.

She wants to know what I think, and I don't want to say. Dare is a work friend. I don't know if friend is even the right word. Dare is a work person. It's a good job. A job where you learn things that can make you money. I don't hold it against her, but Chry doesn't know what that feels like. Her urgency makes me nervous and according to her own New Year's Eve story, it makes Dare nervous too. He was at work on time this morning. I didn't have to cover for him like I thought I would, but after we checked the morning deals, we ate lunch in silence. He didn't mention Chry. He didn't mention anything.

I shrug and change the subject to the pregnancy test I noticed in the bathroom garbage can. "How'd the test come out?"

"Negative."

"Anyone I know?" A small reminder she doesn't need me to play matchmaker or up her sex game. She has all kinds of ways to meet people. I mean she plays in a band. I've seen that peed-on stick before, but I never ask. If she wants to tell me she tells me, and she's told me plenty.

"No. No one you know," says Chry.

"Anyone *you* know?" I smile. I'm just kidding around.

"No." She laughs. "Jeff Somebody. He gave me his number, but I lost it. Mina, I don't care. Not since—"

"Do you think anything will bloom?" I say.

"Between me and Dare? Yes. That's what I'm telling you."

"I mean in the garden. Everything is so dead. I never thought about it until now but there had to have been enough of something living to make all that dead out there. Someone must have cared once."

"Not my uncle. Every St. James Day my grandmother asks him if he's taking care of it. Years ago, when he first moved here, she fixed it up, planted some stuff, but he let it go to hell." St. James Day. Chry has an ocean, a river, *and* a lake. I have a river. And I don't even have that. If I did have a river it would be the Hudson River. The Hudson is not a river, it's a tidal estuary but that's not why it isn't mine. A tidal estuary moves in two directions. It's salty and fresh which is called brackish. If it were mine, I'd tell you what it feels like to stand on its cliffs and watch the sun sink over the other side. If the Hudson River were mine, I'd tell you how it is five short blocks from my house, how the train that chugs up alongside it was always going to be my getaway. How my mother would not let me swim in it, how the currents could carry you away or drag you under. I'd tell you, last and worst of all, it is filled with poison. And though the Hudson River isn't mine it's still here by my side, traveling to and from my town upstate to the New York Harbor through The Narrows beneath the Verrazano bridge to the Atlantic Ocean. To and from the wide, wide world.

I grew up on the cliffs of the Hudson but unlike the amphibious Chry, I never made it to the river, not ever, not once. That's Chry, she has everything you don't times two. She grew up with an ocean and a lake, and she made a river hers the night she took that dare.

"On St. James Day," says Chry, "we eat oysters and drink from the cup of suffering." The story is this: Jesus recruited James and his brother John straight from the family fishing boat and off they went. James and John are sold on the idea of a kingdom beyond our little slice of heaven here on earth, so much so, they ask Jesus if when they get there can they sit right up in first class with him. Jesus says, "You don't know what you are asking. Can you drink from the cup from which I am going to drink?" Without any other details, they right away say, "We can."

What's in the cup?

Suffering. You find this out later.

Meantime it's a smash bang-up day at Arcadia. Arcadia is Chry's grandmother's house on Chry's lake and for the years I've known her, I've known about St. James Day, but I've never been invited. I try to not let this hurt my feelings. I'm told it's very crowded.

This year will be different. Her mom said I should come. After midnight outside the Oyster Bar when I heard all those voices whisper *See-ren-uh*, after Congressman and Mrs. Risk finally showed up, after I made Chry's excuses and we drank champagne and ate oysters, she invited me to Arcadia for St. James Day. I hope she remembers.

Arcadia is only open in the summer. It has porches and turrets and balconies all with windows big enough to fall out of. The front door is wide and heavy and opens in one piece or in a top and bottom half. There are French doors across the back like the ones we have here but they're not falling apart, not by the way Chry describes them. Off the doors is a wide stone terrace that sits over a long sloping yard to the lake.

Arcadia is a dream every day but on St. James Day it's a dream in a dream. There's a huge tent on the back lawn. Rows of round tables with white tablecloths and tall vases of Queen Anne's lace.

The party starts in the afternoon and goes all night. Everyone wears white except G.A., who wears dark purple. G.A. is Chry's Grandmother Anna. Chry doesn't call her Grandmother. "As soon as I could talk, I was like what's with this 'Grandmother' bullshit," is how she put it. I doubt it was as soon as she could talk but maybe.

On St. James Day, G.A. is Queen Anne and the party is her lacy dress like the flowers that grow in the meadows near Arcadia.

G.A.'s father came from Spain to work in the zinc factory on the river near Pittsburgh. The town was Donora, Pennsylvania, the river was the Monongahela. The men who came from Spain could stand the heat in the zinc factory. They kept coming and coming and coming, these men who could stand the heat in the zinc factory on the Monongahela River in Donora, Pennsylvania. Along with them came their wives, either right away or eventually. And along with the men and their wives came St. James Day.

When Chry talks about St. James Day, she talks about Donora. She's never been but she's going, someday soon, she's going to Donora to visit the Smog Museum. When Chry asks G.A. about the Smog Museum, G.A. says, "I'll tell you later," but she never tells her. Chry says she's going to find out for herself, with me. I want to know why I'm invited to this someday trip to the Smog Museum, but I'm not invited to St. James Day at Arcadia. Arcadia didn't always have St. James Day. Arcadia came from the Risk side of the family who were too Protestant to abide saints. But G.A. married in and began to run things so St. James Day came to Arcadia to stay.

On St. James Day they eat oysters and drink from the cup of suffering. The suffering part started the year Chry's uncle stood on a table covered in empty oyster shells and shouted, "Here's, here's, here's…" until the room was silent. "Here's to suffering!"

Everyone lifted their glasses and shouted, "To suffering!" and cheered and laughed and hollered. G.A. didn't like it and she still doesn't. She considers it bad karma. Chry's grandfather died of a damaged heart but that was before the Suffering Toast, so you can't blame it on that.

8

Snow is flying and falling on the harbor. Chry, Dare, Nyro, and I are a pile of coats, hats, mittens, and gloves, a slouching row on the outside top deck of the Staten Island Ferry. White wet flakes whip in the late day gray sky and disappear onto the treacherous chop three stories below. Nyro's face is in motion under a fur-lined suede hunting hat, earflaps down. It was his idea to sit outside, up here on the deck. It was his idea to bunch in close for warmth.

Inside the ferry, a guy is playing guitar and singing Dire Straits. *And after all the violence and double talk, There's just a song in all the trouble and the strife, You do the walk, yeah, you do the walk of life, You do the walk of life* . . . His guitar case is open for people to throw in money. It sounded pretty good, and Chry wanted to stay and listen, but I followed Nyro, Dare followed me, and she followed Dare. And here we are.

Nyro's eyes dive and dart. He's looking for something to entertain himself. I pray he'll find it, so those eyes don't turn on us. I have to think it's how Chry ended up in the river. I barely know him, but I already know this, his extra skill is sensing people's vulnerabilities and amusing himself with them. *He* doesn't know this. He is innocent, which is worse. I contract my energy, keep myself to myself as much as possible so he won't know I'm afraid of this angry sea and sky and of him. That I forgive him this power over me scares me twice.

We watch the Statue of Liberty pass by. She's covered in scaffolding and torchless as presumably every person in New York City knows.

"Where'd she lose her torch?" says Nyro, like the Statue of Liberty is some drunk girl at Limelight who can't find her purse.

"Last I saw, it was cruising down the street in the Rose Bowl Parade on a raft of American Beauties." Saying this reminds me how Chry went missing that day, how she forgot my birthday, how she spent it holed up in Nyro's aunt's laundry room.

"What?" says Nyro.

Chry doesn't say anything. Neither does Dare. They haven't seen each other since they transfigured Tommy's requisite tequila shots into a night of kissing and grabbing all the way past last call. These two midnight expeditions with Dare have ruined Chry. What they've meant to Dare is anybody's guess.

It's been more than a month since their night at the Seaport. He hasn't mentioned it at work, and I don't ask. We keep focused, he and I, more than the others. We watch the trading floor closely, seeing not just millions of dollars transact but the person-to-person transactions too. How the power dips, rises, and slides in a complicated game.

The other trainees don't see this the way we do. We're all the same, just out of college, but Dare and I are different. Unsaid, but I think we're the only ones who have no intentions of returning home.

The Hudson River runs both ways and of course so does the train. But I don't plan on utilizing the northbound track. I'm never going back to where Ford Dealership Heir Baby Boy Boogman is king, back to where my mother, after so many years of working at the hospital, has cleaned up every person in the whole town's shit, back to where the river will kill you with its whirlpools, currents, and pollution.

"What do you mean it was in the Rose Bowl Parade?"

"That's what I mean; it was in the Rose Bowl Parade, on a float, covered in roses."

"Her torch?"

"No, the float."

"Well, what was it doing there?"

"How do I know? Visiting the West Coast before it gets reattached?" It's impossible that Nyro doesn't know the Statue of Liberty's torch has been severed from her hand with plans for it not to be reattached but replaced, but it's also impossible to know if he's having a game or what.

"Huh," says Nyro. "Where are you guys going again?"

"To look at basses. There's a place on Forest Avenue."

"Huh," he says again.

This expedition to Staten Island is my genius on Chry's behalf. I don't plan to spend my days propping up her lovesickness, but she's desperate to see Dare and it's better for me if it's not at a work thing. Yesterday, when we were finished checking deals, Dare said he was going to Staten Island with Nyro to check out some investment of his. I told him we were too. And now we are.

Chry's been talking about taking the ferry to Staten Island for a while now. I asked her what's in Staten Island and she said mafia kingpins and basses. She was interested in the second thing. I wasn't interested in either.

Dare shrugged but that night there was a message on the machine saying they'd be on the three o'clock boat.

"It's weird seeing her without it. It's weird seeing her under construction."

"Nyro, relax. They'll put her back together," says Dare.

"You don't know these guys. The bullshit that goes on."

The ferry is nearing the terminal. Seagulls shriek and swoop from the pilings.

"Do you?" I ask politely. It sounds like he does.

"Yeah. Yeah, I do." Nyro loses his swagger. A first as far as I've seen.

"How?" I say, politely again. I don't normally tiptoe around people, but he is the person who dropped my best friend into the East River.

There's a life ring with the name of the boat, *John F. Kennedy,* on the wall attached to an ancient-looking coiled rope. The ceiling above is lined with orange rubber life jackets behind a grid of wooden slats. They're coated in grime. Nothing appears to have been checked, safety tested, a-okayed since this thing was first launched. Who knows when that was? Kennedy's been dead since the year I may or may not have been born. In short, there's nothing here to save us.

"How?" says Nyro.

"Yeah," I say. "How do you know?"

Nyro raises his eyebrows and stands up. Waves for us to follow, commanding our army of four to the door. He pulls back the heavy handle, slides the door open in its tracks and we follow him inside.

The guy with the guitar is now singing a very stylized version of "Should I Stay or Should I Go." Chry looks at me with an aggrieved face. He'd been doing all right with Dire Straits. We pass in front of the heretic turning The Clash to mush and follow Nyro to the door opposite. No one throws change into the guitar case.

Nyro pulls back the handle on the door to the opposite deck, throwing his spidery energy behind it as this one seems to be airlocked against the blowing wind on the other side. It could be comical, but any comedy to be had at his expense would slingshot back dangerously. Still, Nyro's flicker of weakness and his immediate effort to cover it up, grabs me a little.

We follow him out onto the deck and line up along the rail.

"You have to lean out," says Nyro.

Chry obeys. She leans out, standing on tiptoes and bending as far over the rail as she can.

I do not want to lean out. I can't. Also, I can't not, so I force my body against my will. I lean out.

Dare doesn't lean out and Nyro doesn't insist.

Chry and I lean back in.

Nyro smiles, satisfied we've seen the huge crane that towers above a Staten Island waterfront construction site with the letters, N-Y-R-O. "Rhymes with hero," he says.

And now I see. This isn't the first time I've seen an N-Y-R-O crane. They're all over New York City.

"That you?" I say, though I know it is.

"My dad…it *was* my dad. He's dead. So now it's me. I'm the hero. Supposedly."

Chry is unfazed. Dare is already in the know. I have a lot of questions, none of them polite.

Nyro stares at my brain; his eyes bore a hole in my forehead. "Don't think I can do it?" he says in a mild voice.

"I don't think anything." I say, which is not true at all.

"Don't worry, my mother runs things." He holds his arms out, moves his head from side to side, and lolls his tongue, a marionette with strings attached. "But it's still mine."

The ferry hits the pilings, throwing us off our feet in a pack. We catch each other and manage to stay standing. Then the boat ricochets off the other side, and we repeat the exercise in the opposite direction. We grab the rail in a line and brace our feet, ballet dancers at the barre, as the ferry ricochets back and forth with descending force until the boat is snug in its slip.

Evening falls as we stand in the terminal waiting for the next ferry to arrive so we can board it back to Manhattan. Chry and I spent the last three hours at Mandolin Brothers, and she is hepped up on basses and bass talk. She updated the guy on the Fender she'd bought from him, told him how she'd pried the frets off with a dinner knife and fixed it up with plastic wood and Pettit Poly Poxy, just like Jaco. He wanted to know how the playing was going and Chry said, "I'm a long way off."

He nodded with so much understanding, Chry took a sharp breath in and dropped her shoulders, a physical reaction to his kindness. I felt it too, the kindness in general, and specifically for her. I felt the kindness in the painstaking attention it must take to fill that store with so many beautiful instruments. And beyond that, each of those instruments, a product of skilled effort and love. I felt the way he made it clear it was okay for Chry to just come on by and talk. It didn't have to be transactional. A surge of jealousy washed through me. Everything about Mandolin Brothers was a million miles away from the trading floor where I work. For all our differences, I had never felt that with her before, jealousy. That awful stab of longing and anger. Until that moment, I hadn't thought there was something she had that I couldn't get by working hard, but here was a luxury she was enjoying that *I didn't even know existed.* Chry was seeking things that did not involve transactions. She was reaching for something improbable, maybe even impossible—a stark contrast to the practical applications in my life that I utilized daily to survive. Nyro wants us to sit outside again. He takes us down to the bottom level where cars roll on and off. As the ferry pulls out, there's nothing between us and the churning water except a flimsy metal fence that stretches across the end of the boat. The dark sky, the roar of the engine, the shimmying and banging against the pilings, all of it scaffolds me with fear. Like the Statue of Liberty, wrapped and trapped without her torch, like a drunk girl at Limelight who can't find her purse.

I hold my arms around myself to keep from shivering and am shocked when it's Nyro who says, "You look cold, let's go inside," and leads us through to the ferry's lower level. It's more crowded than I would have guessed. Passengers are dressed up for a night out in the city. This is the smoking floor, and everyone is doing just that. The smell is a combination of pot and cigarettes. Two guys with high hair and leather jackets pass a joint openly.

We follow Nyro to an empty bench. When we're settled in, he takes a joint out of his left coat pocket and a lighter out of his right. He lights it up and passes it to Chry. She pulls hard, making the end glow and crackle. Then Dare. Then me. I take a long hard hit. It sets fire to my lungs and begins to disassemble my scaffolding. When it's my turn again I take another long pull. Then I hold up what's left of the joint like Lady Liberty's torch.

"I lift my lamp beside the golden door?" says Chry.

"Yesssssss," I say, hissing out smoke. "High on the Staten Island Ferry," I say to no one. All of this is a very good idea.

"Oh, we're not finished yet," says Nyro. And we laugh and laugh and laugh until I forget what's even funny.

I slouch down on the bench, rest the back of my head on the polished wood and stare at the fat layer of blue smoke hanging on the ceiling. Nyro pulls out a pack of Marlboros and lights a cigarette. I put my hand up in a backward peace sign, then close my fingers together when he puts an unlit cigarette between them. He rolls the wheel of his lighter to pop up a flame and adjusts it to maximum height. Chry and Dare who are between us, shrink back. We've shed our hats and gloves but we're no less flammable. Nyro doesn't move, just holds the lighter with its tall flame in the middle of us. I hold the cigarette to my lips, afraid to move toward the flame, afraid to move away. I don't know how I got here. I don't even smoke. We stay this way a long time, the four of us. Someone could have painted our picture.

Finally, for the simple fact I don't want to die in a Staten Island Ferry fire, I pull my hair back holding it with my hand in a ponytail, lean across Chry and Dare, and pull the flame in through the cigarette. Nyro releases his thumb and the flame disappears.

He pulls the crushed pack of Marlboros back out and offers one to first Chry, then Dare. They both shake their heads no. They don't want to play the flame game. Nyro shrugs and shoves the pack back into his pocket.

"Where to next?" he says.

Chry and I didn't have a plan beyond taking the Staten Island Ferry with Dare. That we managed to work out a ride back on the same boat was more than we'd expected. Chry's high on basses and Dare and plain high. I'm just plain high. And a little sick from the cigarette I'm inhaling and the stale remainder of the million cigarettes previously smoked down here on the lower floor of the Staten Island Ferry.

Nyro waits for Dare to say something. When he doesn't, Nyro says, "Then it's decided. Come on, this is the best part."

We zip our coats, put on our hats, mittens, and gloves, and follow him up to the front deck where we watch the Twin Towers and all lower Manhattan grow larger and larger until we are underneath it. This time we're braced and ready as the ferry collides with its slip.

9

Me across from Nyro. Chry across from Dare. A thick veal chop on a large white plate each. Heavy silver to the left and to the right. Multiple forks, knives, spoons. We're going to be here for a while. There's a starched white cloth on the table, and a starched white napkin on my lap. In the center of everything, a fat candle lights our multiple wine glasses, the ones holding sparkling water illuminate our faces, the ones holding a deep-hued red wine gleam like garnets. We are alone together in the low light of this crowded restaurant.

We'd waited a long time for the table. Nyro went a block over to Washington Square Park and bought a couple of loose joints and we took turns going around the corner and smoking them. Chry and Dare went first then I went with Nyro. We stood in the doorway of a church and for the second time today, I lit my lungs on fire and left my head. Nyro ground the last of the joint into the marble step with the heel of his Timberlands. Side by side, leaning with our backs up against the church doors, we stared through the bare trees in Washington Square at the Arch, all lit up. The snow we'd seen disappear into the gray waves of the harbor had left a dusting here. We looked out at the sugarcoated city, feeling our place in it. Nyro took my hand and held it carefully. I said we should get back, maybe our table was ready.

At the restaurant when the veal chop arrives, I watch to see which fork Chry selects and take the same one. I've been doing this since the first time her parents invited me to join them for dinner. This heavy silver fork. This heavy silver knife. Both sharp. Dangerously so. All luxury and power. I am famished but I cut the chop in slow small slivers and put them to my tongue between sips of the garnet-colored wine. Over and over. I lose track of the others for a short or maybe long while. Each of us is in our own world, chewing the flesh of the tenderest of beasts, sipping from wine glasses so delicate they could cut our mouths. The noise in the room is a sweet static. Our small table promotes touching. My left knee meets Dare, my right, Chry. Sometime toward the end of the endless veal chop, I feel the gentle pressure of Nyro's foot on mine.

Did I finish the veal? It's no longer in front of me but I don't recall. The waiter pours prosecco into the flutes he's added to our collection of stemmed glasses. The candle's flame refracts and reflects on Chry's brown eyes and lovely brow, Nyro's white skin and head of dark curls, Dare's sandy hair, golden skin and eyes, and, I suppose, my worn penny-colored hair and sea water eyes.

Nyro, who took command of the ordering is saying yes as the waiter tells us the dessert menu. Gelato, yes. Profiteroles, yes. Tiramisu, yes. And they come, one after another. Cappuccino, yes. I take small bites out of each dessert. I let the milky foam touch my lips as I sip the rich espresso underneath. Slowly, slowly, slowly. I do all of this as if I have a thousand years left to live and I do. I am going to live forever.

We spoke words while the food came and went, but I don't remember any of them. Now Nyro is paying the bill and telling the waiter he wants him to call us a cab. I want to ask, *Where to?* But I don't care at all. I look to see if Chry cares. She's staring at Dare. Dare either doesn't notice or pretends not to notice. He is practiced in the art of not acknowledging attention. I know this about him.

Outside Il Mulino, snowflakes are falling again, but now slow and fat. We stick out our tongues to catch them and wait for the cab. It's not far, but by the time the cab bumps down the cobblestones on Franklin Street and stops in front of Nyro's loft, the world is wearing a thick coat of white. We leave footprints on the sidewalk but the snow, now coming down fast, covers them before we get inside.

"When did you move here?" asks Chry. We're taking off our

things. Dare balances on one foot then the other as he lifts his leg and pulls his Timberlands off. He picks them up and places them near the door. Nyro sits on the floor, crosses one long leg over the other, yanks off his boots and chucks them one by one in the vicinity of Dare's neatly placed pair. His wiry frame is deceiving. His arms are like catapults and the boots hit the wall in a set of concussive thuds.

"My aunt kicked me out after the party."

Chry nods, unsurprised.

Dare lifts his eyes to the ceiling; it was to be expected.

"This place is amazing," I say. And it is. Amazing and huge. Now, the second biggest apartment I've ever seen, but nothing like the one on the Upper East Side. The walls are raw brick and the ceiling is open to the original steel beams and wood. It is cavernous and empty except for a kitchen. The walls delineating bedrooms don't reach the ceiling. There's a stereo stack of receivers, tape deck, a collection of cassettes in a rack, and two four-foot-tall speakers. There's a fireplace too, a small brick one, not like the big stone one in our apartment, though the cord of wood stacked on the wall next to it implies this one might really work.

"My room's there, Dare's is there," says Nyro, pointing.

"Wait, you live here? With him?" says Chry.

"Recently," says Dare. He goes to the fireplace, pulls back the screen, takes some logs off the pile and gets to work making a fire.

I sit on the floor and start unlacing my hiking boots, still wondering how we got a table at Il Mulino dressed so casually. I know how. Danny Nyro's name is on every crane in the New York City sky. Money. Maybe not just money, maybe connections but one leads to the other, I've noticed, not the other way around. I put my boots next to Dare's, pick up Nyro's and add them neatly to the line. I take a few running steps and a long slide in my heavy wool socks. I do that a few more times until I'm at the window. The white blanket on Franklin Street is thicker still. The snow is coming down hard.

Nyro goes to the wall and stands in front of an enormous and elaborate gold-framed mirror.

Chry pulls off her black lizard cowboy boots and socks and leaves them where she's standing. She looks left and right, then executes a series of perfect cartwheels across the space until she's at the windows with me. Dare looks up from the fire which is just taking hold.

Nyro spreads his arms wide and takes hold of either side of the mirror. He lifts it off the wall and then staggers under its weight. The physics of his thin, wiry body and the large, heavy breakable object he's balancing over it are not promising. He makes his way toward Dare who jumps up to help him. Together they walk the mirror over near the fire and put it down on the floor.

"Who's up for swim?" Nyro calls, and when Chry bounds across the room and sits cross-legged next to Dare between the fire and Nyro's lake, I wonder if she remembers the last time Nyro offered her a swim.

The fire spits and crackles. "Boy Scout," I accuse Dare.

"Troop of one," he says.

I'm too tired to ask what that means. I stretch out on the floor next to Nyro's lake, put my chin on the small tower of my fists and stare at the fire.

Chry slides her legs out from under her and lies on her stomach too, head on her arms.

I wonder how long Nyro will let us be. If only it could be enough for him for us to lie by the fire, silent, with the snow falling on the city. I wonder how Dare can afford to live here. We don't make much money now. Someday. Someday soon it's going to be us doing deals. Going all over the city with our customers and expense accounts. Me anyway. Where he's going is his business.

"No, no, no, no, no, *no*," says Nyro.

Chry and I look up at him with glassy stares.

"*No*," he says again. And in a series of leaps and strides he disappears into his bedroom and returns with a handful of small brown bottles which he sets up like toy soldiers on the edge of the mirror.

"Time to get happy, campers." He picks up one of the bottles and unscrews the black lid with his thumb and forefinger like a surgeon. He taps the white powder onto the mirror in a pile, then opens his wallet, takes out a credit card and a hundred-dollar bill. He lays the bill on Lake Nyro's gilded edge and chops the powder with his card. *Chop, chop, chop. Chop, chop, chop* until the pile is flat. Then scrape, scrape, scrape until the pile is a series of lines. *Scrape, scrape, scrape* until the lines are neat and equal. He licks the edge of the card, runs his tongue along his top gum, and puts the card back in his wallet. He picks up the hundred-dollar bill and rolls it into a tight tube. Holding one nostril closed with his forefinger, he puts the hundred-dollar straw to his nose and pulls a line of coke up into it. He throws his head back with a loud sniff and takes in a second line through the other nostril. Then he points to me. When I've done my two lines, I hand the rolled bill to Dare who does his two and hands it to Chry.

"Still snowing, ha," says Chry when it's her turn.

We go around again, finish the lines and watch Nyro pour another vial onto the mirror.

"Nobody's going anywhere," says Nyro.

"Snowed in," says Dare.

Nyro jumps up. His skinny catapult frame is powered by the nonstop ideas that run through his head. A series of leaps lands him at the stereo setup where he starts pulling tapes out of the rack. "Fiore, where's that new one you made?" he demands.

"It's in there. Jesus, Danny, you don't have to rip the place apart."

Nyro crouches at the deck and pulls out the tape, inspects it and puts it back in, presses rewind. "Up, up, up," he commands.

We jump up, a combination of coke and Nyro's contagious kinetics.

"Ready? Ready?" he shouts and looks over at us to make sure our hearts are in it. Our hearts are in it.

"We're ready!" Chry and I shout back.

"Yeah, Danny, come on man, press play," Dare shouts across the room and laughs. He looks at us, shaking his head. "He has to control everything," he says and laughs again.

Nyro presses play. Out comes the music. Loud as loud. We dance and jump around the room in a crazy, happy frenzy. The whole tape through, songs I know and songs I don't know, all different but all with the same up and down beat.

"CHRY," shouts Nyro over the music when she nearly falls into his snowy lake. "Don't break my lake."

Chry laughs and pogos as close as she can to the mirror.

"Don't break my lake," he shouts again, and she laughs again. She stops jumping around and stands on tiptoe at the edge of mirror and puts her arms out like she's going to dive in. Dare, who's nearby, plants his feet and grabs her sleeve as she loses her balance. Nyro and I stop jumping, a game of freeze dance, except the music is still going loud. We are frozen in a moment, this wide loft, with floor-to-ceiling windows looking out on the snowy city, Nyro and I immobile where we stand, Chry and Dare in a grip of either safe on shore or drowning, Madonna is singing *Holi—da—ay*.

They fall. Dare falls to the side but Chry is laid out on the mirror.

Nyro and I try to pull first Chry, who is conscious but feels like dead weight, then Dare, who is light and alive, up to their feet.

"Fuck," says Nyro. The mirror is cracked and splintered though the pieces are still all in place.

I ask if it was expensive. It looks expensive.

"What the fuck do you think? Everything is expensive." Nyro throws his arm out wide. Everything.

Chry is making an *ahhhh, ahhhh, ahh* noise and whipping her left hand back and forth. She's shaking her head like she's trying to empty her brains out of it.

"What the fuck is the matter with you?" screams Nyro.

"My fucking hand is what's the matter." Her words are garbled. "And my mouth." She holds the back of her uninjured hand to her lips and when she takes it away there's a mouth print of blood on it. Feeling it pool, she cups her hand underneath her chin to catch the small gush. "I cut my lip," she says. Her teeth are red.

"Come here then, and put some fucking ice on it," says Nyro.

Dare goes to the stereo and shuts down the music.

Chry holds her left hand tenderly in her right, puts them both to her chin to catch the blood from her mouth.

Nyro takes a handful of ice from the freezer and puts it in a delicate china soup bowl he's pulled from one of the cupboards. "Suck this," he says, giving her an ice cube, "and put your hand in here. Easy, though. Don't break the fucking dish."

Behind me, the fire cracks and sputters.

There are two things Chry needs her left hand for, temping and playing the bass.

I can feel Nyro's helplessness from across the room. Dare's impenetrability. Chry's grief.

"Come on," says Dare to Chry.

10

The bed in Dare's room is on the floor, just a mattress and box spring, but neatly made with a Black Watch plaid comforter and a folded Hudson's Bay point blanket laid across the bottom. The only other thing in the space is a gold-leafed Louis XV dresser, with a television on it.

"According to Danny, it was here before they built the room," says Dare, referring to the gaudy monstrosity. "It's trapped now, too big to fit through the door, too valuable to chop for firewood. The TV's mine though. Mets."

Chry has thoughts, ironic thoughts like the ones she's been battling for all this time and thoughts that have felt until this very moment like a lost cause.

Her left hand is turning colors. Dare pulls back the covers on the bed and helps her into the clean white sheets. He lays her head which, as the zazz of the coke wears off, feels heavy on the pillow, though the pillow is soft, a feather nest for the weight of everything. He brings her injured hand up over the comforter and then tucks the comforter around her other shoulder, snugging her in.

Dare sits on the edge of the bed, takes off his wristwatch and crewneck sweater, unbuckles his belt. He unbuttons his Levi's, slides them off and out from under him and loosely folds them, putting them on top of the sweater, the watch on top of that. Chry stares as he stands up in his white T-shirt and chambray boxers and walks across the room to turn off the light. The parts of him are possibly unremarkable but the whole is breathtaking. She's in love with the way he moves.

The space darkens but not all the way—the snowy dawn's white light coming through the windows on Franklin Street leaks into Dare's room from above where the walls end. Chry turns her eyes from Dare as he moves back to the bed and stares up at the milky morning light coming on, at the iron truss and wooden beams that hold up the ceiling.

Dare lies down on the bed near the edge, his back to Chry, and pulls his side of the covers up over him.

For Chry, Dare's stillness is more arresting than his motion. The way his sand-colored hair meets the curve of the back of his neck annihilates the last vestiges of her senses. She is grateful to the pain in her hand, which is grounding her to something she almost remembers. The idea of a person in a body, maybe. She doesn't know why she's grateful to the pain. She rarely cries, despite or maybe because of her name, but more than the trip to Mandolin Brothers in Staten Island, more than the snowy wind of the New York harbor as they crossed on the ferry, more than the pricey remnants of the wine and pot and prosecco and coke, more than all of New York City with its endless offerings of music and mess and people and excitement, more than any of it, is the graceful body of this beautiful boy beside her. And more, more, more than that is her longing to touch him.

Nyro grabs my wrist and twists. The snow has finally stopped, and the next day's light is coming in. We'd been stretched out on the floor between the fire and the cracked mirror, not saying much of anything ever since Chry and Dare evaporated.

But then Nyro, who, as far as I've seen, operates on a kind of limitless trajectory, gathered up the remaining vials of coke and stashed them away. I'm happy to see he has a stopping point. All night he's been doing whatever he wants, with me, Chry, and Dare just along for the ride. Witnesses not friends. Maybe it's the new day, the white morning light, but I see something else. It's possible the night of dinner and dancing has all this time been plain old hospitality. I hadn't thought of that.

The wrist twisting forces me halfway to my feet.

"Ow, stop it, that hurts," I say.

"Don't be such a baby. I just want to fuck you."

"Very romantic."

He's holding my wrist hard. I twist in the opposite direction he is pulling so he won't break it, but then I let him pull me up to him. He kisses me. So tender, it sends a rip of shock through my spine. Until now he's struck me as a bag of synapses without any particular purpose except to keep firing. This still could be true, I pull in close to feel them, this neural network of action. If I kiss this soft mouth long enough, I will know every movement he's ever made. I will know his entire history. And because this is my desire, I kiss and kiss and kiss him. And he gives it away, all of it.

His hand is no longer on my wrist but moving down my back in unison with the other one. The hands asking even as the neurons are offering. Alms. Alms.

He steps back to see me. Steel blue eyes, bright pink cheeks, black curly wreath of hair. He nods, takes my wrist again but this time he doesn't squeeze, and I don't wrench or twist.

"Only just moved in," he says when we enter his bedroom. Except for a queen-size sleigh bed shoved into a corner, an unmade jumble of sheets and blankets, the room is filled with boxes. On one of the walls is a framed lithograph, signed and numbered.

I walk over to it get a closer look at the litho. It's a woman and a man in a kind of dreamscape like maybe they're underwater. "Marc Chagall."

"She looks like you."

"The eyes are blue," I say.

"The hair, though. I noticed it when we met on New Year's."

"The color of an old penny."

"So. It's pretty."

"They used to say, *Seawater eyes and hair the color of an old penny.*"

"Where do you come from where they talk like that?"

"Nowhere." I say, and that's the God's honest truth.

"Come on," says Nyro. We wind our way through the maze of boxes to the edge of the bed. He lifts my shirt over my head and takes off my bra, again he takes a step back and looks. "You really are the girl in the painting. Maybe you're from the sea."

"They say my mother crawled out of the Hudson River and left me on the altar of the Dutch Reformed Church."

"I like that. Better."

"Better than what?"

"Being from known people."

"Okay."

Nyro shoves the jumble of blankets to the bottom of the bed, and we lie on the pale blue sheet. He takes off what's left of my clothes. "In the painting I'm grabbing your ass."

"Is that you?"

"Why not me?"

"Could you not grab?"

"No. No. No grabbing."

And there is none. He touches every part of me until I cannot be still. He keeps on while I touch every part of him.

After all, we sleep. We sleep all day Sunday. In the late afternoon, we get up and slowly get dressed.

I take a long last look at the Marc Chagall. "What's this chicken thing with a girl's head doing in the picture. And what's the red bird?" I ask.

Nyro shrugs. "It's a story from *Arabian Nights*. "Kamar Al-Zaman and the Jewellers Wife, Then He Spent The Night With Her Embracing and Clipping…'"

"Clipping what?" I laugh.

Nyro shrugs again. "That's what it's called.

"Valuable? Must be," I say.

"Yeah, yeah. I guess. It was my dad's."

"Didn't he want it anymore?"

"Nah, he's gone."

"Gone where?"

"Gone off the George Washington Bridge," says Nyro. I'd forgotten. He'd told us his father had died when we were on the ferry though he hadn't mentioned how. "You probably saw it in the news."

Dare comes into the room with a glass of ice water in each

hand, a bottle of Tylenol pinned to his side with his arm. Chry stirs.

"Hey," says Dare.

"Hey yourself." Chry sits up, her head and hand throbbing.

Dare moves his elbow out, lets the Tylenol bottle drop on the bed. He hands her one of the glasses of water and puts the other on the floor next to the bed. He squeezes the cap, unscrews it.

"Proof you're not a child," says Chry.

"Rock solid," says Dare, taps two tablets into his palm and hands them to her. Taps two more out and takes them himself.

"Chrysanthi Risk." Chry holds out her good hand to shake, an introduction.

"Darius Fiore. Nice to meet you."

"We've spent more nights together than days."

Dare nods, he's noticed that too.

It hasn't been that long since Chry told him she loves him and he ran away. It seems like she should regret it, but she doesn't. He's here now. She can't detect any desire to reject her. There must be something to that.

"Good thing it's the left one. I mean, if you're a righty."

Chry holds up her injured hand, dark purple and swollen from her ring finger to her outer wrist. Her pinky is fat and tight. "I am a righty, but I play the bass so it's not great. And I'm already a shitty typist. Zero for two."

"Can you move your wrist?"

Chry swivels her wrist. It's not broken. She can feel in the way he shifts his body that they are having the same thought: This is the second time since they've met that he's had to think about taking her to the emergency room. "I'm all right," she says.

He nods, believing her. "Stay here. I'm gonna shower." He goes to the enormous—and even more hideous by daylight—dresser and pulls out a fresh T-shirt, boxers, Levi's. The room has its own bathroom and like the other rooms the walls don't go all way to the ceiling. Dare disappears into it and closes the door behind him. Possibly locks it.

Chry hears the shower. Considers whether Dare's *stay here* means don't leave the apartment or don't come into the shower with me. Realistically, both, which is not her first choice, but not terrible. Somewhere between her mind and body, she's again grateful for the pain in her hand. It's a relief from her desire. And from that same place, another truth—*that's fucked up.*

The shower goes on for a while. Chry watches the steam rise above the walls. She waits until she can't wait anymore. She leaves the bed and knocks on the bathroom door loud enough for Dare to hear over the running water.

"Yeah?"

"I have to pee." And here they are again, reliving old times.

The water goes off. Dare opens the door, holding his clothes, towel around his waist and gives her an *after you* arm sweep. They brush by each other in the threshold.

The bathroom is marble and modern. A shrine to resting, relieving, and improving the body, Chry thinks. She washes her face with her one good hand, shutting her eyes to the sting-ing soap as she massages yesterday's mascara off her lashes. She looks through the cupboards and shelves for mouthwash but finds none. She's tempted to use Dare's toothbrush and toothpaste but that seems wrong. She opens the door, Dare is dressed and toweling his wet head.

"Toothbrush?" she asks.

"Just mine. You can use it."

Considering they kissed half the night on Pier 17 not that long ago, this should be expected but Chry worries that was more downed tequila than desire to swap fluids. She hasn't for-gotten the New Year's Day feeling of being sent away by him. She won't chance that again, but he said she could use it, so she does.

Dare comes back as she's finishing.

"Shave," he says. "I need to feel better."

"Does it help?"

Dare shrugs. "It doesn't hurt."

"That's a pretty fancy setup."

"It's a family thing. Handed down a couple of generations," says Dare, referring to the gold shaving mirror with a cup and hanging brush.

"Is it real gold?"

"I think so, yeah. I found it in the attic back home, and I liked it. I don't think there's anyone who cares about it enough to count it missing. It was kind of hard to learn to use it." He opens a drawer, takes out the matching straight razor, a stainless-steel blade that flips out from a gold handle, and lays it next to the sink. He takes the brush out of the stand and runs it under the faucet.

Chry is a fascinated audience of one. "What's it made of?"

"Badger bristles."

"Badger bristles," Chry repeats.

"Yeah." He shrugs but warms to her interest. "You have to get it wet." He takes the mug off the stand and shows her what's inside, a puck-shaped piece of shaving soap. "You have to work it," he says, and then uses the brush to make a foamy lather. Chry watches him cover his face and neck with the thick lather. Her head hurts and her hand hurts, but she is content sitting on the counter watching Dare shave. When he's finished with the straight edge, he rinses it, dries it, folds it shut and lays it on the counter.

Chry picks it up, flips it open, folds it shut, flips it open. "A gold knife."

"Not really a knife."

"I think it would qualify."

"For what."

"St. James Day. On July 25th if you cut chicory with a gold knife at noon or midnight, you can open locks, locks and doors, locked doors."

"What's chicory?"

"Cornflowers, they're these blue flowers that grow on the side of the road, up where we celebrate St. James Day anyway."

"Where's that."

"Western New York.

"Oh, well, I'm from Vestal."

"Yeah, yeah, we pass by there."

"Never saw the use of hanging around."

"Mina says the same thing about her town."

Chry holds the folded blade, feels its heft, admires the deadliness locked up inside but made available with the slightest pressure of her thumb. She hands it back to Dare, wondering if that's what drew him to this more complicated way of shaving. There's blood from a fresh nick on the underside of his chin. As he takes the blade, she pulls him close and with the tip of her tongue licks the trickle from the side of his neck where it's about to drop onto his shirt up to the tiny puncture from where it came. She kisses the spot, licks her lips. Pulls her head back to see. "Still bleeding," she says and touches her tongue to it again. Dare lets her, then carefully pulls away.

SPRING

11

Chry's hand wasn't broken but it was badly bruised. We named it ROY G. BIV for the way it was determined to show us every color. As Roy's colors emerged from the initial deep purple, they also went from dark to light. Over the weeks, patterns and designs surfaced and receded. By mid-March it was seaweed green, then a pale chartreuse, like the sky sometimes when it's trying to rain.

By April Fool's Day it was a pale-yellow patch.

Chry's hand wasn't broken but it was damaged to where she couldn't play her bass and she couldn't type for almost three weeks. Somewhere between pale green and dark yellow, she was able to return to the typing pool party which is what she calls her temp life. The agency was glad to have her back, accommodating her with mostly non-ringing phone gigs. Her hand was still stiff. Though she could still play her regular bass, she'd regressed so much on the fretless bass that playing Jaco's harmonics were almost the original million miles away as when she first removed the frets from the instrument. This depressed her.

The subway car we're riding rattles and hums. There are plenty of seats but Chry wants to stand so I do too. We hold on to the straps, surfing the sways of the Number One train all the way to Christopher Street. There we get off and walk through the sweet sunny morning to Washington Square Park. The shops in the Village are mostly still shuttered but we find a deli, and each get a bagel with cream cheese, lox, tomato, and red onion. Hot cups of coffee in blue and white cups with gold lettering, *We are happy to serve you.*

Chry and I, white bakery bags in one hand, coffee in the other, make our way to Washington Square Park. We walk through the big arch on purpose to be auspicious, to the wide round fountain in the center of the park. It's dry, still too early in the season for water. We sit down on the top step of the circled tiers surrounding the dormant fountain with our coffee and bagels and watch the park wake up, feel the light breeze, the air warming with the smell of budding trees and taxi fumes.

Speed chess, pot, hot dogs, pretzels, skateboarders, bike tricks, salvation. It's all on offer in Washington Square Park on a sunny March Saturday, but we're here to find Jaco Pastorius.

Chry pushes her hands into the pockets of her jean jacket. A fool's errand, she supposes, but she has to try. Jaco's been hanging around Washington Square Park. That's what she hears. She knows someone who knows someone who swears they spoke to him. Spoke to him! The guy she knows plays in a band with this other guy who says he saw him. It was really him. Not just Jaco, but his bass too, the 1962 Fender Jazz Bass, three-color sunburst design, the *Bass of Doom*, Chry tells me. Jaco in Washington Square Park, in filthy clothes asking for money, the Bass of Doom strapped to his back. Impossible. But the guy, Chry's friend's friend says no, it's true, it was Jaco, it was his bass.

I don't remember the exact moment Chry's interest became an obsession. I know she came back from summer break junior year with a Fender Jazz Bass. She'd read how Jaco pried off the frets of his '62 with the first thing he could find, a butter knife. There'd been some jazz in the rotation of our dorm-room turntable. I let Chry run the music; they were mostly her records anyway. Over time, I noticed it was more and more jazz and then more and more Jaco and then it was Chry playing Jaco all the time, mainlining it into her veins.

She told me she heard Jaco in her waking head and her dreaming head, she heard him in other people's music, in the movies and on TV but it was the dreaming head that wouldn't let go. It's what pushed her into wanting to learn to play like him, see him play, go to wherever he was.

She hadn't accomplished any of it, so here we are, waiting for Jaco. I didn't ask what she would do if she saw him. It was impossible to think about. My hope is that catching a glimpse will be enough.

There's a band setting up in the dry fountain. Chry straightens her spine, puts her neck forward, and stares. She lifts her sunglasses up to her forehead, stares, then puts them back on. "That him?" I hope it is for her sake, but I also can't help feeling I'd rather it wasn't. Here's Chry, this girl who wants for nothing, but still she wants for everything. Her need is a dark well. There are times I want all of what she has, clothes—no offense to my mom—luscious powerful parents, an ocean, a lake, a river…St. James Day.

"No, but…"

"But what?"

"I think I know that guy."

We stare across the wide empty fountain at four Ramones-looking guys in jeans and motorcycle jackets setting up their band. One is putting together a drum kit, the others unwrap guitars, untangle wires, set up mics and amps.

"Which one, they all look kind of the same."

"The one over there, on the left. I met him when I worked at the *Post.*"

I lean forward and squint. "Is he a reporter? He doesn't look like one."

"What does a reporter look like?"

"I don't know, not that."

"Oh my god, Mina, you should have seen him the morning we met. He had this giant hook around his neck, a giant hook with a fat wooden handle, around his neck."

"Murder by day?"

"I know, right? No, he's a fish guy. You know, the ones that work down at the market by the Seaport. I think that hook is for grabbing crates and stuff."

"He the one who hosed you down?" Even though Chry hadn't been practicing her bass until recently, she was still telling me her life in detail from the top bunk. "I mean how many guys with steel hooks draped around their neck do you meet on the street?"

"Down there, all of them." Chry laughs. "But, yeah, that guy."

Soft air ripples the new green leaves and washes over us, in waves, again and again as we watch the band set up.

We've been here a while and there's been no Jaco sighting, but a band is setting up with four guys who are not the Ramones, but who look like them, and the weather is fine. "We might as well see if they're any good," I say.

"Yeah, not to mention we haven't seen Jaco yet."

"You know we might not see him, Chry."

"I know," she says, but I don't think she does know.

"Well, you wanna go say hi before they start playing?"

"No, because what if they suck, then we're trapped."

Not dumb. Chry thinks of these things.

We watch them finish setting up, as the park comes ever more to life. A girl in a T-shirt with the sleeves cut off and raccoon eyes walking on the step below, murmurs, "Weed, coke, X," without looking at us. We watch her continue her loop around the edge of the fountain, not seeming to have any takers.

"I wonder if she sees that cop," says Chry, pointing to an officer standing near the band.

Sure enough, she swerves and climbs up out of the fountain and heads in the opposite direction.

"Do you think he's going to let them play?" I ask as the cop moves in on them.

Chry shrugs. "It's a free country."

The cop takes a few steps back, crosses his arms and watches as the band kicks in. A small group begins to gather as people in the park gravitate to the music.

"Pretty good," says Chry, her head moving up and down.

We walk across the dry fountain to join the crowd, making our way through so we are right in front. The one Chry knows looks up from his guitar and recognizes her. He smiles and gives her a head bob hello. She gives him a heartfelt wave.

They play a mix of soul, jazz, punk. The sound mingles with the breeze and fills the park. The cop is still here, off to the side, moving to the music like the rest of us, clapping and cheering after each song too.

There's an open guitar case in front of the band. Everyone is throwing in dollars and change. Chry steps forward, throws in a few dollars and I do the same. Vinnie, Vincent, Vin smiles at us—her.

The crowd changes, people drift in and out, some throw money in the case, others just listen for a moment and move on, but Chry and I stay until they stop playing. People dissipate until it's only us and the cop who strolls over in the way New York City cops know how to stroll.

"Pretty good, eh?" We agree. "Know any of them?" Chry points and the cop says, "Vinnie?"

"Yeah, Vinnie. I only met him once but he, uh, helped me out."

"Oh, he's a sweethaht," he says and points to his name badge. "DiSalvo. Anthony. Vin's my baby brother."

"Tony!" shouts Vinnie, coming toward us. "Tony, whadja think?" They hug each other, tight and long. "Whadja think?" he says again.

"You guys sound fantastic. I wish Mom could see it." He turns to us. "I mean, fantastic, right, girls?"

Vinnie lets go of his brother.

"Vinnie, Vincent, Vin," says Chry, "we never were properly introduced." She tells him our names.

"Vinnie," he says. "We decided, remember?"

"Vinnie, how long have you been playing? You guys are really good."

Vinnie looks over at his brother, who says, "Since he could hold a guitar."

There's a long silence which I break by telling the brothers how Chry plays bass. "Yeah? You in a band?" says Vinnie.

Chry tells him her band and the places she plays. Places no one's ever heard of, but Vinnie knows them all. There is a lot of talk between them about guitars, Mandolin Brothers, Staten Island, Chry's two Fender Jazz Basses, the one she plays out and the one she's taken the frets off. "We came to find Jaco," says Chry. "We heard he might be here."

"Heard that too. A friend of mine says he shows up here and West Fourth, you know, the courts there. Says he's a mess, like a bum in rags. I don't believe it. I for sure never seen him. How about you, Tony?"

Tony nods in agreement with the story but says, "No, never seen him."

Chry looks at the ground. She is capable of shame and I think she feels it now, realizing suddenly she came to gawk at a genius down on his luck. She hangs her head even lower as the reality of the morning's search for Jaco sinks in. Then she picks up her head and with wide, sincere blue eyes says, "Jesus, I hope I never see him. I mean my main hope is to see him, but to see him play, in a club or something, not hanging around like a bum in the park."

"Ain't that the truth," says Vinnie.

"Jesus," Chry says again.

"Listen. Listen," says Tony. "I'm in this area a lot. Always comin' through here with the cah. How 'bout I keep an eye out?"

Chry's chest fills so that it elevates her head in a move so dramatic it makes Vinnie laugh. "Yes."

"Here's my cahd," he says and hands one to each of us from a pile he takes from his shirt pocket. "Look, call me anytime. Honestly, you girls running around town. Things happen. Sometimes things happen you can't go to your parents with, ya know? You can call me if you need some help." The card has his name, Anthony DiSalvo, and precinct, address, phone on one side. I turn it over and the other side is in Chinese. Tony says, "I work this stretch through Chinatown." He pulls out his cop pad and pen and asks us our number so he can call us with any updates on Jaco. He hands it to Chry who writes down our phone number and our first names and hands it back.

"Vinnie, Vincent, Vin," she says.

"Okay, ya gotta stop with that."

"Vinnie."

"Yes."

"Thanks for helping me out before, and for, you know, the handkerchief."

"Ahh," he says, waving it away, "fuhgetit. But hey, I gotta a favor to ask you."

Chry nods. "Sure."

"I'm looking for a bass player. Gonna do an all-night ferry run this Saturday, just me, not these guys, and maybe…you? Whaddya say, make some coin?"

12

Chry is short on cash so when Vinnie told her there was money to be made playing all night on the Staten Island Ferry, she said she might like to do that. When he asked her what songs she could play, she borrowed the bass his bandmate was packing up and auditioned right there in Washington Square Park.

She'd been scraping around for money the last few weeks while Roy the multicolored hand wasn't letting her play gigs or take temp jobs. I'd given her my half of the rent and then was surprised to hear her talking to her uncle on the phone, asking him if she could pay him in a few weeks. When she got off the phone, I asked her why not at least send my half and she said she's using that to live on. This pissed me off—she's the one whose family has fountains of money.

I almost never talk to Dare about Chry, though I know she wishes I would. She wishes I'd find more ways to bring them together. I try not to hold the things she doesn't understand against her, and she doesn't understand her love longings are not equal to the person I need to be at work.

But the day after I found out she was living off me for the time being, I did talk to Dare about her. I told him she took my half of the rent and kept it instead of paying her uncle who we sublet from. Dare said that's how it is with Nyro.

Nyro's mom, or the business or whatever, owns the Franklin Street loft, and Nyro lives there for free. Dare pays rent to Nyro and Nyro keeps it. He was embarrassed to tell me this and I know why. We ate our lunch in silence for a while. Then he said, "Why is life like a shit sandwich?" I told him I didn't know, and he said, "The more bread you have, the less shit you have to eat."

I laughed and then wanted to say something else, something

about what things cost and how no two people ever seem to have to pay the same price, but I didn't know how to talk about it without bringing up specifics about Chry and I'd betrayed her enough. She was losing her mind for the long string of days she'd been waiting for Dare to call.

Dare and I fell back to our silence, eating our for-the-moment non-shit sandwiches in the cool, dark conference room, the morning deals checked and ready to be sent to the back office in a pile between us.

When we finished Dare said, "I guess we better go rewrite the board," and we gathered the remnants of our lunches and headed back out to the bright lights and the low afternoon hum of the trading floor.

Saturday night, Chry and I are on our way to Staten Island. Again. The ferry's nearly empty but Vinnie said not to worry, this is when people are going into Manhattan; later, after the clubs close, the crowd will be coming from the opposite direction. Chry is playing the bass with frets, which is the only one she really knows how to play. I'd come to help her by carrying the amp on the subway and then across Battery Park to the terminal where Vinnie was waiting.

When he saw us, he slung his guitar over his back and said, "Gimme that." I handed him the amp and was tempted to turn around, get right back on the Number One train, and to West Seventy-First Street. I didn't want to ride the Staten Island Ferry all night. And here was Vinnie, with his shoulder-length dark hair and soft brown eyes looking safe as Christmas, but according to Chry, he was wearing an iron hook around his neck the day they met. I don't think he's a serial killer or anything, just everyone knows the mob runs the fish market and he *is* from Staten Island. Isn't that where they all live? I don't know what constitutes a friend exactly, but I suspect not letting Chry spend the night on the Staten Island Ferry with a fishmonger musician, no matter how sweet his face, comes under the category of friendship.

We're on the top floor of the *Gov. Herbert H. Lehman* ferry. It's identical in every way to the *John F. Kennedy*, down to the cruddy, unhelpful-looking lifejackets in the ceiling. Chry and Vinnie are set up in the same place we'd seen the guy playing "Walk of Life" when we were snowed in on Franklin Street. They took a while to warm up; we were almost past the Statue of Liberty and it was still sounding pretty rough, but soon after that they caught on to each other's groove, and by the time the boat was ramming the slip on Staten Island, they sounded good. They were growing confident with each other. I could hear the trepidation falling away and the trust building. They got better and better as the ferry filled with riders on their way to the city, and then as it was making its way back to Staten Island, it was clear this was going to work. They were throwing off something contagious. Passengers were pulling change and stray dollars from their pockets and dropping it into Vinnie's guitar case.

I'm sitting by a window, listening to Chry's joyful state. I've been her audience for such a long time now, I can hear how she's feeling through the music. I'm relieved to be watching the lights and sights of a mild spring night on the harbor from inside instead of on a deck bench in a snowstorm or worse, leaning over the rail at Nyro's insistence. This boat, the *Gov. Herbert H. Lehman*, and the one we'd been on that cold afternoon, the *John F. Kennedy*, are the only boats I've ever been on. After four years of rooming together in college and now being on West Seventy-First Street, Chry thinks she knows everything about me. She doesn't and I don't blame her. There are things I keep to myself. Like the fact I can't swim. I can't swim, so this favor I'm doing for her is a bigger favor than she understands. I thought that one time back and forth would be it, but here I am signed up for an entire night. In fairness to my mother, who could be blamed for not teaching me to swim, I have always been terrified of drowning. She did what she could. Our two-bedroom Cape was clean and bright, with organized drawers and a little bookshelf in my room for treasures from the trips to the library she'd squeeze in between shifts. The sheets on my bed were always fresh and tucked tight with a red, white, and blue patchwork quilt. The room had a bright blue carpet and fresh white curtains with a ruffle. I was always safe in that house. And even though the cliffs of the Hudson River were a short walk to the end of our road, I was safe from it too, so high up and with a mother who made it clear that looking out over the vast ravine was awe-inspiring and also a very different thing than actually submerging a body in that dangerous river.

My mother, Rebecca Berg, fixer of cuts and breaks and 105 fevers and anything else that came through the Hudson Valley Hospital emergency room, saver of abandoned babies, sewer of red, white, and blue quilts, Becky Berg, keeper of secrets I didn't need to know, told me only one thing about the day I was found on the altar of the Dutch Reformed Church. She said I nearly drowned. I wonder why she chose this one horrific fact. Was it the only fact she knew or was it the least worst one? I wasn't found in a basket bundled in a pink silk blanket whose monogram would someday reveal my true lineage the way lost babies in books are found. I was found eyes closed, lips white, blue umbilical cord still attached. I was found half-submerged in water and just about dead in the baptismal font.

Becky Berg is a believer, so she says the story differently than how I receive it. She says I was kept alive by the holy water in that font and brought to her, who'd been waiting for me, a woman who'd been praying all along for this very arrival.

We ride and ride the *Gov. Herbert H. Lehman*. Out and back, out and back, until I don't want to know how many trips this night will take. I close my eyes and listen to the sounds of the boat, to Chry and Vinnie who are getting better and better as the hours wear on. Their playlist repeats after about ten songs or so, but the music gets tighter. Back and forth across the harbor we travel. The Twin Towers recede and loom, recede and loom. The Statue of Liberty, torchless in her scaffolding prison, stands by.

After midnight, the ferry only runs on the hour but Chry

and Vinnie keep going, waiting for the late, drunk, and generous crowd returning from a night in the city.

I fall asleep, dreaming nothing. For how long I can't say, but a commotion sits down next to me—loud talking, the thud of bodies flopping on the bench, and all with a boozy smell so strong it gags me to consciousness. Awake and asleep, I'm so disoriented I almost shout, but my voice stops in my throat as I comprehend the two large men next to me. They're too close. I keep my eyes closed, not wanting to engage. Chry and Vinnie are still playing, same as they have been all night. I want to believe they won't let anything happen to me. Chry at the very least.

I open my eyes but keep them straight ahead. Stiff with fear and already up against the window, I can't move away. I want to call for Chry but don't want to let these guys jostling next to me know I'm afraid. I close my eyes, try to fully wake up as I pretend to sleep; maybe these two thugs will find somebody else to sit too close to.

The hot boozy breath is nearer still. I try not to let my eyes flutter, try to keep up the ruse that I'm sleeping and don't want to engage. Then I hear the same word I heard New Year's Eve in Grand Central Station, downstairs in front of the Oyster Bar.

Sirena Fuggitiva.

"Jesus, Tony. Give her some space."

"Ray, ya gotta see her though."

"You're scaring the crap out of her."

"Sweethaht, it's okay, it's me, Tony, Vinnie's brother."

I flash open my eyes, simultaneously relieved and furious. "You scared the shit out of me!" I say and give him a push on his rock-hard arm with both palms.

The other guy pulls and I push until there's enough room between us for me to believe they're just saying hello and not actually accosting me. After we're situated, with them at a socially acceptable distance, the second guy leans across Tony, and says, "I'm Ray, the other brother. Sorry for the intrusion. Overserved and overfriendly but mostly harmless."

Ray is a big guy, same as Tony, but leaner, less a body builder than a runner. They are undeniably brothers, looking more like each other than either of them like Vinnie. They have the same friendly eyes as Vinnie, aquiline noses, large talkative mouths, but unlike Vinnie's rocker hair, these two have a short clean-cut look like maybe they're both cops.

"Mina," I say and smile because after scaring the shit out of me, I feel safer than I have all night. Mostly I trust cops. My mom's years of ER stories are filled with a thousand small mercies, and anyway it was the cops who resuscitated me that first day when I was left to drown in a pool of holy water. I get why not everyone does, but I do and here's one, maybe two of them, keeping me company on my all-night voyage.

"See," Tony says to Ray. "What'd I tell ya. Just like Nonna says." His speech is loud and slurred. The way he's referring to me in front of me is crazy rude but he's not scary, just drunk.

"Tony, chill man."

"Look, it's her. And now here she is on the ferry," Tony shouts, then says quietly, "Pretty coincidental, don't you think?"

"Ton—"

"Sirena Fuggitiva, Sirena Fuggitiva!," he shouts again.

"I'm sorry," says Ray. He shakes his head and laughs.

"It's okay." And it is because Tony has spoken this word I've been wondering about since I heard it on New Year's Eve. And the way he's saying it to me is so worshipful I can't help but enjoy it a little bit. "Why is he calling me that?"

"Sirena, she's, uh, she's like a story…"

"Sirena!" says Tony.

"Tony, shhhh," Ray says to him and then to me, "It's a story they tell about a mermaid that guards the harbor. She lives underneath the Verrazano Bridge, in The Narrows there. That's all. If you acknowledge her, she will keep you safe but if you ignore her, she'll destroy you."

Ray tells me this with a mixture of embarrassment and belief, a lilt of the outer boroughs in his accent, the Rs not quite making their full execution at the end of his words but not as heavy as Tony and Vinnie.

"So why is he calling *me* that?"

Ray shrugs. "White skin, green eyes, red hair, the way you were sleeping, you looked a little mythological, you looked— look—the way they describe her."

Tony drops his head back and closes his eyes.

Ray and I look at him like a set of parents watching their baby drifting off to sleep. Chry and Vinnie play on. Nothing about the hours they've been at it suggests any kind of waning.

"Come on, let's get him situated," Ray says as Tony's head lolls back awkwardly. We get up and with maximum effort arrange him so he's laid out on the bench.

"You think it's okay?"

"Yeah, he's a cop. No one will give him a hard time and I mean—" He waves his arm to indicate the place is nearly empty.

"You a cop too?"

He shakes his head.

"They were saying that New Year's Eve."

"What?"

"That. Sirena. But whispered. At the Oyster Bar. But in the air, you know? No one was speaking, it was coming from, I don't know, the walls."

"Yeah, New Year's, that's right, yeah."

"What's right?"

"Oh, they do that."

"What?"

"I'll tell you."

13

I let Ray DiSalvo take me out through the heavy sliding door to the upper deck, to the same side of the harbor Nyro had insisted we see, the side that looks out toward the Verrazano Bridge. The bridge's suspended steel cables light the night in upside-down arcing swoops. The road the cables support, which crosses The Narrows between Brooklyn and Staten Island, is lit up too. The air is a biting, salty wind.

As much as I don't want to be on this deck, it's a relief to get away from Chry's playing. I'm tired of it. Being on this boat all night, even though I slept for part of it, has exhausted me. It was too much to ask. And now this, the outside deck in the cold night, also is too much to ask. My fear of drowning is as much a part of me as my arm.

Ray offers me his coat, but I tell him no thanks. We sit down on the bench, our sides touching. The wind comes at us in a series of slaps which I receive like the Sunday morning sermons I only ever half-believed. Always with my mother. She'd leave purified, the feel of the communion wafer still on her tongue. I'd leave with the same unnerved feeling, both delivered and furious. Ray takes his coat off and drapes it over both of us, ignoring my wanting not to be warm.

"Not a cop. Not in the fish business," I say.

"Not a cop. Not in the fish business."

"Not telling?"

"Don't feel like it," he says. "How about you?"

"Eurodollars." He tilts his head like he's getting ready to ask me a question which I'm used to. No one knows what Eurodollars are, which is the main reason I say it.

He nods, noncommittal.

"You know what a Eurodollar is?"

He nods again. I suspect he's lying. Maybe not. Then he says, "Now, about Sirena Fuggitiva."

"About Sirena Fuggitiva," I repeat back to him and wait.

Ray DiSalvo of unknown occupation tells me this:

On the 28th of December in the year 1908 at 5:20 in the morning there was a long, terrible silence, then a noise like a thousand bombs going off. It was an earthquake. The epicenter was dead in the middle of the Strait of Messina, the strip of water that separates Sicily from the mainland, the part of Italy called Reggio Calabria. Nearly the entire city of Messina was destroyed—90 percent of the buildings wrecked, seventy-five thousand people killed. There was death and destruction on the mainland side from Scilla to south of Reggio, but not nearly as bad as the Sicilian side where Messina had been reduced to rubble.

In the moments after the destruction of Messina, the few survivors left rushed to the seafront to escape the buildings as they continued to crash and fall.

What came next was incomprehensible. A long, loud hissing noise; the water was leaving. It receded for half a mile, and then, it returned. One, then another, then a third tidal wave. The waves killed more people, destroying everything in their reach; the Calabrian side of the Strait of Messina did not survive the disaster after all.

There were two girls among the survivors, Adriana and Audenzia. Adriana from the hillside on the edge of Messina, Audenzia from a town across the channel, in the upper part of Reggio Calabria, Scilla. They met in the months after the disaster, on a ship sailing from Palermo, Sicily, to New York City. They were on the ship's lowest level—steerage class.

Not yet seventeen, Adriana was dark-skinned with dark eyes and hair. She loved to sing, had a beautiful voice, and an uncanny memory for music. She sang the masses on Sunday but for Adriana, more than the Sunday hymns, she sang the music of Mozart, Puccini, Verdi, the music of the opera—her father's first love and hers too. The stories and songs of opera had always been a part of her life. The night before the earthquake, she'd gone to see Verdi's *Aida* at the Vittorio Emanuele II Theatre. It had been a wonder, a spectacle, the opera itself, the theatre, the town of Messina still lit and festive from the Christmas celebrations and overflowing with visitors who'd come to the city to see the opening night of *Aida.*

That night, after the performance, Adriana could not sleep for the excitement of having experienced Verdi's masterpiece. The evening itself had been spectacular, but the music had been something else; it had reached into her heart and held on. She lay awake reliving the notes in her mind. Overcome with happiness and wonder, she never went to sleep and in the early morning hours, before the household was awake, she got up, dressed, and went out on her bicycle for the day's bread. The baker wouldn't be open for another hour, so she took the long way through the lemon grove. The lemons had been harvested but the air was still filled with their scent and if she rode up high enough, she could look out to the sea.

Adriana was on her bicycle in the lemon grove when the earthquake hit and her family's villa, which had stood for generations, rose up out of the ground and then folded in on itself, killing her parents and her brothers in their beds. Adriana, thrown from her bicycle, flew and tumbled and fell. She tumbled and rolled, and the bike tumbled and rolled until they came to rest, the mangled bicycle on top of her. She lay in the lemon grove, injured and in pain, while others rushed to the water. When the earth and sea were finally still, Adriana stood to find her left leg no longer fully served her. From that moment forward she had to learn a new reality, a reality with a leg that wouldn't support her. Her bike was ruined but she couldn't ride it anyway. She walked with a slow step, drag, step, drag, step, drag.

Audenzia had eyes the color of the pale green sea and hair the color of a well-used copper pot. She too was young, like Adriana, but different in that she had already exerted the full power of her will. Audenzia had been arranged to be married to a wealthy exporter who had seen her walking the cliffs of

Scilla and was taken by her long waves of copper-colored hair. But Audenzia would not, could not, marry this old man; she had already promised her life to a fair-haired boy from Palermo who'd come to Scilla to apprentice with her father. They had kept their love and plans a secret, even while her mother, grand-mother, and aunts worked for months on her wedding dress for the arranged marriage. The dress would be magnificent—bead-ed silk, cerulean blue like the color of the sky, made with hours of tiny loving stitches by this team of women.

Audenzia would never wear this splendid creation; this she knew because she was going to sneak away with the fair-haired boy from Palermo. *Fuitina*, they call it, the trick young girls use to marry for love against the wishes of their families. She runs away with her lover and when they return, the town knows she's no longer a virgin, so the parents have no choice but to let the couple marry. She would wear a black coat on her wedding day, not the cerulean beaded silk dress with its masterful stitching.

But then, the earthquake, the tidal wave. The fair-haired boy from Palermo was swept out to sea and the mother, grand-mother, and aunts gone too. The dress Audenzia would never wear survived the disaster, which she saw as a sign. Of what? It's hard to say, for she was too far out of her mind with grief to interpret signs. She gathered up what money she could find and took the sky-blue dress, the work of all the women who'd raised her, carefully packed it in a sturdy leather valise and went to seek out the boy's family in Palermo. She thought they might take her in. She wasn't his widow, but almost.

When the mother in Palermo opened the door to Audenzia, she recognized her by the description the son had sent in his letter, the letter that said he was to be married. The mother called the family, shouted their names, one by one, the sisters, the grandmother, the father, the uncles. When every single member of the household had gathered, the mother threw her head back, then thrust it forward, and spit. It landed in Audenzia's eye as if she'd been practicing it since the arrival of the news of her dead son. The mother, satisfied, slammed the door.

Audenzia's mind, which had been ebbing and flooding in waves of grief and longing, receded. Anyone could see it by the wild look in her pale green eyes. She took what was left of the money and the cerulean dress that had been made for her but not allowed for her, packed safely away in her sturdy leather valise, and bought a ticket for America. She boarded the ship with a sack of Tarocco, the blood oranges that grow in the rich volcanic soil that surrounds Sicily's volcano, Mt. Etna. Tarocco, named by the farmer who sliced one in half and beheld the sweet-tasting, aromatic, mixed-colored pale and garnet fruit. "Tarocco!" he cried, calling to mind the mystery of the tarot deck Sicilians use to play cards. Audenzia held a tarot blood orange in her palm and it whispered its story to her. *From violence comes beauty, from destruction comes perfection, from the ash of her life in Scilla comes a new life in America.*

There's a mirage that lives above the Strait of Messina, a fata morgana, named for Morgan Le Fay, the shape shifter, enchantress, witch, and sister of King Arthur. The mirage is a magical city, a castle in the air. Adriana and Audenzia had both seen it with their own eyes. This is what they first talked about. The conversation they had when they found each other on the hot, crowded lower level of the ship to America. Adriana saw Audenzia's eyes were wild, but she wasn't afraid, just as Audenzia was unbothered by Adriana's pronounced limp. They didn't talk about the day they were betrayed by the ground beneath them. They didn't talk about the wave. They talked about the castle in the air. They talked about New York City.

As the days on the ship stacked one against the next, they absorbed the things they needed to know for their arrival in America from the other passengers. They learned they would have to answer questions. A woman with a lacy-bonneted baby taught them English words, *Hello, yes, cousin, Brooklyn.* An elderly man told them about the stairs. About the doctor. He said they would have to walk up a flight of steps and everyone would watch to see if something might be the matter. He said you couldn't be lame. You couldn't be wild-eyed. He said that at the top of the stairs a doctor will make a mark with chalk if something isn't right. The chalk mark means no. You cannot enter America. The chalk mark means go back.

The girls practiced a trick with the valise to get up the stairs. They both held the handle, with the suitcase between them and walked in a way that disguised Adriana's limp. As they walked, Adriana sang the arias from the operas she'd grown up with. Softly she sang the music which held her story and her heart. It reached past Audenzia's grief and longing to the strong mind that was buried too deep to calm her wild eyes.

As they traveled across the Atlantic, they ate Tarocco, the tarot blood oranges from the volcanic ash of Mt. Etna, and practiced the walking trick with the suitcase. It passed the days, buoyed their spirits, and lifted their confidence.

The day came when their ship passed through The Narrows that separate Brooklyn from Staten Island, the passage to America. They stood close to each other, holding hands as they entered the harbor. They watched New York City come into view with the other passengers crowding the deck. Adriana sang in her soft way, not Verdi this time—she was too nervous, too excited—she sang a song from her childhood, from long before the morning she rode her bicycle through the lemon grove…*Brilla brilla una stellina, Sun el cielo piccolina, Brilla brilla sopra noi, Mi domando di chi sei, Brilla brilla la stellina, Ora tu sei piu vicina…Twinkle twinkle little star…* She sang the familiar words over and over soothing both her and Audenzia's frightened hearts.

When they reached Ellis Island, they were ready to climb the stairs. But at the entrance a man asked them for the valise. *No, signore. No,* they protested but he would not let him pass. People behind them began to push, shout for them to give him the suitcase. Someone spoke to them in Italian, told them their suitcase wasn't being confiscated, just held as they proceeded upstairs. There was a promise. It would be returned to them before they entered America.

The suitcase was pulled away. The girls gripped each other's arms for support. Adriana's throat was too dry to sing, but she whispered the only thing she could make her mouth say, *Brilla Brilla una stellina, Ora tu sei piu vicina*—Twinkle, Twinkle little star, Now you are closer.

She held Audenzia tight and she could feel Audenzia holding her. She felt her strength and power and knew Audenzia was using her very soul to keep her standing. But when she looked over, she saw her pale green eyes and they were wild. They began the climb, one step, then another, then another, and they had hope. With all their practicing, Adriana's legs were stronger. They were going to make it up the stairs without the valise. Adriana's leg, the good one, began to ache from the hard work of climbing. They were almost to the top. Adriana looked again at Audenzia and her eyes were still wild but also fierce. She thought that for all the earth and sea had taken from her, it had also given something back, this friend who would see her through.

She stumbled. She didn't know how or why, just that the combined force of the best of their abilities wasn't enough. She stumbled and they fell together. They fell and fell and fell. At the bottom of the stairs, she was reminded of the day in the lemon grove when she had lain so long underneath her broken bicycle. She couldn't get up. But Audenzia was up, pulling her. Audenzia pulled at Adriana who was on her hands and knees.

She crawled while Audenzia pulled her back up to the top of the stairs where the doctor was waiting for them. He saw Audenzia's wild eyes and made a white chalk X on her coat. Possibly mentally unstable. She felt it on her shoulder. Then he drew a circle around the X. Definitely mentally unstable. She didn't scream or plead or rush at him. She wept. Tears came for the first time, for her fair-haired boy, gone, for the promises he made and did not keep, for the woman who she thought might love her but only spit in her eye, for the destruction, for the castles that float in the air over the Strait of Messina. She wept for her resolve, now gone.

The doctor turned to Adriana and leaned forward, not un-kindly. He reached his hands to her which she took, and he lifted her up to standing. When she appeared to have her balance, he took his piece of chalk and made an L on the shoulder of her coat. Lame.

The promise had not been a lie. The sturdy leather suitcase with the cerulean wedding dress was returned to Audenzia on her way out the door through which she had come. Audenzia and Adriana were returning to Palermo on the same ship that had brought them to America.

They stood on the deck where they'd held hands and Adriana sang, *Brilla Brilla una stellina*. They looked out to The Narrows through which they entered the harbor a few days back. Audenzia held up her thumb and forefinger and squinted toward the horizon to mark the space where Brooklyn and Staten Island nearly touch. *Non tornero*, she said. I will not return. *Non tornero, non tornero, non tornero*, she repeated it over and over with a composure Adriana had not witnessed before, the wildness gone from her eyes, gone from behind her eyes.

It's hard to know when the mind deceives, the fata morgana for instance, the mirage of a city in the sky over the Strait of Messina seen through the centuries by so many, so real, and yet not real. The distance over water, another deception, is farther than it appears.

As Audenzia whispered, *Non tornero*, Adriana tried to think of a song to calm her, but no song came.

As the ship approached The Narrows, Audenzia turned to Adriana, *Prendi il vestito*, take the dress, she said and then she was leaning over the ship's railing and then she was gone. The passengers screamed and pointed. Adriana screamed and pointed but the ship would not stop for a foolish girl who thought she could swim to freedom. The passengers watched the copper-colored hair moving in the waves. They saw Audenzia disappear beneath them, then reappear, disappear then reappear. They watched and shouted until she did not reappear.

Adriana returned to Palermo. She had nothing except the suitcase with the sky-blue wedding dress. Neither of which she would have any reason to use. She sold the dress—sewn with extreme care and experience by the women of Scilla, a year in the making, never worn—for a large sum of money. This is how she set up a small shop near where the ships leave Palermo for America. She sold travelers their last taste of Sicily, scoops of gelato served on brioche buns. And as her customers sat in Adriana's gelato shop, she told them about Sirena Fuggitiva, the exiled mermaid, who lives at the entrance to New York Harbor. She said look for hair the color of an old copper cooking pot. She warned them to call to her as they passed through The Narrows, to acknowledge her because anyone who grew up with the mirages on the Strait of Messina knows these mysteries need to be recognized. Call to her, call to Sirena Fuggitiva, and she will protect you and help you reach your destination. Don't acknowledge her and like Scylla and Charybdis—the maidens turned to monsters that live on either side of the Strait of Messina—she will destroy you.

"So that's the story the grandmothers tell. They say she's the reason they made it through to America; they called to her and she protected them. They warn us to say her name when we look out to The Narrows where she lives, but more importantly if you say her name at midnight on New Year's Eve, she'll stand by you all through the coming year." He shrugs, an amused believer.

"But I was downstairs in Grand Central Station, nowhere near The Narrows."

"Yeah, sure, right there in front of the Oyster Bar. That's a whispering gallery. Sound waves travel up and across those vaulted ceilings so you can hear a person across the room like they're standing right beside you. I guess they used to go there to celebrate, the grandmas, back when oysters were cheap. They'd whisper her name into the walls at midnight for luck in the new year or for the fun of the trick of it, or probably both."

"You believe?" I ask.

Ray shrugs again and smiles. "You know what they say, it's better to be lucky than good."

14

We work on Wall Street, but we don't have any money which is why we come here. Not dump enough to be dive, not sweet enough to be swank, just some nasty Swedish meatballs congealing in a chafing dish. They use the free food and cheap beer to lure us types in and here we are.

It's Friday night so the guys with houses and wives are on their trains to Long Island, New Jersey, Connecticut, somewhere a million miles away from a week of yelling and drinking and fine dining. All gone to their weekend lives, leaving no one to pay for our drinks but ourselves. It's the same crew the night we drank on Pier 17. Chry again too. I told her the brokers didn't like our friends showing up and drinking on the company tab. This probably isn't true, but it might be. I explained that the nights out were as much a part of mine and Dare's work as writing prices on the board and checking deals, that we needed to be liked by them so we could get on a good desk. Dare wanted Swaps; I wanted the Japanese Desk. The brokers working these desks were the moneymakers in the room and we wanted on. Hanging with them after hours mattered as much as anything. This is true. She asked me if Friday night counts and I said no, also true. I told her where to meet us, that Dare would be there.

Even though we are the extreme bottom of the food chain at Merton Marston, we've organized ourselves into our own pecking order. It should be me first, then Dare, then Bryan, Hal, and Steve, but the boys won't put me over Dare so we're more like co-captains.

Miller Lite is the happy hour special so that's what we're drinking. It's early June. The chewing gum on the pavement is starting to soften, emitting a whiff of the city's warm weather unfresh smells, giving notice there's a hot, possibly unbearable summer coming soon. The air conditioner wheezes and huffs, spitting more dirt than air. Our bottles of Miller Lite sweat on the table, Swedish meatballs harden on our plates. Chry's stationed herself up close to Dare. He is a mystery to her. When they're together I don't want to have anything to do with whatever's going on between them. Her desire is a freight train that compels me to move away. Dare doesn't stop it, rather sidesteps, seemingly not wanting to break a sweat. Chry would normally find this scenario too maddening to bother with; this is new.

Hal asks Chry where she works and she says she doesn't work anywhere, she's temping.

"You're tempting?" He smirks.

"Temping, tem-ping, dumbass," Dare says.

"There's not a tab anywhere?" says Bryan, annoyed and coughing up sweaty dust-filled dive bar air.

"Actually, there is," says Steve. "Joe Serf's got some guys in from the London office, they're up at Windows. I saw him before I left work and he said we should come up, help out showing these guys a good time."

"What the hell, Steve?" says Bryan. "When were you going to tell us?"

"We spend the whole day trapped in the stratosphere. I didn't feel like going all the way back up."

Windows on the World is on 107, a bunch of floors up from us.

"So, don't go," says Dare. "We'll go."

"I'll go," I say. "Chry'll go."

Chry confirms with a nod.

"Okay, okay, okay, what the hell else we got to do?" says Steve and we gather our stuff to head back over to One World Trade. We leave a pile of crumpled bills on the table, not stiffing the waitress but not exactly making her day either.

Out on the street, the sky has gone gray. The June heat is receding and it's trying to rain.

The Windows on the World express elevator is out of order, which means we need to take the regular express to the seventy-eighth floor and the local from there. I don't exactly feel like going back up either, but I don't want to go home and no way Chry is not following Dare this Friday night, no matter how many miles up in the sky that might be.

Up top, we see Serf at the bar with the London guys.

"Nice view," says Steve, still annoyed. "Very panoramic." It's normally the harbor, the Statue of Liberty, Verrazano Bridge, the whole shebang, but now it's just the inside of a rain cloud.

"Pretend you've died and gone to heaven," says Serf.

"Sorry, shag," says one of the guys in from London. "Don't plan on seeing *you* at my final destination. No offense, mate." He gestures his chin toward two women in high hair and heels, at the opposite end of the bar. "Them maybe."

He motions for the bartender to lean in, tells him to send over some drinks, put them on the tab. He leans back, says to Serf, "You don't mind, mate?"

"Happy to assist," Serf says, slapping him on the shoulder.

This is Windows on the World. There's no loud demands or forced shots like that night at the Seaport, but Serf's on the hook to entertain his out-of-town guests, so when the high-haired girls wave a thank you, drink their drinks, and leave, he turns to us to add something to the festivities.

No one is immediately forthcoming. Serf is undeterred; if we can't entertain, we will be the entertainment. "Yo, dead-weight," he says.

He means us. We collect checks but we don't close deals.

"Broker Poker."

Broker Poker is a trader's game, but it can be executed a lot of different ways. The general idea is to play people below you in the power game against each other. The object is to drain their dignity.

"Who's coming to dinner with me and the lads, here?" says Serf, to entice us to play. "Le Cirque. Okay? I know the free lunches are the best meal you get all day. I'm supposed to bring one of you anyway, directive from upstairs; they like New York and London to play nice. Supposedly you're the future." He lifts his eyebrows to indicate how unlikely he finds the idea of us having futures.

"We could draw straws," he says. He picks up his glass and takes a long drink, puts it down on the bar and adds, "but what fun would that be? Now there is something more random than random. Deadweight? Anyone?"

I wait for someone to answer. I don't want to play, be played, but when no one speaks, I say, "Monte Carlo."

"Correct," Serf says. "Monte Carlo. Mina's been reading her options book. She deserves to come along based on that alone. You know there's a seat on my desk opening soon which I'll be looking to fill with one of you idiots and so far as I can tell, *this chick is kicking your asses.* What about you, what do you know?" He throws his chin at Dare.

"When there's a high degree of uncertainty about the available facts, you would use it. Like a lucky guess," he says.

"A lucky guess," repeats Serf, confirming and accusing at the same time.

"Unfortunately, a chick is not my first choice for tonight's dinner or," he clears his throat, "the activities planned for after." He looks at me. "The lads have come all the way from London to see some American tits." He shrugs. "So probably not you, unless your tits are in play."

"Charming," I deadpan.

Serf laughs and throws up his arms as if to say, *Hey, I didn't invent this life I'm just here to get my slice,* then, "So. Broker Poker, Monte Carlo. You too, babe." He points at me. "We need an honest sample." He points to Chry. "Not you."

Chry stares daggers. She will not demean herself to respond. Serf doesn't notice or care; this is why I don't like her hanging around my work things. She gets to express herself where I have to play along.

"How shall we proceed?" Serf says and looks at me.

"Take all our names and put them in a hat."

Serf sticks his hand out at the bartender with a gimme motion. "Pen."

The bartender hands him a pen. Serf rips up a couple of bar napkins and writes our names on them, then grabs a bowl of peanuts off the bar and dumps them out. The bartender takes a rag, wipes them into his opposite hand, and throws them in the trash.

"Our random selection," says Serf, flourishing his arm. He swishes his hand in the bowl and takes out three cocktail napkin scraps. "Mina, Bryan, Dare."

"Very scientific," says Steve. "This is how my future's getting decided?"

"Your future was fucked the day you decided not to read that options book. Right, Mina?" says Serf and winks at me.

Steve rolls his eyes.

Serf puts the names back in the bowl and takes them out, one, two, three. He does this over and over again, each time contorting his body in a different way—under the leg, behind the back, eyes closed and on and on while one of the London guys makes tally marks and snickers between long pulls from his glass of beer.

Finally, Serf calls out, "Dare, it's you buddy."

Dare doesn't hear and Serf calls out again, "Fiore, you're in. Night out with the boys."

Dare, who hasn't been paying close attention, looks over and says, "Hey, Serf, thanks but I can't. I have some place to be."

I can't believe Dare is telling him no. I mean he doesn't run the Swaps desk or even the Japanese desk, but Serf has a big account list, does a lot of big deals; saying no could hurt Dare's future.

"Your funeral, buddy," says Serf unfazed. "Hal, you having dinner with the queen tonight too or can you join us?"

"I'm in."

I tell Chry and Dare I'll meet them at the elevators. There's a woman in the ladies' room with a table of supplies: tampons, hair spray, mouthwash, and hand towels. I splash water on my face again and again, trying to right some of the wooziness. We've been drinking for hours. When I come up for air, the attendant is by my side with a towel. I take it from her, and she recedes. I dry my face and stare in the mirror. White skin, pale green eyes, hair the color of an old penny, an old copper cooking pot. *Sirena Fuggitiva.* Could I be? Her body never was found. If she had a daughter and that daughter had a daughter, and that daughter left her daughter in the baptismal font of the Dutch Reformed Church in Upstate New York. It could be. I could be. I look and look. Think about what an asshole Serf is, how I refuse to let him humiliate me. Refuse. Tears come. I put the hand towel down on the sink and wash my face again.

When I pick my head up, once more the attendant is by my side, holding a fresh towel for me to take. I try to thank her, but I can't make the words. I rummage through my purse for some change, or even dollar, but I only have two twenties, neither of which I feel able to part with. "I'm sorry," I say. "Thank you. I'm sorry."

She nods, stoically.

"I'll see if my friend has some change."

She nods again, expressionless.

Outside in the hallway, I stand for a moment to gather myself. A girl from nowhere, but lucky to be alive. My story is for me and everyone in my town but that's where it will stay. Even Chry doesn't know how I was saved from drowning in holy water. She would never understand. Her history goes back and back and back—a father, from a wealthy Pittsburgh family, now a New Jersey congressman; a mother from New Jersey royalty, which I would have thought was a joke but is most definitely not. She has a Civil War great, great, great uncle, an American Revolution ancestor, and on and on. I don't have a past before the day I was born, whichever day that was. This feeling isn't fair to my mom—we are each other's family and that includes our Dutch ancestors who came to the Hudson River Valley— but it is fair to the mom I imagine, the monster who crawled out of the river to drop me in a vat of holy water.

Sirena Fuggitiva. I hear it again like the night in Grand Central Station. I whip around and unlike New Year's Eve there's an actual person standing behind me. A person whose smile says, *Yes, it was me who just said that.*

"Ray?" I barely recognize him. He's dressed so differently from the night we met; he's wearing a gray chalk-stripe suit, starched white shirt, and pale blue tie. His hair, blown wild the night we sat outside on the ferry, is combed and neat.

"I didn't mean to scare you," he says. "I'm sorry."

"Wha-what are you doing here?" I ask. I don't mean to be so shocked, it's probably an insult to him, he's just the last person I expected to see.

"I work on the fiftieth floor."

"Oh?" Second surprise.

He smiles again, wide.

"Dai-Ichi Kangyo Bank."

He laughs at my face because my mouth is wide open, too appalled to speak. He is Ray from Dai-Ichi Kangyo Bank, one of Merton Marston's biggest customers.

"I told you I knew what a Eurodollar was."

"I'm sorry. I..."

"It's okay," he says, with a kind smile. We both know what he's forgiving me for. The assumption I'd made about him.

"Hey, it's okay," he says again. "It was more fun to tell you the Sirena Fuggitiva story than talk about Eurodollars. Don't you think?"

I nod. I do think but I doubt anyone else at Merton would agree. Not even Dare, who is cool enough to tell Serf no. I don't think he'd say no if Ray asked him to dinner.

I cringe, remembering the way I'd bragged out the word *Eurodollars* like he was some, I don't know... I'm the one who comes from nowhere.

"I better get going," says Ray, "but it was nice to see you."

I nod, my mind spinning, too overwhelmed and surprised to manufacture words.

"I'll see you soon, I bet." He smiles again.

Chry and Dare are at the elevators waiting. My head is so full of Ray and his brothers—one a banker, one a fish seller, one a cop—that it's not until we're all the way downstairs and out on the street that I remember I never went back to tip the attendant.

Dare hails a cab and we pile three across the back seat.

Chry asks me what's the matter. I tell her I forgot to tip the lady in the bathroom. She says it's okay, that I can give her double next time, but I don't think it's okay at all.

We ride in silence. I'm disoriented. Ray DiSalvo. The lady who gave me a towel to dry my eyes, twice. "Where are we going anyway?" I ask, realizing I have no idea.

"Party on Franklin Street," say Dare.

I ask him if that's why he didn't go to Le Cirque with Serf and the guys from London.

"I said no because he was being a complete asshole."

"You mean about not letting me come."

"Yeah, about that."

Chry turns so Dare can't see, throws me a *this is why I love him* look.

I ignore her, say to Dare, "I don't need you to stick up for me."

"I wasn't sticking up for you. I just don't want to spend my Friday night with an asshole."

"And there's a party at your place?" I say, pointing out the real story. I don't need his heroism.

"Not my place, two floors up. Stew Crew."

I don't know what the Stew Crew is, and I don't ask. Neither does Chry. I assume she's thinking what I'm thinking—we'll find out soon enough.

As we ride the freight elevator up to the Stew Crew party, I'm reminded that I haven't seen Nyro since the night we were snowed in here. He could have gotten my number from Dare, but he never called. I didn't want him to call anyway. He's dangerous, with a cruel streak. But I think about the night we were snowed in—all of it, from riding the ferry to the next day's white light coming in over the walls, our naked bodies being good to each other.

"What's the Stew Crew anyway?" says Chry as the big freight elevator stops on the fourth floor with a bump.

"I think there's, like, ten of them, stewardesses for Pan Am. I only met a few; they come and go at all hours. Nyro seems to know most of them, but he's around a lot more."

Dare pulls back the handle, throws his weight behind the heavy elevator door, and slides it open.

Separating us from the pulsing music and crowd dancing is Nyro.

A version of Nyro.

The version of Nyro if he were a stewardess for Pan Am, wearing a women's navy blue suit, with a crisp white shirt and a blue and white scarf tucked in at the neck. His black curly hair is arranged and tucked neatly under a matching cloche hat; his full makeup is expertly applied.

Nyro, the Pan Am stewardess version, is holding hands with a female version of himself, a woman equally as tall and thin except with long, sleek black hair, and wearing what is obviously one of his suits.

Nyro throws his arms wide. "Finally! What the hell? Been waiting for you guys to show up for hours. This is Penelope."

"Lovely to meet you," Penelope says in a British accent and a voice several octaves lower than what must be her natural register. Maybe not. They are disorienting, these two.

Chry moves closer to Dare. Her subtle way of letting the room know that as far as she's concerned, they're a couple. And though her shift can't be more than a step to the left, it leaves me feeling completely alone. I should have put that twenty in the restroom lady's basket.

Nyro's women's wear hasn't constricted his movement. He springs up and away. His companion follows.

Chry, Dare, and I look at each other.

"I stopped being surprised a while ago," says Dare.

"Jesus," is all I can say.

"He makes a good-looking girl," says Chry.

I don't argue. Ray DiSalvo is Ray from Dai Ichi Bank. Nyro is a stewardess. No one is what they appear. Including me, from passing as a girl who went to a good school and works on Wall Street, when all I really am is a baby left to die in a pool of water, no matter if it was holy or not.

Nyro comes sprinting back toward me, moving fast but constrained too—a gazelle in a girdle. He puts his hand on my ass and pulls me in close. "Hi, Mina," he whispers. "Welcome to the Stew Ball."

I push his chest away so I can see his face but let him keep his hand on my ass. He is drunk, wired, and very, very happy.

"Nyro. Danny." It's all I can say. The eyeliner. The eyeliner so expertly applied is the thing I can't grasp.

He takes his hand away, steps back, and shrugs. He takes a leap back into the festivities, then turns back to me. "Shhhhh," he says, putting a finger to his lips. "Mom can't know."

I ask Dare to help me back down the elevator which is heavy to operate. He tells Chry he'll be right back and takes me down. We walk a half block to Hudson Street, and he flags down an uptown cab.

"Sure, you don't want to stay?" He opens the cab door for me.

"It's okay, Dare."

He pauses before slamming the door shut. "Don't worry about him, Mina. He's...I don't know. He's got everything... and nothing. You know?"

I shrug. I don't know. "Thanks, Dare," I say. "See you Monday."

SUMMER

15

When the weeds in our garden gave way to wildflowers, no one was more surprised than Chry. "Looks like G.A. really did plant a little piece of Arcadia back there," she said, when it became clear that the green shoots and stalks rising through the tattered straw were going to be Queen Anne's lace and chicory, the flowers of St. James Day.

Queen Anne's lace, because it grows in the fields and along the roads in the height of summer. Queen Anne's lace, because each flower is an explosion of tiny white blooms, the queen's lacy dress, with one tiny purple bloom in the center, Queen Anne herself. They are Chry's grandmother's favorite; she is Anne, and she's the Queen. Chry loves them too because she loves her grandmother and because she loves summer at Arcadia. *They're as wild as they are dependable. They don't mind being picked and kept. No one asks them to come and stay all summer, but they do anyway. You can call them weeds and they won't even care.*

Chicory, because it grows in the fields and along the roads. And chicory, because if you cut it with a gold knife at noon or midnight on St. James Day, it has the power to open locks and doors. *She's a maiden who told the god Apollo to get the hell away from her. For revenge, he turned her into a flower that lives for only one day. She blooms bright blue in the morning, fades as her face follows the sun, and dies in the afternoon. It's no use to try and pick her to bring home and put in a vase, she'll die before she lets you.*

Queen Anne's lace and chicory are growing in our back garden, with its crumbling wall and wrecked stone patio, up through the weedy mess on the other side of the rattly French doors. They are there thanks to G.A.

"You're coming this year, right?" says Chry after she's told me about the wildflowers of St. James Day.

"Yes," I say. When she asks me why I've never been before I don't tell her I'd never been invited.

We're on our way to New Jersey, stopped in traffic in the Lincoln Tunnel. There can't be enough air in this tunnel for the people on this one bus, let alone all the other cars and buses. I can feel the Hudson River trying to penetrate the tiled walls and ceiling, water-stained with decades of river effort. I hold my breath. When I can't hold it anymore, I take a series of short gasps, hoping whatever it is I'm taking into my lungs is more parts oxygen than carbon monoxide. How will I know when the air becomes straight poison? I won't.

It's the third of July and I'm going home with Chry for the weekend. She's too brokenhearted to notice I'm in a tunnel panic. She'd asked Dare first, to come with her to her mom and dad's annual Independence Day bash, but he'd said no. Nicely. He told her he had plans. She said fine, no problem, but then he told her he wanted her to know he hoped they could be friends. He didn't want a girlfriend.

I'm the second choice, *a close second*, she'd said in a laughing apology that held so much sorrow and sincerity, it was like she'd handed me a shard of her heartbreak. Don't be mad, she'd said. I wasn't. I couldn't stand the sight of Chry brokenhearted. She didn't know what to do with herself. I didn't know what to do with her either.

For all the time they'd spent together, especially after her staying out all night at the Stew Ball, I'd figured at some point they'd swapped bodies. I thought they would have closed the deal but Chry, who continues to tell me every detail of her life, hasn't said anything about it. I'd told her about my night with Nyro, not everything, but that he'd surprised me with a kind calmness when it was just me and him. I told her I liked him.

Even after four years of college together, I'd never been to Chry's house on the hill above Sandy Hook. I spent vacations with my mom. I didn't have money to travel and anyway I want-ed to be with her. My mom and I both knew I wouldn't be back much when the time came for me to leave for good. Becky

Berg, she loved me hard and I loved her the same. She loved me enough to know I couldn't make a life up there on that stretch of the Hudson River.

As we come out of the tunnel and wind our way around the ramp that takes us to I-95 South, Chry says, "Welcome to New Jersey! Home of The Boss, South Side Johnny, the one and only Jersey Shore from Cape May to my own beautiful Sandy Hook." She pauses, takes a deep breath and continues. "Birthplace of baseball, Frank Sinatra, Bugs Bunny…and. The. Lightbulb."

"Congressman Risk's daughter knows all the facts," I say.

She shrugs. "The basics, any Jersey Girl worth her weight knows 'em."

"You never really struck me as a Jersey Girl, Chry."

"I am. I'm a Jersey Girl just like the song… Except no one's in love with me." She tries to laugh but it comes out as a hoarse whimper.

The bus carries us out over the New Jersey railyards. Across this part of the Hudson River is the long view of the Manhattan skyline, shimmering in the summer sun. There's the diagonal slice of the Citibank building, the Empire State Building, the Chrysler Building, at the tip, the Twin Towers, home of Merton Marston Forex, Inc. One of those towers is mine. I haven't conquered it yet, but that's the plan. I cringe to think about the night Serf embarrassed me in front of the London guys, like a grown-up version of Baby Boy Boogman trying to put his foot on my neck. But right away, I uncringe. Fuck them. Also fuck Dare. Fuck him for making my roommate so goddamn sad and fuck him for his help. Don't need. Don't want.

Chry asks me if we should take the kayaks down to the Navesink River to watch the fireworks and I tell her no. She shrugs and looks at her dad. "It's as good a view from here as anywhere," he says. As good a view is right. Their house is on the top ridge that runs parallel to the bay side of the curve of beach Chry grew up surfing, Sandy Hook. The house is a wall of windows and out the windows is everything. In the far distance, New

York City. In the near distance will be the fireworks over the river.

Chry's dad had picked us up at the bus depot. We wound up and up and up this small mountain sloping to the sea. What is the opposite of fear? The higher we went, the more I felt the air and vistas. I felt the comfort I grew up with on the edge of the Hudson River, where it's so wide open you can watch the sun rise in the morning, cross the sky, then sink into the west. In other words, you can see the world turning. You can track the daylight's part in one earthly revolution. Yes, the opposite of fear. I could live up here, high up over the world. One day, I might.

The fireworks start after nine. Chry would prefer to be on the water but she lets me have my choice. Sitting in side-by-side chaise lounges, turned away from what Chry refers to as the Bight and toward the part of the sky over the Navesink River where the fireworks will be. The New York-New Jersey Bight. Chry tells me this is the piece of ocean their corner of the world lies up against, the patch from the end of Long Island to Cape May.

We've greeted and mingled with the Risks' friends. Some of them are familiar from New Year's Eve, all of them *ooh* and *ahh* over Chry, how grown up she is, how beautiful. They are also kind to me but with what I suspect are practiced cocktail pleasantries. After we'd said hello, Chry excused us and we came out here. She swiped an icy cold bottle of Cliquot on the way. The bartender protested but Chry stared him down. The transaction, such as it was, didn't include glasses so after Chry sent the cork over the edge of the porch and let the froth dump into her mouth, she handed the bottle to me. We swigged while the sky boomed. When the fireworks were finished, so were we, with the Cliquot, anyway.

Here we are, Chry and I, side by side, the sun rising and falling across the Bight, the guests coming and going, the world booming and busting. Chry is making a go of the family fes-tivities with her hurting heart, a valiant effort. I don't mention

Dare—what good would it do? But I admire her for the last part. I could see how a girl could love Dare. I practically do myself, truth be told, but the roadblocks were there from the start. One, we work together. Two, my best friend loves him. Three, I would never give him the chance to tell me no, which makes us something more than he and Chry will ever be. In a way.

Chry wipes the wet mouth of the empty bottle of champagne with her sleeve. When it's dry, she lifts her face to see if anyone inside the glass doors is paying attention, then pulls a small brown coke vial from her pocket.

Blow? I move my mouth to make the words and the surprise but don't say it out loud. "Where'd you get it?"

"Your boyfriend."

I make a face like I don't know what she's talking about.

"Nyro, the night of the Stew Ball," she says, as if I'm an idiot for not knowing who my boyfriend is.

She gently taps a ring of coke onto the rim of the bottle, looks up again to check the crowd inside the house, then holds one nostril and snorts the coke with a quick circular motion of her head. She licks the bottles mouth, first outside then sticks her tongue inside, making just enough motion to lick up any stray granules. She rubs her tongue across the front of her teeth and gums and says, "Now you." She dries the top of the bottle where she'd been licking and snorting.

Chry tees up another circle of coke, looks over at the party again, and says, "Come here. It's not going to make the trip." I get up, snort, and lick just as Chry had. She holds my arm, her grip strong, when I almost lose my balance.

We go back and forth a few times in this new Chry invented style of pulling coke up our noses until Chry, says, "Jesus, Mina, we gotta get outta here. I can't let my parents see me like this."

"Would they know?" My mom's an ER nurse; she would know. She'd told me a thousand times there'd be no point in trying to pass anything by her. I never did.

"Would they know? Just Say No," Chry says and laughs. "My mom worked on the Congressional Wives Against Drugs campaign. She was on the cover of the *Star-Ledger* with Nancy Reagan. And my dad. And me." Chry looks through the window at the room beyond, sees her parents and what's left of the party. "Half those people in there," Chry gestures, "are big donors, maybe all of them. You don't even know, Mina. Everything is like quadrupled—failing, succeeding, minding your own business. You don't know. I mean, they're in there slugging back their drug of choice like there's no tomorrow, and we're out here doing the same thing." She shrugs. "Anyway…we have places to be." She jumps up quick, stops, puts her finger to her lips dramatically, then tiptoes to the door like a cartoon character, opens it and slips inside.

She returns with a set of keys. "I asked the guy making drinks to tell them we went out." She shrugs. "I've done my part in the greetings, chitchat, and formalities. They're just going to have to deal with us being gone for a while."

In the dark garage, Chry chucks the spent champagne bottle into one of the trash cans before we hop up into her jeep. We'd been a million places in this vehicle our senior year in college when she'd received it as an early graduation present, but she keeps it here in New Jersey since it's a pain to park in the city. We unzip the soft top the way we did on those first warm nights of senior year.

"Music. Need to find music," says Chry. Then, "Shit." Then, "Wait here."

I sit in the passenger seat of the jeep in Chry's dark garage, surrounded by shadows of a life of doing things, not wanting things. Next to the jeep, a sailboat on a trailer parked where a car might be, a gaggle of bikes in one corner, beach chairs hang on a wall next to a line of surfboards.

She returns before I finish my inventory of the shadows of Chry's life, lived up here at the top of the world. She hands me another bottle of ice-cold Cliquot, which she's wrestled off the bartender. "Hold," she says, and reaches under the seat for the garage door opener, presses the button, chucks it back under the seat, and backs the jeep into the driveway.

"Shit." She throws the jeep in park. "Mina, find that clicker." I hand her the bottle and lean down, feel around under the seat for the remote. I find it. I also find a crushed soft pack of Marlboro Reds, three quarters, a dime, and the flat square foil of a condom with its telltale raised round ring. I hold it up for Chry to see. "Square peg, round hole."

"That is not mine," she says, "and those aren't mine either," meaning the Marlboros.

Inside the glove box is a flashlight, some maps, and a pair of sunglasses without a case. I add the newly excavated treasures and shut the garage door. Chry hands me the champagne, throws the car into gear and continues backing down the driveway.

I am afraid of water. Lakes and rivers and oceans. And estuaries and straits. But beyond wondering which body of water will complete my original destiny, to drown, I'm not afraid of anything. Chry bombing down winding roads with a head full of blow on top of her being drunk is crazy fun. When we're out of earshot of the house, she turns the radio all the way up and sings as loud as she can into the windy ocean air.

"Where are we going?" I shout over the wind and the music.

"To find some live music," she yells back.

At the bottom of the hill we cross the Navesink River. Chry turns down the radio as we pass through a street with a neat row of houses but cranks it back up as she bangs a left onto Rumson Road where there are only mansions set far back and surrounded by tall gates.

"New Jersey royalty?" I ask, still yelling.

"Open it up," she shouts back, ignoring my question.

I take the foil off the champagne, untwist the wire.

"Don't point it at me!"

"Sorry." I point the bottle in the direction of the passing mansions and ease the wire crown off the cork. With both thumbs I push the cork out of its snug little home. It pops faster than I expect and flies out of the car thankfully in the opposite direction of Chry's head.

"See," she says, laughing as I dump the spouting froth into my mouth, just as she had on the terrace. "You could've killed me."

"What doesn't kill us makes us stronger!" I shout into the night, holding both arms out, champagne bottle still gripped in my right hand.

"What the fuck, Mina. Keep that philosophical bullshit away from me."

"It's what they say."

"Keep 'them' away from me too."

We are laughing and screaming into the night, our hair blowing back as Chry careens the jeep along the two-lane road. "So, this is Jersey!" I say.

"This is Jersey. My hometown."

Chry crosses a little bridge then heads right onto Ocean Avenue.

"Where are we going!?"

"Temple of Knowledge." She holds out her hand for me to give her the champagne so I'm not sure if she's calling the Cliquot the Temple of Knowledge or if we're going to a temple where there's knowledge.

I hand her the bottle. She takes a swig and hands it back, then wipes her mouth with the sleeve of her jean jacket. "Madam Marie. She tells fortunes." We drive for a while, the ocean on the other side of the car, the other side of Chry. "Then we'll find some music," she adds.

The scenery becomes increasingly deserted and decrepit; there are rundown houses and buildings, everything more and more disheveled and sad and…dangerous.

Finally, Chry parks the jeep in a spot facing the beach and says, "Let's hurry, before she closes."

Two men on the sidewalk, their heads hunched together, look up. One lifts his chin, a kind of hello, the other is oblivious. I look away, not wanting to make eye contact.

Besides the lines, or I should say circles, of coke we did earlier, the cold air rushing our faces in the open-topped jeep kept us alert, but it feels good to be free of it. Chry hurries past the hunched men. I follow her down a sidewalk toward the beach.

The scatter and smell of garbage on the street gives way to salt air and the sound of midnight waves shushing and crashing.

We arrive at the Temple of Knowledge, Madam Marie's fortune telling booth, but the tiny building is locked and dark, its neon signs, *Readings* in one window, *&Advisor* in the other, turned off for the night. Chry pulls at the handle shaking it in frustration. "Come on, come on," she says through gritted teeth. I'm jacked up on coke, Cliquot, the drive, and finally the fear of this dilapidated town on the edge of the ocean, so watching Chry attempting to will the Temple of Knowledge into opening is unnerving.

I put my hand on her arm, "Chry, stop."

She throws me off. "No. I won't. We came all the way here."

"Need some help?" A voice we can't see.

"Madam Marie?" says Chry into the night.

"No," says the voice. "But I'm over here."

"Where here?" says Chry

"Around the corner."

Chry, having just shaken me off, grabs my wrist and pulls me toward the voice. There, on the other side of the boardwalk railing, leaning up against Madam Marie's little building under a giant blue eye is the voice embodied.

It's a girl around our age. Her head is wrapped in a dark paisley scarf, and she's wearing one oversized gold hoop earring and long necklaces in multiple shapes and sizes.

"Fortune teller or trying to be Miami Steve?" says Chry.

The girl laughs. "Nothing wrong with wanting to be Miami Steve, but I tell fortunes, the late shift."

"Officially?"

The girl shrugs and laughs again. "Officially, sure."

"Look, I came to see Madam Marie," says Chry.

"Well, she's not here."

"What's your name?"

"Sandy."

Chry smirks at this. "What's your real name?"

"Sandy to you, since you wished it."

Chry tilts her head, amused, though I still don't get the joke.

"Okay, okay, you can tell me my fortune." Whatever this girl's name is she's earned Chry's trust. She climbs up and sits on the railing and I do the same. "I have two questions," she says.

"Forty dollars."

Chry rummages through her pocket carefully so as not to reveal exactly how much is in there and extracts two rumpled twenties. She reaches them out to the girl under the giant blue eye.

"Not yet; when we're finished."

Chry holds the money in her fist and the girl says, "Ask me anything."

"Is Bruce playing at The Pony tonight?"

"No."

"Are you sure?" Chry's as surprised as I am at the quick reply.

"Uh, yeah, I'm sure. He's playing Wembley Stadium in London tonight. It was on the news."

This seems like an enormous waste of a question but Chry accepts it as a fair transaction. And I suppose the girl copping to a source from the temporal world is a testament to her honesty.

"Second question?" she says earnestly.

Chry drops her shoulders, looks down at the weeds and scrub, picks her head up and says, "Will we be together?" She waits for an answer and when the girl doesn't respond she says, "Do you know who I mean?" At our backs, the whole wide ocean, reaching and retreating in soft bursts of sound. Soothing for Chry probably but not for me. Never for me.

The girl reaches over and picks a tall weed. She stares at it then breaks it in half. She breaks those halves in half and rolls them in her palms. After a long minute she opens her palms and considers the ragged pieces. "I see you together," she says finally. "Side by side." She looks up at Chry who is leaning so far forward on the railing I can see the muscles in her arm working to keep her balanced. "Love isn't always how you think it's going to be—fireworks and kissing on Ferris wheels," the girl continues. She closes her eyes and turns her face out to the night air coming up from the rolling waves. "Have mercy on the brokenhearted," she says finally.

Chry's breath accelerates and her head moves in small rapid nods. "Thank you. Thank you," she says.

"You're welcome. You can leave the money there, on the boardwalk. Sandy, the late shift, tell your friends."

On the way back to the jeep we pass the spot where we'd seen the two men with their heads huddled together, but now there is only one, passed out in a patch of litter just off the sidewalk. There's a pop, pop, pop of firecrackers off in the distance, a whistle, and the soft crack of a bottle rocket.

"Do you think she means me? Have mercy on myself?" Chry says.

I don't answer. I don't know what she means.

The Stone Pony is only a few blocks away. Chry pulls the jeep to the curb, takes the key out of the ignition, unlocks the glove box, and takes out the crushed pack of Marlboros. "Why not?"

"Why not."

Inside we push our way through the crowd. At the bar, I order two Budweisers, while Chry sticks a cigarette in her mouth and asks the guy next to her, in a beach tan and a tank top, for a light. She takes the cigarette out of her mouth and puts it between her lips and uses the glowing tip to light it. She hands it to me, and I hand her a bottle of Bud, ice cold and wet with condensation.

Southside Johnny is ripping it up, covered in sweat and singing his heart out. We go all night, drinking and dancing and smoking Marlboro's until we finish the pack, until the band shouts good night, until there's hardly anyone left in the club. The bartender shouts out the classic last call, "You don't have to go home, but you can't stay here."

We stumble out onto the sidewalk, singing Southside's last song loud into the night, Chry in her perfect alto, me so bad it makes us laugh, previous fear of this unfamiliar place now drowned in beer and music.

"Uh-oh," says Chry and stops. I see what she means. Across the street there's a guy in the driver's seat of the jeep, smoking a cigarette. Muscular with burnt blond hair, he's wearing the sunglasses from the glove box. I look back at the club, but the door is shut and no one we'd been jumping around with inside is anywhere in sight.

My body shoots adrenaline, not that different a feeling from snorting rings of Nyro's coke, the last of which we did hours ago. "Should we call the cops?"

"Just say no." Chry reminds me that the company of the police would not only be detrimental to her reputation, but her mom and dad's as well.

"You'd think Sandy to You might have warned us," I say.

Chry takes out her keys. "There's nothing else we can do." She sets her face with a determined look and marches with authority to the jeep. I follow, mimicking her false bravado.

We cross the street and come up on the jeep from behind. "You need to get out of there," Chry shouts.

"You gotta get out of that jeep," I yell, thinking that between the two of us we might sound like a mob.

He holds his arm out over the side, flips open a blade. His arm hangs limply but he's gripping the knife hard.

"Listen, motherfucker! Get the fuck out of my car!" Chry yells now, louder still.

No response.

"I said get the fuck out of my car, you goddamn motherfucker!"

Nothing.

I think about Vinnie's brother, Tony, and how he said there could be a time when you need help, and you can't call your parents. This would be exactly that sort of time, but he's a New York City cop, nowhere near Asbury Park, New Jersey.

Chry is seething. My chest is pounding. I am wishing hard. It's a crap strategy, wishing, but it so recently worked for Chry, who materialized the answer she wanted from the inside of a Springsteen song, I decide to try. I am wishing this guy would find something better to do than come between us and getting back to Chry's house.

"How much?"

"What?"

"How much you gonna pay me to leave?"

Chry and I are out of cash. I consider the perils of negotiating a price, then driving this guy to an ATM machine.

Chry shouts, louder than ever, "Fuck you, motherfucker!"

"What the fuck are you doing, T. J.? Get out of that fucking jeep, asshole!" A guy is shouting as he comes around the corner in front of the jeep. "I been looking for you all night." This one is tall and dressed in a long sleeve T-shirt and surf shorts. "For crissakes, she's not fucking worth it."

Have mercy on the brokenhearted.

Blue and red lights, the whoop of a police siren.

"Jesus. Now we're fucked," the guy who'd just shown up hisses.

The cop car parks diagonally across the road and two officers come out. T.J.'s brought his arm in the car, though it's not clear if the knife's been put away.

"This your car?" says the cop with threatening authority as he jumps from his cruiser.

"It's not his."

The cop walks over to the jeep, one hand resting on his gun holster. "Get out of the car. Let's go."

The other cop, he too now out of the cruiser, has his eye on the friend. "Listen, he's just had a bad night," the friend says.

As the first officer turns his head, the guy in the jeep lifts the hand holding the knife in a fist pump.

Everything breaks loose. Two cops, the guys, struggling against each other. Chry and I watch, not sure if the police have even noticed us yet. In the end, the cops have one guy each on the ground with knees on their backs and hands on their necks.

Chry, who's been holding her keys like a weapon, says, "Mina, now!" We run and jump into the jeep. She throws it into reverse and backs down the deserted street in a crazy zigzag. She takes the turn at the end of the block in reverse, then throws the jeep into drive and floors it.

"Be careful!" I scream as she careens close to a parked car, but she misses it, and we drive on. We go the whole way up Ocean Boulevard keeping under the speed limit. Neither of us speak.

By the time we are passing by the gates and mansions, the sky is beginning to lighten.

"Chry, pull over."

"We have to get home before my parents wake up."

"Pull over."

She pulls the jeep to the side of the road. I take the flashlight out of the glove box and shine it on her. "Chry!"

"What?" she says, pushing her hair off her face.

"Blood."

"What? Where?"

I run the flashlight up from her face down to the seat and back. "All. Over."

Chry looks at her hands. "Oh my God! What the hell? Oh my God!"

"That guy must have been sitting there bleeding all night." The steering wheel is covered, the gear shift, the dashboard, the seat, everything is covered in blood.

Chry's face has finger streaks where she'd pushed back her hair, like the day she spent working at the *New York Post* except instead of ink, it's blood.

16

I am going to St. James Day at Arcadia. Finally. I thought delivering Chry home to her parents soaking wet from the ocean in the early hours of the day after the Fourth of July might disqualify me. Something in the way they credited me for things going well made me wonder if the opposite would be true. And then I knew for certain. That morning when Chry made a right to the Sandy Hook beach instead of a left up the hill to her parents' house, I was sure if we got caught, it would be on me, Chry returning home covered in blood. It never bothered me until that moment, the idea that they were counting on me to make sure she got home in one piece, but it did then. A lot. I hate that it was part of the price of being Chry's friend.

I stood in the sand while Chry swam in the waves. The sky was pale pink, the water, green. She had begged me to join her. For my own sake, she said. She still doesn't know I can't swim.

She'd found a broken bucket and an old towel near an over-flowing trash can. She filled the pail with seawater and brought it to the jeep. She used the rag to swab the mess of blood from the seat and steering wheel and every place it had spattered.

We are all going to Arcadia for St. James Day, not just Chry and me, but Nyro and Dare too. Chry felt so reassured by Sandy to You's prediction that she and Dare were destined to be together that she relaxed her urgency toward him. It worked. Two vertical lines stopped appearing between his eyebrows at the mention of her name.

One by one our spots had been secured. Mine was on July 5th morning when we managed to get the jeep in the garage and ourselves in our beds before her parents woke up. Dare's was because Chry wanted him to come, and Nyro's so it didn't look like it was Dare she wanted as much as a fun group of friends.

Chry and I are packed and ready, waiting for Nyro and Dare to pick us up for the trip. There's a long buzz from the outside gate. I take a last look around the apartment to make sure I haven't forgotten anything. Through the French doors, our little backyard is a bath of sunlight and the Queen Anne's lace and chicory are blooming in a wild weedy rapture.

Chry sees me staring. "We have to be sure to tell G.A. I bet even she wasn't expecting that."

I go to meet what must be Nyro leaning on the buzzer while Chry does up the three locks on our apartment door.

"Okay, we hear you, we're coming!" I shout, lugging my big suitcase and bag down the hall. I leave the outside door open for Chry to follow, pull my load up two steps to the landing under the brownstone steps and there, smiling, with his arms up and entire body leaning on the gate, is Nyro. Loafers, madras plaid shorts bagging on his skinny frame, wrinkled pink Brooks Brothers shirt untucked and Ray Ban Wayfarers. His head of black curls is as wild as ever.

He pushes his lips into a space in the wrought iron for me to kiss.

"Are we romantic?" I say.

He shrugs. "When we feel like it."

"I don't know, Danny." I smile. "Last time I saw you, you were flying the friendly skies."

"I contain multitudes."

I stand on the other side of the gate. "Should I let you in?"

"I wouldn't."

Chry comes up behind me, drops her face on my shoulder. "Nyro."

"It's me. Let's go, we're double parked." He steps away from the gate so we can open it and Chry and I follow him to the street.

Dare has the trunk open of a bright blue Beamer. He's wearing long khaki pants and a Combat Rock T-shirt. "This your car?" I say as I throw my bag in. For all the time we spend together I realize there's a lot I don't know about him.

"Nyro's dad's."

"Nice color."

"Lapis blue," says Nyro, coming up behind me.

"Your dad's awfully generous with his shit," I say.

"Not in this life, he wasn't," Nyro says, and now I remember again that his dad is no longer living. He lifts a middle finger to the sky. "Thanks for the car, Dad."

This act of Nyro holding a middle finger to the heavens silences us, and we take our places in the BMW. Nyro driving, me in the front passenger seat, Chry and Dare in the back. Even Chry, who has the exquisite habit of overriding conversational weirdness with a combination of ignorance and acuity, doesn't speak.

We drive through the streets of the Upper West Side to the ramp for the George Washington Bridge. We wind our way around in slow traffic until we are up on the bridge where we continue to crawl as we cross over the wild and mighty Hudson precipitously far below. As we near the center of the bridge, Nyro slows the car to a complete stop and puts the flashers on. Horns screech and honk behind and around us. An instant cacophony. Long screams, short blasts, low bass tones, high-pitched squeals of anger and distress.

I twist in my seat to see a look of calm determination on Nyro's face, his chest rising and falling with purpose.

"Buddy, I can take over. I can drive," says Dare, with a compassion beyond the usual exasperation, humor, and watchfulness he exhibits around Nyro.

"For the millionth time, Fiore, I'm not your buddy."

A semi rumbles by, a long, tall monster, spewing exhaust and long blares of a horn.

"Jesus, Nyro, come on," says Chry. "You're going to kill us."

I have his eyes in mine. I try to transmit something that will get him to put the car in gear but at the same time doesn't also say the only thing that matters is us not being hurled off the bridge into eternity through a hideous headline-making crash. I hold him in a stare, my eyes saying I care about him as much

as my own life. I don't know if it's true, but I try to make it
true. I transport a message, a reminder of the night we were
snowed in on Franklin Street. The morning when the white
light came in and covered our side-by-side naked bodies and we
were something new.

I hold his dark blue eyes with my seawater green eyes,
mocked for all those years, along with hair the color of an old
penny, mocked for not belonging to anything anyone could
recognize, found in a puddle of holy water, a sea creature who
can't swim. I hold his eyes in mine and try to tell him something
I hadn't told anyone in New York City. *I'm nothing too.*

"Okay," he says, and puts the car in drive, pulls forward, and
we finish the trip across the river.

We go up the Palisades Parkway on a wave of relief and now,
I can feel it, a slice of friendship. Up, up, up the other side of
the river from mine. Funny, I never dreamed of getting to this
side, just wanted a way down, down to New York City. A dream
that came true, I remind myself.

And now we are heading west to Chry's family, west to Arcadia, west to St. James Day. We're invited for the week. I didn't
know how Dare and I would get the days off at the same time
but early in July we got our desk assignments, both our first
picks, me, the Japanese Desk, Dare, Swaps desk. We spent the
next few weeks training our replacements. We asked permission, separately of course, to take a week off before we started
our new jobs. All this is remarkable, Dare and I getting our
first-choice desks and getting a week at Chry's lake, if Nyro
doesn't kill us before we get there.

Route 17 follows the lazy turns of the Susquehanna River.
Below us, fly fishermen cast their lines, the midday sun sending
sparkles and shimmers on the ripples in the water. We have the
windows down with Dare's mixtapes playing loud, and sweet
fresh air is rushing in. When we stop for gas, Chry goes into the
station's little market and Dare gets out to pump. Nyro catches
my eye and shrugs.

"That where it happened?"

He nods. "Left the car in the road. They found him with a broken neck, dead, washed upriver at the mouth of Spuyten Duyvil creek. They'd been looking the other way, to the south of the bridge, for some reason. It flows both ways, you know."

I know.

"Spuyten Duyvil. It's Dutch. For Spit of the Devil, or Spite of the Devil, depending on who you ask," he says. "Spit or spite."

I nod.

"So that's perfect."

Farther west on 17 we pass signs for Vestal, New York.

"Hey, Dare, should we drop you home?" Nyro yells over the music.

"No thanks," he shouts back.

"The Vestal Virgin," says Nyro.

Dare shakes his head and laughs. I look back at Chry. She's been trying to get Dare to give it away since the night they met.

17

I yell over the motor that we should turn back. Chry doesn't answer but 180s the boat at full throttle. Terrified, I grip the rail to keep from flying off the back. The sky turns pale gray as we race home through wind, chop, and spray. Lines of white caps move in all directions.

Chry's 180 forces Dare and Nyro, who'd been standing in the bow, to sit down hard, right up next to each other. A wave crashes over and drenches them. They shout, rubbing the water from their eyes and whipping their hair off their faces in duplicate motions.

Chry barks for Nyro to move to the seat opposite to balance the boat. He stands and another wave cracks on the bow and sprays them, but Nyro manages to take the seat across from Dare.

"Slow down!" he yells over the wind as we approach the dock and the nearby sailboat, which is rocking violently in the crisscrossing current. Earlier, when we'd motored our way out, it was moored so placidly we could read the name on the stern, *Wand'ring*.

Chry pulls back on the throttle and tries to steer away from the sailboat, but the wind and waves are too strong. I hunch down in my seat, my heart exploding in my chest, the very thing I fear most, happening. Nyro moves next to Dare again, leaning over the edge to fend off the *Wand'ring* which is now a wild animal on a leash, pulling and jerking.

Chry turns the wheel hard. The wind twists and moves the sailboat away.

We slide by, a near miss, but something explodes with a *crack*.

"What was that?" I shout, too focused on watching Chry steer the boat onto the lift to turn and see what happened.

"The mast," shouts Dare.

"Shit. Okay, okay, we have to get this boat up," says Chry.

The sky is now iron-dark; Nyro and Dare take turns crank-ing the lift, then we all race down the dock. Rain pummels us we tear up the lawn to the house.

"G.A., G.A.!" Chry yells as we rush through the door, kick-ing our shoes off in the entrance. "We need to get her and us into the cellar," she says. "I've seen the sky like this before. "G.A., it's a bad storm!" she yells into the house again.

We all run around the house shouting for Chry's grand-mother. She's not on the first floor. We pound up the stairs. One, two, three, four of us halt at the doorway to her bedroom. She's on a fainting couch, looking out the window at what should be the lake and sky but is now only dark, driving rain.

"G.A., you have to come down to the cellar," Chry says, panting.

"No, darlings. You go please. I'd like to watch."

"G.A., you're crazy," Chry says, laughing. "But you really do have to come."

"I most certainly am not mentally unsound, but I will insist you four get to the cellar immediately. I'll watch from here."

What G.A. says goes. This is deep law at Arcadia. Chry doesn't question her, though I ask her if it wouldn't be a better idea to watch away from the window.

"Yes, wise. Thank you, Mina. Now go down to the cellar. I'll see you when this blows through."

We all four pound down two sets of steps, first to the main floor and then into the cellar. It's a mess, a shipwreck. Years of house things are jam crammed around and layered with dirt and dust. The whole back wall is racks and racks of wine, also layered in dust.

"Make yourself at home," says Chry, motioning toward the wine. "My grandfather's collection. He spent years building it."

We wander over to the rows of wine racks. Nyro picks up a bottle and blows off the dust. He nods his head, turns to Chry with raised eyebrows. "Wow."

"Yeah. It's a classic tale. Save and save and for what? I re-member when he died, the bottles coming up all day, the next day, the day after that, the night of the wake, after the funeral, bottles and bottles and bottles moving up into the light to be drunk, opposite of being down in the dark to be saved."

"How 'bout now?" says Nyro.

"Good a time as any." Chry shrugs. "Could be our last day on earth. We just need to find a corkscrew."

The cellar is impervious to the whistle and wail of the storm we'd escaped. I can't help worrying about G.A. but she'd been so sure, and Chry so obedient and now unworried as we wander the dusky cellar, poking around the vast jumble.

I root through shelves of old serving platters and dishes and a pile of silver candlesticks, trays, and bowls, all tarnished black. There's a chair like the ones in the kitchen but with a broken back. I pull it over to see if maybe's there's a corkscrew up on some high shelves.

At my new eye level, I find a bunch of empty cigar boxes. I hold one out to Chry.

"My grandfather smoked cigars." She laughs. "I mean, duh," she adds, indicating the upper shelves piled with boxes. She pauses; looking at the boxes her eyes go dreamy. "After a long day playing in the water, or in the woods, I'd have dinner, then a bath. I'd run the halls in my summer nightgown, snooping in closets and drawers, touching every stray thing I found— an empty perfume bottle, a piece of red felt holding a row of sewing needles, golf tees, concert tickets. I'd peek into my grandparents' room with the fireplace and the fainting couch, the door would be open, letting the breeze come across the upstairs rooms. He'd be there in his wingback chair pretending to be sleeping, his cigar burning in the ashtray next to him. I'd tiptoe through these golden shafts of evening light until I was right in front of him and yell, 'Boo!' He'd make a little jump and say, 'They told me there were ghosts, but I wouldn't believe it.' I'd say, 'I'm not a ghost, Grandfather. I'm a girl.' He'd hold his heart. 'Thank God. Thank God,' he'd say. 'I thought you were a ghost.'"

Above the cigar boxes is another high shelf. This one is piled with dozens of different-sized glass jars filled with seeds.

"What are these?" I say to Chry, picking one up.

She drags another broken chair over to where I am and stands on it.

I unscrew the lid. A medicine-y smell overtakes us. We gag, though after the first whiff, it's not too bad. I lick my finger and touch it to the seeds in the jar, pulling out three. They're light brown and covered in white spikes that disintegrate when I rub my thumb against them. I squeeze them flat, but they don't crumble. I open more jars. They're all the same.

Chry picks up a seed and stares at it. "I think...I'm pretty sure...these are seeds for Queen Anne's lace. I think. You know how G.A. planted the garden on West Seventy-First Street? We have them, right? Growing out back?"

I shrug. "Yeah, but it's a little patch. You could plant a meadow with what's here."

We mirror each other's perplexed look and jump down off the chairs. Something. There's something private about these seeds stashed away so high.

"Danny, Dare, find anything?" Chry calls, covering for our secret.

"Nothing for opening wine, but we might need this," says Dare, holding up a long, heavy-duty flashlight. "Depending on the storm."

"A solution!" says Nyro, emerging from the shadows of a large wooden wardrobe, cracked and warped, its wood-inlayed deco design ruined with mold. He comes into the light, slashing the air with a machete, shiny and sharp. "What's this for, Chry?" He makes large swiping Xs as Dare, Chry, and I take steps away.

"Slashing your way through the forest."

"What forest?"

"The whole north end of Arcadia, off to the side of the house. The room you're in looks out on it. My dad used it to make a path for me when I was little to this very cool place deep inside...where he'd played as a kid." She pauses, embarrassed. "He said I should be on the lookout for fairies, which are small and fly, and gnomes, which are the size of an ice cream cone and walk like gentlemen."

"Hard not to love the girl with a magical forest," says Nyro.

"True," says Dare and smiles.

Chry turns her face to him and stares.

"Hey, watch this magic," says Nyro, holding the machete loose at his side. He walks back through the racks of wine, then whistles low. "This is some collection," he says as he studies the bottles, his face empty and strange. It's as if he's trying to find a way to have them all in the short time we'll be staying here, like he's deciding if drinking as much as possible would be as good a heist as pulling up a truck and carting them away. "Okay! Here we go…" He pulls a bottle off a low rack and comes forward to present it to us. '64 Dom Perignon. "Stand back. Let the magic begin." He takes off the foil, untwists the wire and carefully removes it, and, holding the bottle at the neck and pointing it away from us, takes the machete and in a quick swoop of the blade catches the edge of the cork and sends it flying into the cellar's recesses. He holds up the bottle victoriously letting it bubble and flow, then tips it into his mouth. We throw our head backs and let him pour the delicious bubbles into our mouths as if we all just won the World Series.

"Here's to the girl with a magical forest!" He holds the bottle aloft in salute.

"To Chry!" we all say.

"To me!" says Chry.

At the top of the cellar steps, the door opens, making a rectangle of light. It's G.A. telling us the world is safe again. "Chrysanthi," she says. "Come see."

We clamor up the steps to find G.A. standing stock still in the kitchen with a mild expression on her face and staring down at the lake, at the damage, the mess. "My goodness," she says, "this is extremely inconvenient." The iron frame of the dock has been lifted and corkscrewed into the sky like a roller coaster to nowhere. It's wooden slats, busted and broken, are a mass of floating debris. The roof of the boathouse is gone, and the walls are partially wrecked, but the boat is still on its lift next to the mangled dock, unharmed.

18

The next day there's a lot of hoopla because it had been a tornado. Its path of destruction was intentional and narrow, like the worst person you ever met pursuing their own worst instincts. Some of us get mowed down, some of us are bystanders: A line of houses in town with their front porches ripped off, a row of docks and boats shredded next to a row left untouched.

Nyro, Dare, Chry, and I stand on the wide stone terrace, holding cups of coffee steaming in the clear cool morning, not saying anything. Maybe we're all thinking the same thing—the path of suffering is random and exact. Maybe not them, but I am.

Inside the house, G.A. is making phone calls, all no-nonsense, firm but polite. St. James Day is Thursday. Things need fixing. Things need to be perfect. She is a general gathering an army.

The garage at Arcadia, like the basement, is a century of necessary and unnecessary things, but with items less dusty and more recently utilized—bikes, water skis, tow ropes, marine-grade fittings and fasteners, garden tools. It's a jumble, unlike the garage in New Jersey, which is organized and stacked, though the black jeep we'd taken to Asbury Park is parked inside.

"How'd that get here?" I ask.

"My dad comes back and forth in it all the time, and sometimes he flies home and leaves the jeep here."

"He comes by himself?"

"A lot. My mom's not so crazy about Arcadia. Or G.A."

"Your grandmother? Really?"

"She likes her fine, she's just not into following her rules. I can't remember the last time she's been here on St. James Day.

She refuses to be told what color to wear. She says she doesn't look good in white."

We pull four rickety bikes from behind some sails and other boat stuff and attempt to pump up the tires. Only two have tires that will both hold air, so we tell Nyro and Dare we'll see them later and leave them sprawled in the morning sun, laid out on a couple of chaise lounges on the terrace. Dare had asked G.A. if he could help with the storm cleanup, but she firmly told him no, he was her guest. Nyro hadn't offered.

Chry and I want to see what there is to see. There had been swaths of damage, but no death, so we weren't being ghoulish, just curious. We pedal out the driveway leading to the road under a bright blue sky. My bicycle squeaks and scrapes with the rickety sounds of old parts brushing against each other. *Pedal, pedal, click, thunk.* The shoulder of the two-lane road is wide and flat and lined to forever with the Queen Anne's lace and chicory I'd been hearing so much about. Chicory, that blue-eyed maiden who told the god Apollo to get the hell away from her, so he turned her into a flower that lives for only one day. *Pedal, pedal, click, thunk.* If you cut chicory with a gold knife at noon or midnight on St. James Day, it will open locks and doors. I picture G.A. collecting Queen Anne's lace for seeds, feel the secret of them up on her high cellar shelf.

We work our legs up the hills, catch glimpses of the lake at the top, then watch the view disappear as we hurtle down. Everything about Chry's family's speedboat is dangerous to me and the storm was terrifying, but cresting these hills with their wildflowers, sweet air, and long views, pedaling to the rhythm of my breath and the clacking of this bicycle that already knows the way, has taken this stretch of road before—all of it is bone-deep peace.

We ride up on a green-gold hay field flattened and covered with storm-soaked pink housing insulation, the handiwork of yesterday's destruction. It clings to the landscape like a Van Gogh painting covered in wet confetti.

"Whoa, whoa, whoa." Chry skids to a stop and drops her

bike. She jumps the flower-filled ditch and sprints into the field. "It's like a giant chewed up all the Barbie doll clothes in the world and spit them out," she shouts back to me.

"Freaky," I say, but don't move.

If Chry feels you're resisting a plan, it's like rocket fuel for her, but I don't feel like hanging around. This field is partly pink when it's supposed to be only green gold. Someone must care.

"Mina, check this out!" She holds up a big white plastic pillow.

I stay put.

She runs back toward me. Her stride is graceful, even though she's carrying a fat white pillow under one arm and something under the other.

"You take this."

"I don't know, Chry... It probably blew here last night, maybe someone's looking for it."

"It's nothing, don't worry. Better you take it than it gets buried in this field forever," she says and pushes it on me.

Chry tightens the other treasure, what I now see is a wooden box, under one arm and grips her bike's handlebar with her free hand. I do the same with the squishy white rectangle.

"Really?" I raise my eyebrows.

"Really." She smiles and pedals off.

We sit opposite each other on the twin beds in her room. My room too, for the week I'm here, but it's been Chry's for a lifetime of summers at Arcadia. Like the rest of the house, it has wide-planked, polished honey-colored floors. The walls are covered in old-fashioned wallpaper, cream with stripes of small, pale blue flowers. There's an oil painting in a heavy gold frame of a sailing race, a line of boats with their sails all leaning in the same direction. The furniture is mahogany, heavy and dark. The beds are made up with white chenille spreads—quilts with elaborate designs in faded blue and white—folded at their ends to pull up on cold nights.

Chry hands me the box. It's wide and flat, about ten inches across, six inches high, polished and smooth. On the top is a design made with inlayed wood.

"A rose compass," says Chry, eyes shining, "like downstairs, in the front hall." She traces her finger on the rose compass design. "When I was little, I'd ask G.A. why it was in the floor crooked. She'd say, 'That's your point of view, darling. North is north.'" Chry loses herself and stares off with her lips curved in a gentle smile. Then she remembers where we are, that I'm here, and laughs at herself for relating another dreamy memory. She shrugs a shoulder, as if to say, *Who could blame me?*

The box is locked tight. I shake it. Something inside shifts but it doesn't clank like it's filled with gold coins or gobs of jewelry. I gently try to pry the lid off, but it's fixed tight. There's a tiny gold keyhole. Where would you even put the key that fit in there to keep from losing it?

"Should we smash it?" I say. It doesn't seem right but I'm curious.

"No. It's too beautiful. What if it's an antique? What if the box is worth more than what's inside?"

"You're right."

"St. James Day," Chry says with a nod, indicating a solution so final no more discussion is needed. She laughs again, this time to acknowledge the absurdity of this magical fix. She walks over to the closet and stashes the box on a high shelf. "So, we're not tempted."

"Where are we going to find a gold knife," I ask, ashamed of my practicality in the face of Chry's summer magic.

"I know someone with a gold knife," she says.

I do too. Dare. She'd told me about it, how she watched him shave with it.

Neither of us speak, thinking about that long night, the fun of it burned deep into both of us. We had talked about that part, the fun, but now I see how personal it was for her.

She and Dare had spent the night together. She'd watched him shave. Meanwhile Nyro and I had our night. I'd do that again; it wasn't love, but possibly a *kind* of love. I don't know.

The curtains lift with a breeze bringing in lake air. It smells fresh, like everything that ever lived and died gave itself back to the water, sky, and earth until all that was left were the clean white bones.

Chry takes the white plastic pillow I'd brought in and works the rusted zipper around three sides and then flaps the top open. It's a wedding dress. She lays it out on the bed, and we stare at the thick matte silk with embroidered flowers covering the bodice and sprinkled out across the skirt and train. There's a veil, also spattered with flowers. Its demure neckline and cap sleeves are from another time. "Wait here," she says.

She returns with a large dangerous-looking pair of scissors and, without flinching, sets them on the dress. It's equal parts fascinating and devastating. The elegant, if old-fashioned, cap sleeves, peplum-type overlay, and almost the entire skirt and train, are relieved of their duties.

Watching Chry attack the dress with her long, sharp-bladed scissors, I wonder what happened to Sirena Fuggitiva's cerulean dress. I rarely pray. Almost never, but I clasp my hands, try to silence the sound of steel scissors on silk with the words in my head. *Please let this never happen to that dress. Please let it be found and worn by someone whose beloved did not die. Please. Please. Please.*

19

The woods at Arcadia are Chry's sweet secret. Her dad made the path that wound through them when he was a kid, then opened it back up with Nyro's machete when Chry was old enough to venture in by herself. At the far edge, there's a wide clearing with mossy ground cover and a wide ring of mushrooms. The mushrooms are like in a fairy tale, but they're real: white stalks, red caps with white dots. Chry was told never to touch them and never, ever, to eat them. She never ate them, but she did touch them. She made them into umbrellas for the woodland creatures she created out of sticks and leaves. She picked them and pulled out their stems, turned them over to make boats for the pools of water that form where trees grow together.

She takes us there. We follow the path into the woods, the sounds of motorboats and lawn mowers transmuted into a distant buzz, sunlight coming through the trees in long rays as Chry tells us her childhood tales. "I used to think they could kill you, but they won't kill you—that's not the main purpose anyway—they're for daydreaming. I only ever picked enough so I wouldn't get caught. I didn't want to disturb the fairy ring; it protected me. I liked to lie in the middle of the circle looking up at the clouds moving through the sky and the trees swaying in the breeze making the light move."

And here we are, Nyro, Dare, Chry, and me, lying in the clearing on the mossy earth staring up at the tops of the trees and moving light just as she had as a child. I'm asleep and awake, dreaming of the exact place I am in. We humans, for once, are quiet, even Nyro. And for the moment, I don't know anything else so there's nothing else to dream about. We lie and lie and lie in the circle beneath the sky and dream dreams about only this. I respectfully decline the universe's standard offer of the future. Instead of moving forward in time, I let it circle me. There's only this sky and the memory of this sky, nothing else.

I feel a shadow across my face. It might be the sun moving past the trees or the trees themselves, alive and moving in the breeze, but it's Chry, standing over me. "Time to go," she says.

I nod. Everything is a circle, nothing ends, just answers to questions, questions to answers, questions, answers…

20

G.A. hands Chry a box which she takes, holding it like a nuclear weapon or a baby. It's identical to the one she found in the field, but it isn't that one. One of the two of us knows this—me. I can see from where I'm sitting that the box from the field is still up on the closet shelf where she'd stashed it.

Chry had changed her mind about asking Dare for his gold knife and had asked G.A. for one to cut chicory at noon or midnight on St. James Day. This is what passes for normal conversation at Arcadia, and anyway, Chry remembered from some year gone by that there was a gold knife in the house somewhere. When Chry asked if there was, G.A. had said, "Yes." She said she would look and here she is handing a compass rose box to Chry whose face is knit in confusion.

We'd been sitting on our side-by-side beds, Chry playing an invisible bass, practicing, practicing, like always. There wasn't room in Nyro's Beamer for the actual bass. I'd been rereading my options book for work. I don't need to know this stuff right away, but I will eventually. The derivatives markets are only getting bigger. The old drunks in the back row of the trading floor might be happy brokering Eurodollars until the end of time, but the new crop, the ones who came up right before me, with their Hermès ties and Church's of London shoes, know there's bigger, better money elsewhere.

"It's a compass rose, like the one downstairs in the entryway," says G.A.

"Yeah, yeah, I see. Where, uh, where is it from?" says Chry.

"The man who did our floor made these for me with the extra wood, three of them. One for me and one for each of my sons."

"Do you have the key?" says Chry.

"Ah yes. Somewhere. Wait here. I've hidden it and...let me see."

Chry widens her eyes at me.

"It's not the same box; the one you found is still in the closet. I can see it from here," I tell her when G.A. leaves.

G.A. returns holding a very long and delicate gold chain with a tiny gold key on the end, so tiny she has to hold between her fingernails.

"And there's a gold knife in here?" asks Chry.

"Yes, yes, I think so. A gift to my husband, to open oysters." Chry and I exchange looks. This is the key to the box that holds the gold knife to cut the chicory to open the box that she found in the field.

"Now let's see that box," she says and Chry, who's been holding it like it might explode since G.A. handed it to her, offers it up with both hands. G.A. inserts the key and turns it with a surprisingly loud click. We laugh. She carefully puts the key on its long thin chain around her neck.

"Go ahead, Chrysanthi."

Chry lifts the lid.

G.A.'s face stills, the anticipation of the St. James Day treasure she was expecting drained away.

"G.A., you okay?" Seeing her grandmother turn pale, Chry closes the lid, puts the box on the bed and says, "Come on." She takes her arm and walks her to her bedroom. I follow. In the bedroom, Chry helps her grandmother onto the fainting couch.

"Thank you, darling."

"Sure, sure." Chry pulls up the big wing chair, sits down and waits while I stand in the doorway like the child ghost Chry once pretended to be.

"They were looking for it in Pittsburgh," G.A. says. "There were safe deposit boxes at three different banks. They scoured the apartment... Your father wanted to have it appraised with the rest of the estate."

"And it's been here this whole time?"

"It's like I was hiding it on purpose, but why would I have done that?"

"It's your crown," says Chry, "from your wedding. I've seen it in the pictures. I guess you could do whatever you wanted with it." Inside the box had not been a gold oyster knife, but G.A.'s bridal tiara.

"Yes. Garnets, pearls, interestingly a row of diamonds that detach to make a necklace, all set in platinum. My husband bought it for me to wear for our nuptials. Something new. I had a veil attached and it was quite beautiful. We had a perfect day, a beautiful write-up in the society pages."

"Did you ever wear it again?"

"No, never. It didn't seem polite. I felt that…" For the first time since I've met her, G.A. seems old and frail. There's something she wants to say. We wait but nothing comes. Maybe because she can't remember or maybe because I'm standing here.

"A crown is…a crown is a foolish thing." She turns in a quick motion. "I must check on the work. The boathouse should be finished soon." She reignites, getting up from the sofa. "You have it, Chrysanthi. I want it for you, my only granddaughter. But don't worry, I remember now, it doesn't have any power. Not anymore. Just something fun."

We listen to her quick sure steps click down the hall. Chry holds the open box, showing me the jeweled heirloom. "Mina," she says, "I don't want this," but she closes the lid respectfully.

"She didn't give you the key."

"I don't care."

"Well, maybe it would open the other box, from the field."

"Oh, shit." She shakes her head. "What is going on? I don't know. I'll ask her for it later."

21

On our third day at Arcadia, Nyro makes pancakes. Dare isn't surprised when he offers to cook for us, but Chry and I are. "Honestly," she says, "I thought you were too selfish."

Nyro doesn't reply just shrugs cheerfully.

The pancakes are delicious. When Chry and Dare aren't looking, I catch Nyro's eye and mouth the words, *I could love you.*

"Don't do it," he says back in full voice.

"Don't do what?" says Dare.

"Don't have any more. We're going swimming off the boat in a little bit."

My breath catches in my throat. The dock's been too wrecked to swim from and the boat's been trapped on its lift in a construction zone, so I haven't had to answer to the fact that I can't swim. The sailboat, a Thistle, I'm told, is still on its mooring with a wrecked and broken mast. G.A.'s been too busy to care what we're up to during the day, which has involved non-water-type things like lying around in a circle of red-capped, white-spotted mushrooms on a mossy clearing in the woods. We've also been working on having something white to wear for the St. James Day celebration.

Turns out Chry knows how to sew. G.A. had taught her a little bit at a time over all their summers together. The wedding dress she had found and massacred was too big for her, so she reworked it on an old black Singer sewing machine tucked away in the corner of G.A.'s big master bedroom.

I watched her from the fainting couch. I'd asked if could lie on it and Chry motioned, *Yeah, yeah, no problem.* G.A. flew by the doorway in the fast-motion way she had of moving through the house as she prepared for St. James Day, then stopped dead and tilted her head back, observing me in her spot on the couch and

Chry on her sewing machine. "Lovely, yes. Lovely girls, so glad you're enjoying your time here," she said.

When she was finished, Chry held the dress up. "Should be perfect."

"Looks perfect," I say back. I can't get past my queasiness over the destruction of the dress, haunted by the dress of Sirena Fuggitiva's. I've heard tornadoes can carry things for miles, so maybe this one once belonged to someone in another state or maybe it belonged to someone *nearby*.

"So now we have to figure out something for you," says Chry.

I knew everyone wore white to G.A.'s St. James Day party, but I'd forgotten to pack something and so had Chry; besides, she didn't even have anything white to wear until the dress she was holding up in front of her flew into her life.

She'd remembered to tell Dare, the day she got up the nerve to call and invite him and Nyro to Arcadia. She had laid out the week, how it would go, and had told them everyone wore white to the party.

We'd been occupied here with getting up late, then doing this and that until the afternoons, when one of us, usually Nyro, would go downstairs and embark on our nightly effort to shrink the wine collection. We'd lain around the living room, doors open wide, the lake breezes coming through the screens with that same white-bone smell of everything that had ever lived and died since the glacier that carved the lake, mixed with the smell of the house's old books and long, silent winters.

Chry would pick something from the record collection, which was lined up across a long low shelf. You couldn't guess what she would pull out of the sleeve and lay on the turntable, but it was a lot of jazz, Pat Metheny, Weather Report, or another incarnation of Jaco, until Dare would get up and put on something else, The Police maybe. Then Nyro would get tired of that, and put on the Stones, *Hot Rocks 1964-1971*, turned up loud. It was the closest thing he could find to maybe make himself happy from the frayed and battered records.

I eat Nyro's pancakes slowly. I do not want to go swimming out in the middle of the lake. I can't. My face flushes hot. I shift my eyes away from Chry, rest them on the framed needlepoint sign on the wall above her head: *Steel lightens your work, brightens your leisure, and widens your world.* Her grandfather bought Arcadia with steel money.

"Look," I say. "I start my new job next week. I have to read some stuff."

"Same," says Dare.

"You both started new jobs and you both have to read some stuff?" Nyro says skeptically.

"Yeah, Danny, yeah, we did. Promoted. Both of us." I nod.

"Well, congratufuckinlations," he says not unkindly. "Chry, you and I can still go, right?"

A bolt of fear comes up from my gut. Chry out on a boat with Nyro by herself, the guy who once, in theory, didn't mind watching her maybe drown.

I shoot her a look. She shoots one back. My look says, *You need a chaperone.* Her look says, *You fucked him, that seems a lot more dangerous then tooling around in the middle of the lake I grew up on.*

"What's left to learn? Something more random than Monte Carlo?" she says, impressing me with her memory of the night we all went up to Windows on the World. Though I wonder, for a minute, if it was necessary for Chry to remind me how shitty I felt that night.

I shrug. "Rereading. Same stuff."

Nyro looks up. "What the fuck are you people talking about?"

"Option theory," says Dare, chopping his words to shut Nyro down.

"Monte Carlo, something more random than random," I say quietly. I lower my voice even further. "It's kind of hard to grasp, that's why I need to reread the material." False. It *is* hard to grasp, but I don't need to reread the material.

"Hey, Dare," says Chry changing the subject. "Can we borrow your gold knife? St. James Day is almost here, and we have a lock to open."

Has she forgotten about G.A.'s key? Or maybe it's not St. James Day *unless* you're opening locks and doors.

"I don't have a gold knife," he says, uncurious about the rest of Chry's question.

"Your razor, didn't you bring it?"

"Oh yeah, that is gold. I don't use that anymore, just your boring ordinary safety razor these days."

Chry and Nyro leave to put on their bathing suits. When they return Dare and I watch them walk down the lawn and wade through the water where the dock is still missing. Chry, waist deep, pulls on the big wheel of the lift and lowers the boat while Nyro watches. When it's low enough, they climb up on it, work the cover off, and eventually back out, Chry driving slowly to avoid the Thistle still broken on its buoy.

"Did you even bring the book?" I ask Dare.

"Nah, I just didn't feel like swimming right now."

I tell him he can borrow mine. He says sure but he's going upstairs for now, going back to bed maybe.

Up in our bedroom, I make both my and Chry's bed, hang up some clothes she left on the floor, and straighten my side of the room. I pick up the options book and leaf through the pages. I know it cold. I'm not sure if Dare does but I don't mind sharing; we're not competing anymore. We're on different desks and we can help each other. I walk down the honey-floored hall to his room, picturing Chry as a little girl ghost flitting around in her white nightgown.

Dare calls for me to come in when I knock. Like all the bedrooms at Arcadia, the walls in here are covered with old-fashioned wallpaper; this one has a pale green background with big pink roses. The room has twin beds the same as ours, but Dare has it to himself. Nyro has his own room too. He sits on the bed near the open window, back up against the headboard, a blanket covering his outstretched legs though it's warm in here. It's on the other side of the house from ours, so the air doesn't float up in soft wind off the water. In here, it's still and smells like pine and loam. The only movement comes in sound—that soft summer insect hum.

I sit on the edge of the opposite bed holding my book.

There's a concert poster tacked up with pushpins on the wall between us. It's a jaunty grinning skeleton wearing a hat and playing guitar inside a ring of roses. Grateful Dead, Watkins Glen Summer Jam, July 28th, 1973. It's the only randomly tacked-up thing in the entire house, so unlike the oil painting of sailboats in its heavy gold frame in our room. I imagine this is Mark's room, Chry's uncle. I can picture G.A. leaving this poster up out of a softness for him, the way she must have come to West Seventy-First Street and planted wildflowers.

"I brought you the book," I say, holding it up to prove my errand.

"You can leave it."

I put it on the nightstand between us.

For the first time since we've met, with no task, no trading floor buzz, no booze, no Chry to take up all the feeling, I am overcome with shyness. I fold and unfold my hands, lift my hair up onto the back of my head, twist it, stick the end through and pull it into a loose bun. "I suppose you don't need to review either."

"No."

"Didn't feel like swimming?"

"No. You?"

Out the window are the tops of pine trees. The room is getting warmer. I can feel the sun rising higher in the sky. "I can't swim," I say. "I don't know how to swim."

Dare looks out toward the pines, adjusts the blanket on his legs. "It's weird, how these things come up and make it difficult when you least expect it."

"I should have told her," I say. "I mean, I knew we were coming to a lake. I'm just so good at not swimming, I don't bother to think how it might go."

He nods. I flip my feet up and lie down, cross my hands over my chest, my shyness evaporating. "How'd you get the job at Merton, anyway?"

"They recruited me out of college. I couldn't go home. Not that I wanted to."

"Why not?" I pause. "Vestal Virgin," I say, though I'm not sure why.

His chest rises and falls in a sigh, then he says, "What there is to know is this…" He stops, considers, then continues. "I was batting .357 my senior year in high school and I had speed; there were scouts."

I interrupt him to ask didn't he play football and he tells me, yes, football and baseball.

"I was in our kitchen shooting the breeze with my grandmother and watching her roll out dough for Easter Bread when my father called, wanting me to come down to the store. It's an appliance store, he still has it. I drove down there and found him sitting in his office. He had his elbows on the desk, fingertips pressed together in the shape of a steeple. He said, 'I'm hearing those scouts left town because they found out you were selling drugs.' I said, 'Yes, sir, that's true.' Then he said my name, 'Darius.' Just like that, so gentle I began to relax. 'Darius,' he said it again the same way, 'Are you telling me they left town because they heard you were dealing drugs.' 'Yes. Yes, sir,' I said. 'What drugs?' he said, still soft, like he was reaching down into his heart to understand what would make a kid with his whole future ahead of him do something like that. 'Pot,' I said." Dare stops. He goes on. "My dad picked up his Kiwanis Service Award paper weight and with the precision of fifteen years of pitching to me in the backyard and his own three in Double-A ball, hurled it, smashing this once perfect nose—" He puts his finger to where it goes crooked. "—into adulthood where it would never look or work the same again."

"So, no going home?"

"No going home. But, hey, who knew my business acumen would land me on Wall Street."

"We're doing good, aren't we?"

"Yeah, we're doing good."

I sit up, swing my legs over, and jump up off the bed. "Come on, they'll be back soon, let's go. Why sit up here like an old man?" I try to snatch the blanket, but he grabs it and pulls it back over his legs with a quick ferocity that surprises me.

"No thanks," he says, calm again.

22

A huge white tent, white folding chairs, tables covered in white linen—everything is set for St. James Day. It's the kind of miracle that money can buy. G.A. had commanded an army of construction companies to repair the dock and boathouse in four days. They'd dropped their contract work to help. Everyone in the world for a hundred miles in every direction knew that St. James Day must come, and it must be perfect.

Chry had also performed a miracle, a thieving kind of miracle. She'd produced a sail from one of the many recesses of Arcadia, either the jumble of the cellar, the garage, or quite possibly the boathouse. We'd been prohibited from going in there since it was a construction site but that wouldn't have stopped her. From the stolen sail she cut and sewed a dress for me. I worry that once the mast on the *Wand'ring* is fixed someone will be looking for it, but she said no, the boat to this sail is long gone. I chose to believe her. It's a simple dress, ingenious really, using the stiffness of the fabric to add to the dress's dramatic style. She'd used me as a live model sewing with a giant curved needle and heavy-duty thread since the sail fabric was too bulky for the sewing machine.

Chry's dad came in last night from New Jersey and her uncle Mark arrived from Los Angeles. Dare and Nyro had driven up to the Buffalo airport to get him while Chry worked on my dress.

We are out on the terrace early morning. Congressman Risk and Chry's uncle Mark are in faded shorts and sweatshirts shucking oysters. The lake is perfectly still, a pale pink sky mirror of the morning light. Chry and I sip from mugs of coffee, both of us up early at her behest. She puts down her mug and holds her hand out to her dad. "You too, Mina," she says, so I do the same.

He puts oyster shells, each with its gray, recently deceased inhabitant into our outstretched hands. Chry slurps her oyster, then pitches what's left into the can with the other spent shells. "Happy St. James Day!" she shouts. I cup the rough shell in my palm, hold it up to my lips, and suck down the raw oyster and its salty bath, just as Chry had done. I lick the seawater off my fingers, pitch the shell into the can, and shyly call out a Happy St. James Day.

"To suffering!" says Chry, a rebuke to my timid St. James Day greeting.

"To suffering," her dad and uncle say in low voices, looking over their shoulders.

"They don't want G.A to hear," Chry says to me. "She doesn't like the suffering toast. And. They're. Afraid. Of. Her."

Mark says it again, louder, though he still doesn't shout it. "To suffering!" He lifts his shucking knife for emphasis, his *gold* shucking knife.

"Hey, where'd that come from?" says Chry.

"What?"

"The knife."

"What do you mean? It was my dad's, the original."

"Well, how come you have it?"

"Why wouldn't I?"

"G.A. was looking for it the other day."

"Okay, well here it is." He shrugs and sticks it into the hinge of the oyster in his hand, slides the knife along the edge, makes another cut and brings the shell bearing the doomed creature up to his lips. He pauses to take in the anticipatory moment, then slurps it into his mouth.

Chry and I walk down the sloping lawn and out onto the dock to look at the party set-up from the lake. Everything is perfect—the boathouse is returned to its original state, the dock too looks like no tornado ever happened. We walk to the end, look down through the clear water to the flat rocks on the bottom. I can stand here, tippy toe anyway. Turning back toward the grounds of Arcadia, the tent, tables, and chairs, everything, is ready; next comes the army of workers to set up the white porcelain dishes and silver vases of Queen Anne's lace. Chry closes her eyes, breathes in, a feeling and a memory of a feeling. I do the same, a first time feeling.

When we get back to the terrace, there's a sheriff's deputy sitting with his feet up, shooting the breeze with Chry's dad. The congressman offers him an oyster off the shell like he'd given us, but the deputy waves it away, so he slurps it down himself.

They're talking about the traffic, where the cars will park, and what time the sheriff's department will be here to help. The sheriff nods at Jamie Risk's questions and directions. They're easy with each other. When the coming details of the day are ironed out, the conversation stalls, but the deputy stays there, feet up, hands behind his head.

"Anyway, Jamie," the deputy swings his legs down and stands up, "we'll make sure your traffic runs smooth."

"Thanks, Marty. Appreciate it." Chry's dad turns to us. "Chrysanthi, you girls want to help open these?" He looks at Chry. "You'll have to take over one day."

She says yes, but only if she can use the gold knife.

"Here," says Mark. "I've been at it all morning." He hands the knife to Chry. "Just make sure it gets put back right."

Chry's dad hands me a regular oyster knife and both of us a clean dishtowel. "Grab one out of the cooler," he says. We each pick out an oyster and hold it with our towels. Following his instructions, I slip the knife into the hinge, move it down both sides underneath the top shell, then move it along the bottom shell to cut the muscle. I pull the top shell off, pitch it into the bin, and offer the bottom shell up to Jamie Risk, to show him my success.

He smiles. "That's it, Mina. You can eat the first one, but the rest go on ice."

I slurp down my prize, chuck the shell, pick up another, and get down to the business of Risk family traditions, shucking oysters on the morning of July 25th.

Noon or midnight, I think as I stick a plain old non-gold knife into an oyster. G.A.'s key, I think, as I move it from side to side.

I help until the job is finished. My hand aches but it feels good to be on the family end of St. James Day at Arcadia. The party will be thrilling, I know it, but in a way this is something even better.

Chry's dad collects the towels. "This stuff will stink up the house if we don't take care of it right away."

In the kitchen Chry, still holding the gold knife, says, "I need this."

"What for?" says her dad.

"To cut chicory, so I can open something at noon or midnight."

"Honey, that's just a made-up thing."

This defeats everything Chry has told me—Arcadia is magic, St. James Day is magic—but she doesn't seem to mind and she doesn't wilt under her father's denial. When he puts out his hand and says, "I need to wash it," she gives it to him. He goes to the sink with the slow deliberation of someone who is buying time. After washing the knife, he takes a fresh dish towel out of the drawer and dries it, then goes over to the liquor cabinet above the refrigerator and, one by one, pulls the bottles down and puts them on the counter. He stands up on his toes and reaches his hand into the back of the high cupboard to feel around where he can't see. Out comes a compass rose box. That makes three. Two everyone knows about, and one only Chry and I know about.

"This knife didn't get put back last year." He tries to pry open the cover with his fingers, but like the others, it's locked down tight. Without hesitating, he takes the gold knife and slips it under the lid above the keyhole. It pops it open. 11:47. Close enough to call it magic. I steal a look at Chry, who is watching as deliberately as her father is moving. I gesture with my chin to the clock, it's almost noon. She mouths the word, *Midnight*. There are so many practical reasons why this is all dumb. The gold knife is now in the box we theoretically need to open another box. A plain old oyster knife would open ours. G.A. has a key to at least one of them and chances are it could open all of them. Jamie Risk takes a white velvet pouch from inside the box, opens the drawstring, and puts the knife in. He puts the whole thing back and closes it up, then stashes the box where he found it and returns the bottles of scotch, bourbon, vodka, and gin, one by one.

&

The St. James Day Celebration at Arcadia is here, and it is as beautiful and perfect as Chry said it would be. She and I make our way through the crowd in our white dresses and wait our turns at one of the bars under the tent. "Tanqueray and tonic," says Chry to the bartender, a fit older woman with a pretty, lined face wearing black pants and a white blouse.

She stares.

"Please."

"Make that two," I say, squeezing in next to Chry.

The bartender doesn't speak. She looks at me uncomprehendingly, then back at Chry. She is in an obvious struggle to overcome some overwhelming incident but it's just us, one decked out in a remade wedding dress and one sewn into a stolen sail. When she regains her composure, she says, "You're Chrysanthi, all grown up... I've been working your grandma's summer party since forever. I'm...uh...Cass."

"Cass, yes, hello," says Chry. "You work at the Breeze Inn, right?" Chry turns to me. "All-time best french fries ever."

"Yes, I do work there, own it actually—"

"Oh, of course, I'm sorry. I've always wondered, how is it in the winter?"

"Oh, it's not the weekend crowds like the summer, that's for sure. We have our regulars. There's always a fire going in the Franklin Stove. More cozy than crowded, you know?" Cass has relaxed, but she stiffens again, as if remembering whatever it was that had originally darkened her face. "Did you say Tanqueray?" She cuts the word hard at the end.

"And tonic. Two."

After she mixes the cocktails and hands them to us, she says, "Your dress? It's…familiar."

"Oh, you wouldn't have seen it in the store or anything. It's made by me from an old wedding dress." Chry smiles big, letting her know she's not the kind of elite asshole who's above repurposing an old dress.

"I see." Cass blinks and shakes her head, as if she's ridding herself of whatever's in it.

"Thanks," says Chry, turning away blind to the heavy air between them. I follow her but glance back. Cass's mouth is a hard line.

Nyro comes up beside me. He's wearing a white shirt with the sleeves rolled up and white shorts. He leans in, schussing and crunching the sail I'm wearing. He kisses my ear, near the top outer edge and it sends a current to my legs. "Later, the face, then the body," he says, his lips grazing the place he just kissed.

"I won't tell anyone," I say.

"Won't tell anyone what?"

"You are in possession of a beating human heart."

"Mmmm…good. It's better for me that way."

Dare comes through the crowd. He's wearing a white shirt like Nyro, white pants, long though, not shorts.

"Where's your dad?" Nyro says to Chry. "I haven't had a chance to talk to him about the Weehawken project."

Chry shrugs. She could care less about the Weehawken project, but I half wonder/half guess what a boy who owns all the cranes in New York City and a New Jersey congressman might talk about on St. James Day at Arcadia.

By the time the suffering speech comes around, everyone is woozily, deliriously happy.

Chry's dad and her uncle Mark stand on the table piled with used-up oyster shells. Mark whistles sharply and calls out, "Everyone, everyone. Hey, people," until it finally gets quiet. "My brother, the saint…" he says and makes an exaggerated gesture toward Congressman James "Jamie" Risk.

The saint lifts his glass. "To suffering," he calls out to us all. "To suffering," we shout back. And now I have shouted "To Suffering" at the Risk family's St. James Day Celebration, a party I had only heard about in stories. If anyone asks what I did on my summer vacation, I can say I celebrated St. James Day at Arcadia and that it was perfect, better than Christmas.

It's two thirty in the morning and there are still voices downstairs. Chry disappeared after the suffering speech, forgetting or not caring that we were going to open the box using chicory cut with a gold knife at midnight. I came upstairs after I lost track of her. Out the window, conversations rise and fall, occasionally staccatoed with laughter. A quarter moon slides into the lake.

When Chry was young she had a nine o'clock bedtime on St. James Day but no matter how much the party was raving on, G.A. would come to her room to say good night and tell her the tenth miracle of St. James. Chry tells it to me when she tells me stories to help me fall asleep, when she talks about St. James Day. She tells it to me as a gift, a gift to a girl who is afraid to fall asleep. I think of it now as I stare out at the sinking moon, afraid of the gunshots and knives falling into piles that may or may not come as I drift off. I'm afraid to lay my head down without Chry.

A man returning home from his pilgrimage to Jerusalem goes up on deck one night after dinner to sit on the edge of the ship and feel the cool evening breezes. He falls. As he is falling, he calls to St. James to save him. His friend throws him his shield and shouts, "May the glorious apostle, James, whose help you invoke, assist you." The drowning man grabs the shield and uses it to stay afloat. With the help of St. James, he swims for three days and three nights, following in the ship's wake until they reach port. When he arrives safely, he tells everyone how St. James helped him by holding his head. Miracle Ten.

I don't know how many miracles there were, if there were ten or ten thousand. I only know this one story of St. James, this story that says if you call to him, he will hold your head until you arrive safely at port. I ask St. James to hold my head as I say the story to myself, playing all the parts, G.A. telling Chry, Chry telling me, me stilled into dreaming.

I wake up before morning. The house is dead as a stone. The bed next to me is empty, still made.

I put a sweatshirt on over my pajamas and creep down the back stairs. In the darkness is a mash-up of party remnants. Today, the twenty-sixth of July is St. Anne's Day. G.A.'s day. It's not a big deal, but Chry says G.A. brings it up to soothe the sad feeling of the best day of the year come and gone.

I find the oyster knife I'd been using yesterday in the kitchen drawer. For all the searching for a gold knife, for the appearance of a gold knife, come to find out any old knife will do.

Back up in the bedroom, I close the door tight with a quiet click, then reach up on tiptoe for the box on the high closet shelf and take it down. I slip the oyster knife underneath the lid, the way Chry's father had done, so like the way he'd shown me to slide the knife into the oyster and cut the muscle you could feel there. I slide the knife and pop the latch.

It's empty except for a piece of notebook paper, folded into quarters, the left edge is ragged where it had been ripped out of a spiral binder. I unfold it carefully, smoothing down the creases, and read the neatly copied lines.

> Let me not to the marriage of true minds
> Admit impediments. Love is not love
> Which alters when it alteration finds,
> Or bends with the remover to remove.
> O no! it is an ever-fixed mark
> That looks on tempests and is never shaken;
> It is the star to every wand'ring bark,
> Whose worth's unknown, although his height be taken.
> Love's not Time's fool, though rosy lips and cheeks
> Within his bending sickle's compass come;
> Love alters not with his brief hours and weeks,
> But bears it out even to the edge of doom.

If this be error and upon me prov'd,
I never writ, nor no man ever lov'd.

Shakespeare. A sonnet. Found in a compass rose box lying in a field next to a storm-blown wedding dress. Finders keepers, losers weepers. I hate this. Where is Chry? And now a siren. On and on. It screams and shrills into the pre-dawn darkness, into my bones. I open the window to look for signs of Chry, then leave it open, letting the cold air and blare of the siren in. What is a wand'ring bark? It is the star to every wand'ring bark. It being love. A bark? Like a dog? Love is a star. Love is a star that follows a barking dog. And wand'ring. Wand'ring. Like the Thistle. I turn the ragged page over. There's something on the back, just two words. It's the same handwriting but more scrawled, emotional, as if it were trying to break out of the confines of the sonnet.

I fold the paper and return it to the box, then the box to the shelf where Chry had first stashed it. I climb back into bed, burrow under the blankets, and try to talk myself to sleep.

23

When I wake again, it is fully morning. Chry is here, sitting on her bed, still in her St. James Day dress. There has been a drowning. A boy was standing on the bow of the boat while it idled in neutral; his friend threw it into forward gear full speed and the boy was thrown off and run over. There were five of them, three boys and two girls. One girl wouldn't stop screaming. She was screaming when the sheriff arrived, screaming on the rescue boat, screaming in the car on the way to the hospital, screaming up and down the halls of the hospital. No words, only screaming.

There's no swimming allowed. The gratitude I feel for this small mercy blackens me. Survivors can be ruthless.

Nyro and Dare drive back to New York. Their goodbyes are careful and somber and who can blame them? They want no part of a drowned boy. Nor do I. I'm aching to leave with them, but I tell Chry I'll drive the jeep back with her on Sunday. Her father will fly sometime later; his travel details are vague and beyond our concern.

Two mornings in a row, Chry and I walk to where we can see the swimming beach and watch volunteers and rescue workers attach heavy ropes to huge iron triangles, each with a row of black spiky iron flowers—grappling hooks. They're dragging the lake for the body.

On the afternoon of the second day, they bring the boy onto the beach. The wind is blowing, and the sky has streaks of dark and light gray, wanting to rain. Chry's dad, her uncle, and the sheriff's deputy who'd been working on their boat, tie up to the swimming dock. The sheriff's boat ties up behind them and two more deputies get out onto the dock and walk over to where the Risks and the deputy are standing.

They lift the boy up out of the boat. He's wrapped in white sheets and lying on a blanket the men grip tightly.

They walk him down the dock and across the beach to the black Suburban with *County Coroner* written on the door that has been parked in the lot since the search began. They put the boy into the back of the Suburban and drive away. Then it's just people getting back in their boats or standing in small clusters, heads down. Jamie and Mark Risk drive their boat slowly around the beachhead and over to the dock.

Chry and I are back at the house by the time the boat pulls onto the lift. We watch the men mess with the cover and crank the boat up. The wrecked *Wand'ring* is motionless on its buoy in the flat water. Instead of walking down the dock, they slog through the chest-high water as if they forgot the dock was fixed. They walk to the shore and file up the stone steps, one after the other, then walk across the lawn to the house, two across, with identical gaits. At the back door, they kick off their wet shoes, leaving them in a pile on the terrace. Dripping water across the kitchen floor, they come and sit down at the table with Chry and me. Chry's dad looks at her square with serious eyes and nods. Check, she's still here, undrowned.

She nods back. Once again I find myself resting my gaze on the kitchen sign: *Steel lightens your work, brightens your leisure, and widens your world.*

Mark gets up, takes two tumblers from the cupboard and a bottle of whiskey from the cabinet above the refrigerator. He pours himself and his brother half a glass each. They both take a small sip, then Mark knocks the rest of his back in one go and pours another. Chry gets up, retrieves two more tumblers from the cupboard and puts one down each in front of her and me. Mark pours whiskey into our glasses and we knock it back in one gulp, same as he had.

Chry's dad opens his mouth to speak, but no words come out. Twice more he does this, then he drops his arms on the table with a thud, lays his head on them, and begins to cry. Mark stares at him, then pours himself another double shot of whiskey.

24

It's just so goddamn strange, you know? So, so, so, so god-damn strange."

"What's strange, Mark?" Chry keeps asking him, but he won't say. Just that it's so goddamn strange.

"What's strange?"

"That boy dying. Cass. None of us caring, I don't know."

"What's she got to do with the boy dying? Who says we don't care?"

"He's hers. Her son and you know…" He trails off. He's been drinking all day as far as we can tell. After our double shots of whiskey, Chry and I had gone back to bed and slept late into the afternoon. We'd come downstairs to find evening had arrived without anyone noticing. The sky is a mass of slate-colored clouds and the house is cold, shut up against the impending weather. Chry's father and G.A. are talking quietly at the kitchen table.

"Those two." Mark jerks his thumb toward the kitchen.

"What about those two?" says Chry.

"You know." Mark, who had been slumped back on the sofa, sits forward.

"No, Mark, I don't know."

"You know." He leans an elbow on one knee and drunkenly puts his head in his hand.

"I don't." She grabs his arm and squeezes, trying to penetrate his slurring words. "What do I know?"

He looks at us, then looks back toward the kitchen. His head wobbles precariously on the flimsy scaffolding of his arm. "Nothing. I'm going to bed."

The hand not holding his head is loosely gripping the same tumbler from this morning's whiskey with a splash still left in the glass. The bottle is presumably empty. With the classic deliberate motions of a drunk thinking they're fooling the room, Mark puts the glass down on the coffee table. Tilting and pitching like a toddler, he makes his way toward the front hall steps, avoiding, it seems, the back steps which would take him past his brother and mother. From the hall he shouts, "North is north." It's been a week since I arrived at Arcadia and first heard that chestnut of G.A.'s wisdom.

"Jamie!" Mark yells, "Ja-a-mie. There's a package here. I forgot to tell you. Jamie. Package!!" Chry shakes her head. There's a crashing noise—Mark falling up the stairs. No one goes running. "I'm okay," he shouts.

A good long while after Mark has crashed his way to the top the stairs and Chry has turned on a living room table lamp, casting her in a soft pool of light, and G.A. has gone up the back stairs to bed, Chry's father comes in to ask for help.

"Look, I know it's late. This came yesterday," he says, holding the brown package Mark was yelling about. "It's the new forestay for the Thistle. It's a two-man job."

"Dad, we're leaving tomorrow," says Chry.

"I know, it'd have to be early. That's best anyway, when the lake is calm; I'm thinking six or so, right around sunrise."

"We'll do it," I say. "We can help."

25

The knock comes early as promised. A few light taps, silence, then three hard unapologetic raps. Chry doesn't move. I wait. Three more hard raps.

We were up late. Chry had been uncharacteristically charged-up and wakeful as she talked me to sleep. I only ever know the next day if I've made my trip to the unconscious without gun-fire, bombs, and lightning strikes. And in the morning, when the realization comes that I've gone to sleep undetonated, I am always grateful to her. So, I slip out from under the covers and scuttle over the cold floor to speak to her dad.

"Chry's asleep," I whisper loud enough for him to hear me through the door. When he doesn't respond I say, "I'll come. I can help."

"That's fine, Mina. Meet me at the dock."

I put on jeans and a heavy sweatshirt—one, because it's cold, and two, so there can be no chance I'll be asked to go in the lake. A lake that has already claimed one life this week.

There's a dense morning fog and a mesmerizing low gray light; last night's secrets are on the other side of the world. The *Wand'ring*, though just off the dock, is barely visible. Chry's dad pulls the dinghy off the shore; it makes a light scraping sound as it crosses the smooth rocks. I roll up my jeans and carefully make my way over the slippery mossy stones that lie beneath the ankle-deep water. I remind myself that it is *nearly* impossible to drown in this shallow water. Chry's dad steadies the dinghy and I step in, sitting down hard as the little ship rocks with my weight. He hands me a box that he'd left sitting on the dock. "Forestay," he says. "Don't drop it." His voice straddles the razor's edge of humor and need. He gets into the dinghy without rocking it as I had, the expertise of a lifetime navigating this simple operation. He takes up the oars and dips and pulls. There's a rhythmic splash of water and squeak of the oarlock. We could be anywhere as we set forth through the fog.

He doesn't strain. He's not in a hurry.

"Wand'ring," I say. I've been thinking about this since I unlocked the poem in that sliver of night between the celebration and the drowning.

"Yes. I named her. Years ago."

"Like wand'ring bark?"

"Yes." He smiles.

"So, I don't know what a bark is." I too am walking the knife edge of humor and need.

"Sonnet 116. Shakespeare. A bark is a ship. *It is the star to every wand'ring bark.* Love is the star; love guides we wandering ships." He smiles again, genuine. "I'm glad you're here, Mina. With us this week…and here now. I appreciate it." His rowing slows as we move out past the dock. "Love," he says again. Smiles again.

I had not told Chry there was a poem in the box. I had not told her there was a handwritten sonnet on the front with two other words scrawled on the back. I had not told her those words were *Marry me.* I could ask about them now but I'm afraid to say them here in this pale gray mist, where no one can see us. If I say there was a dress and a compass rose box and a Shakespeare sonnet and *marry me…* If I say these things there is a chance, a very, very slim chance, that I won't return from this errand to fix the mast on the Thistle sailboat named *Wand'ring.* I know this is crazy thinking. Chry's father loves me like a daughter, but a parent loving a child isn't always what you might imagine. I know that a girl in a small rowboat, a girl who cannot swim, has something to fear.

As we approach the Thistle, Chry's dad maneuvers the dinghy around to the front. He attaches the hook of the dinghy's line to a metal eye under the Thistle's bow. He pulls the line until the dinghy is right underneath, then hoists himself up and begins unsnapping the pale green canvas cover. When the cover is pulled out and rolled back, he comes over to where I am, in the dinghy, still attached. "Pull yourself toward me," he says, which I do, hand-over-handing the rope until I'm right up underneath him. "Now the box," he says. "It's deep out here; if that thing goes in, it's gone." I hand up the box. "Now you." He reaches down to me and I stand and reach up. We grab each other by the wrists, lock in, and he pulls. My lightness surprises him. I feel him feeling it.

The boat's been crippled since the storm. I feel empathy toward it, so broken in plain sight and it answers me back by rocking me like a cradle on the quiet water.

Chry's dad and I work together to remove the damaged forestay. He, at the bow, quietly calling directions, me at the transom, obeying. When the broken forestay is removed, he attaches the long main piece of the replacement up toward the top of the mast. Then he threads the connecting piece, the pigtail he calls it, down through the stem.

"It attaches underneath. I should be wearing gloves for this—ahh, son of a bitch."

"What? Are you okay?"

He holds up his hand, showing me blood. "It's all right. Jesus that hurt," he says, then leans over and puts his bleeding hand in the lake. "I got it on though." He turns his head back toward me and smiles victoriously. "We have to seat the mast now. You up for this?"

I nod.

I do what he tells me, hold the mast steady, move it forward, then back. He grunts as we try to get it in straight and leaves bloody handprints on the brushed aluminum.

When the mast is up, he takes off his T-shirt and dips it into the lake, wrings it out, then swabs the bloody prints off of it. He dips the shirt back in to rinse it, then wrings it out again, all traces of blood now gone. He lies down on one of the Thistle's bench seats.

I lie down on the other. The boat rocks gently, the water making soft slapping noises against it, the lines and their fastenings clinking lightly, the air soft. I close my eyes, let the low rocking and soft slapping work my body, and wonder if I could ever make peace with the world of water.

"Now that the mast is up, I may have to chain myself to it." Chry's father reaches his hand toward me.

"I can't swim," I say, sitting up.

"If there is a person, one person, who would never let you drown, it's me," he says, also sitting up. "I would never hurt you, never let anyone hurt you."

He moves toward me, takes my hands in his, and slides himself onto my lap. He does this slowly but faster than my brain can comprehend it. He leans forward and kisses me, opening my mouth with his tongue. He kisses me long and soft, and I kiss him back for a while. I can feel him hard against me. I push him away with as little commotion as possible, the way he'd gotten into the dinghy without rocking it. "I can't swim," I say.

"I know."

"I can't swim," I say again.

"I know." He pushes back onto me, lays me down, moves his hands down my hips, inside my Levi's.

"Bombs go off in my head when I try to sleep. Lightning crashes, buildings collapse."

"That so?"

The thing that I'm trying to say is he is killing me. I will die from never sleeping again without Chry and he is taking her from me.

"Please. No." I don't beg him, shout, or slap. I want him to love me the way he always has.

"Oh, Mina, I'm aching." His whisper is a plea.

"Please, no," is my plea back.

He gets up fast. Moves to the bow and jumps off, swims out, then back, pulls himself up into the dinghy. He hand-over-hands the line, pulling the little boat up next to the big sailboat, and shouts up to me, "Come on, let's get you out of here."

26

C hry drives the jeep home to New York City while I stare off at the trees and mountains along Route 17 or pretend to sleep.

"It's always hard to leave," she says, mistaking my silence for something else.

We pass the sign for Vestal. "The Vestal Virgin," she says, repeating Nyro's taunt about Dare in the same snide way. She hadn't liked him leaving early. I didn't tell her he was hiding sores on his legs the way I was hiding my inability to swim. I had seen them that day in his room.

Now, of course, I have another secret.

Chry's never cared about secrets, keeping hers or wanting to know yours. Really, she just wants what she wants. An appealing feature in the end. She had her stories and she'd tell them if you wanted to know. She didn't have an appetite for intrigue or psychoanalysis in the way most of the girls at school seemed to have. She didn't crave the drama the others needed to *identify* themselves. Chry was secure in her stories. Why wouldn't she be?

I want to ask her where she was the night of St. James Day, but my heart is a glass shard that I can't risk dislodging.

Over and over in my head, I play the loop of what happened on the *Wand'ring*, as the jeep wends its way along Route 17. All across New York, the loop plays. I lie down on the bench. When he kissed me, I kissed him back. I felt the warmth of him pressed against me, the pleasure of his tongue in my mouth, the feeling of this man, who is so much to so many, giving everything to me. A hundred, five hundred times, I tell myself the story of a girl who did not say no soon enough. I work it into a feeling like the sharp edge of the knife, like my glass-shard heart. I have lost the part of myself that was an honorary Risk, a second daughter. Gone. In its place, sharp objects.

By the time we reach the Catskills, I have a plan. I'll dissolve nearly the entire memory, leaving only one thin slice, which was his attitude as we walked from the dinghy to the house: *Nothing just happened, everything is fine.* The plan is to remember only his last words, launched cheerfully at Chry and me as she backed the jeep out of the driveway, "Safe home."

There's traffic at the entrance to the George Washington Bridge and it is going on forever. We are finally on the bridge itself, but still creeping when Chry says she wants to tell me something. I'd spent the entire trip not asking, and now here she is saying.

It's about where she disappeared to the night of St. James Day. I had been waiting for her to open the compass rose box sitting on the closet shelf. I had known something happened to make her forget our plans.

"Mina," she says into the car's silence. "Nyro and me."

They'd gone down to the cellar for a bottle of something and found some more DP, two bottles, perfect for taking to the fairy garden to drink. They each carried one up through the party, and Nyro brought the machete, to whack off the cork or clear the path to the mushrooms, whatever the need might be. They'd walked out the front door with the champagne and that crazy-ass knife without anyone noticing. We are at the center of the bridge, the spot where Nyro stopped the lapis blue BMW and nearly killed us, and she's telling me how they'd gone into the woods with two bottles of Dom Perignon and a deadly weapon. I ask where Dare was, because last I heard, she still had a thing for him, last I heard, she was buying Sandy to You's story of their side-by-side life.

"He told me no, okay, Mina." Chry slaps her hand on the wheel for emphasis. "Dare and I were down at the dock. It was almost midnight and I was trying to unlock him. I had my hands on him, and he said it couldn't be that way for us right now. I asked him when and he told me 'Never.' He said he was sorry."

"So, then what happened?" I work to keep my voice neutral.

"First of all, listen. Is this weird? I mean you guys aren't together in any way, right? I mean that's my understanding."

"We aren't together in any way," I say, swallowing the shattered glass combination of fury and relief. The car inches forward on the bridge as my gut churns. I open the window to breathe, but there isn't any air, only truck-spit black smoke mixed with the river's brackish midsummer slag. *Appreciate this.* I talk myself off the edge of the void. *You need this.* These people are not yours. *Better to know now.*

Chry's tale of fucking Nyro, fucking all night on the mossy grass in the woods at Arcadia, blindsides me, but it doesn't make itself useful the way I'd hoped it might. It doesn't dissolve the memory I was trying to rid myself of by the time the jeep arrives at West Seventy-First Street. And it doesn't absolve my guilt.

Still, I push it away, all of it. I dig ditches all through the month of August, burying small scraps of Arcadia in each one and by September it's more like a story about something that didn't happen to me but a girl like me.

FALL

27

The congressman is on the phone saying hello politely and asking to speak to Chry.

"She's out," I say.

He pauses. "Mina, there's a hurricane coming. New York City schools are closed tomorrow. So is the World Trade Center. I want you to come to our house. There's going to be flooding. I'm worried with you girls in that downstairs apartment. I think you should evacuate."

"I'll tell Chry."

Silence. I learned this trick at work. Let the silence go on for as long as it takes. If you wait for the other person to speak first, you'll learn something, or at the very least, you'll have the upper hand.

After a while, he says, "Would you have her call me?"

I tell him yes and goodbye.

Chry comes in. "I got it," she says and shows me her new VHS tape still in the plastic. *Modern Electric Bass.* "Jaco, himself. Showing you how he does it." She talks and talks like before we stopped talking. "Jaco," she says again, "showing you how he does it." She talks about this Jaco Pastorius instructional video the same way she first talked about Dare. How Nyro had dropped her into the East River and Dare had saved her from freezing to death, how they'd spent the night in Nyro's aunt's laundry room. How she would have fucked him then, but he wouldn't, how she loved him for not trying to fuck a half-drowned drunk girl.

She doesn't unwrap the tape, saving it, I think, for when I'm not here. It's personal, between her and Jaco. She puts on a record.

"Oh yeah," I say. "Call your dad. He wants you to evacuate."

Chry punches her home number into the phone and I sit

at the table with a cup of tea, trying not to listen to her talk to
the congressman. The wind rattles the windows. Our ghost of
a garden dances and blows. The chicory is still standing but it's
dark brown and dead. The Queen Anne's lace is dead standing
too, tall brittle branches with claws where their flowers used to
be. I gather from their conversation that something's happened
to G.A.

When Chry hangs up the phone, I ask if we should evacuate.
She says no and I agree. For her part, I don't think she wants
to be separated from her Jaco VHS tape; for my part, I have
nowhere to go. She tells me G.A. isn't doing well. She's in a
facility. She had a bad fall. There's a hairline fracture in her hip.
"My dad gave me the number, says we can call her but don't
expect much. She's talking in circles."

Chry dials the number and puts it on speaker so we both can
hear. Neither she nor G.A. know I'm not family anymore.

"A hurricane's coming," says Chry when she gets G.A. on
the line. "Hurricane Gloria, the storm of the century."

"We had a storm at Arcadia," she says. "A tornado. The dock
twisted up like a rollercoaster, the boathouse roof, gone. All
right before St. James Day but I fixed it. You couldn't stop me
back then."

"G.A.," says Chry, laughing, "that happened this summer."

"Yes, of course, dear," she says. "I saw the whole thing from
my bedroom."

"Yeah, we were in the cellar, remember?"

"I do, Chrysanthi. I remember. You had a lovely time with
your friends."

"G.A., can I ask you something. Can I ask you something
about all those seeds?"

"Seeds! Yes, I collected seeds in the fall. I planted them in
Mark's New York City apartment."

"You did. I live here now! Mina and I live here. Your flowers
bloomed all summer. The Queen Anne's lace and the chicory."

"Chicory. For opening doors."

"But, G.A," says Chry. "Why *so many*?"

"So many what, dear?"

"Seeds!"

"Well, because of the crown," G.A. says, as if the answer is obvious.

"What about the crown?"

"It's a tiara, actually."

"Yes, the tiara. We found it this summer," says Chry.

"Hmmm, all right, darling… Garnets. Garnets are for love. That's what Stuart said. Garnets for love and sex."

"Oh geez. Did you say sex? Oh crazy."

"Love and sex and babies. Stuart wanted eight. He made me promise. Katherine wouldn't but I would. I said I would."

Chry looks at me, her face animated. She covers her wide-open mouth with her hand and bugs her eyes. Composing herself, she says, "Who's Katherine?"

"Stuart's first."

"Before you?"

"Yes, before me, before I promised. Garnets for the pomegranate seeds that commit you to love, like Persephone. You know her, Persephone?"

"Hades kidnapped her. She ate the seeds and had to stay in hell half the year."

"Yes…Chrysanthi, you have your father's knack…" She drifts off.

"Garnets. In the tiara," Chry prompts.

"Yes, I was in the society pages—my wedding picture with the tiara. Stunning. I had a baby the next year—James. When I saw that face…well, I had no trouble imagining seven more. But then, oh then, when Mark came, three days it took him, a bloodbath. I lived, but I knew I wouldn't live through another one. I decided I couldn't have any more babies…but I'd promised…but I wanted to live. I set about keeping myself alive. Not for me but for *them*." The last part, the declaration, wears her out.

Chry waits, then reminds G.A. what they're talking about. "So…the tiara…garnets."

"Yes, well, I was keeping myself alive not having any more babies…"

"With the seeds?"

"With the seeds."

"And the tiara?"

"Oh, my goodness, Chrysanthi, I sold that thing years ago. I couldn't get it out of the house fast enough. They paid me a small fortune but of course your grandfather is never to know. I invested the money, some of it, some I gave to that poor woman in town, sweet girl, she still serves us drinks on St. James Day. Oh, but didn't that money grow and grow. I had to hide the statements from Stuart."

"Well, then what was the tiara doing in the compass rose box?"

"They were looking for it everywhere, to have it appraised," she says. "I couldn't let that happen, now could I? Shhhhh, don't tell Stuart." She laughs. "They searched all the safe deposit boxes, but I knew they wouldn't find it. I had a copy made. Synthetic garnets, cubic zirconium, platinum-plated copper. It's a very good copy, but it's not real."

The crown is fake.

Chry and I look at each other, remembering her confusion when she'd rediscoverd it. There she was on top of life at Arcadia, yet the truth about the crown had somehow eluded her. Now here she is a million miles away and she tells us the story with perfect clarity.

"Collect the seeds if a storm is coming," she says, clear as a bell.

Hurricane Gloria comes and goes. We don't evacuate. The apartment doesn't flood. Everything is fine.

28

Chry and I write notes, passing a yellow legal pad that I can't help thinking she swiped from one of her temp jobs, back and forth. We're in the Periodical Reading Room at the New York Public Library. The big one on Fifth Avenue with the lions out front. This incredible room is for the sole purpose of *reading magazines*. What a world. The chairs are wooden but curved and comfortable. The desk lamps, three across on the long tables, give off golden circles of light. The lamps are attached to the tables, reminding us we're not to be completely trusted. There are so many things I love here. Everything is priceless. Everything is free.

We'd walked down from Seventy-First Street in the vivid October afternoon. Chry wanted to do research. I said I'd come along; we hadn't seen much of each other these last months. She'd been taking bass lessons in the evenings; she was in even more of a hurry to conquer the fretless bass than before. I had a new job at work. It was different, harder, but more exciting. I'll be getting my own accounts soon. Dare is on the desk beside mine and our chairs sit back to back. We still eat lunch together, except instead of being sequestered in the conference room we just rotate our chairs a quarter turn and eat side-by-side on the trading floor. He gave up liverwurst sandwiches. I asked him why the change; he'd been such a die hard. "I contain multitudes," he said, which was weird because that's what Nyro said was his reason for dressing like a Pan Am stewardess. I know. I know. Walt Whitman. I went to that good college on the Hudson River. *Do I contradict myself? Very well, then I contradict myself, I am large, I contain multitudes.*

While Dare and I eat lunch we study the prices on the board we've so recently been promoted from, discussing the day's events, both of us helping each other and trying to learn. After lunch, the trainees come out and rewrite the prices, just as we'd done. It's nice not to be them.

Both of us, I imagine for our own reasons, put our week at Arcadia somewhere else. He never mentions it to me, nor I to him. So much happened that week that I want to remember and so much that I have no choice but to force myself to forget. As for Chry, she accepted Dare's no, and I guess he was relieved, but I think he misses her. There was something in the way they were with each other, so much to talk about, always laughing.

Chry is so desperate to conquer the fretless bass she stopped playing her other one altogether. She backed out of so many gigs, her bandmates threatened to replace her and then did. She didn't care. She stopped talking me to sleep. Not all at once, but little by little. One day she said, "I can't keep it up, Mina. You should see a psychiatrist if you can't fall asleep without a bomb going off in your head." It was happening infrequently, but when it did, I'd jolt awake screaming and drenched in sweat. There was no hiding it from her.

We've been in the Periodical Reading Room all afternoon. We'd walked across the park and down Fifth Avenue, bustling with people enjoying the bright blue sky and autumn gusts. Every part of this day, so far, has made me think it's possible, after all, to have a golden life.

I read an article in *Vanity Fair* called "John Paul Getty Jr. Comes Clean" and skim the cover story in the same issue about Princess Diana, "The Mouse That Roared." So much money and all these problems. I don't believe it.

Next, *People Magazine*. I don't think gossip magazines improve your life, so I only ever read them at the doctor's office, which I haven't been to in a couple of years. There's an article about John Hinckley, the guy who tried to kill Ronald Reagan, finding love at St. Elizabeth's Hospital for the Criminally Insane. He is possibly even engaged to a former society lady who killed her ten-year-old daughter with a shotgun. They're described as the wealthiest and whitest people there, so like a match made in heaven or something. Chry's tongue touches her top lip in concentration. She's wearing wire-rimmed schoolboy glasses and her hair gathered in a high messy bun.

What are you looking for? I write on the pad.

Info about seeds.

I want to ask if she's planning a garden for next spring, but I know it's not that. She'd gathered a grocery bag full the night before the hurricane on her ailing grandmother's say so and it's been sitting on the top of our refrigerator ever since.

What do you want to know?

Chry puts down her pencil, takes off her glasses, and stares at me.

She writes, *Wild Carrot, Daucus carota, is an abortifacient. For two thousand years women have used them as a contraceptive and to terminate pregnancies.*

I lean back in the chair, cross my arms, look at the words, and then her.

She writes, *A lot of the information was lost during the Medieval Witch Trials, the midwives, healers, herbalists passed it down generation to generation but once they started getting burned alive, the information was lost.*

Wild Carrot? I write it underneath.

The seeds. You're supposed to chew them to release the oils, then wash them down with water or wine or I guess anything. A teaspoonful every day the week before you ovulate, during ovulation, a week after, as a contraceptive. Or, if you haven't been doing that, right after you have sex and for a week after.

?

G.A.!

?

Wild Carrot is another name for Queen Anne's lace. That's why she had all those seeds!

Oh, whoa. I widen my eyes and write, *Wow.*

Wow is right.

So, is that what you came to find out about your grandmother?

Yeah and about me.

About you how?

I'm pregnant.

Chry puts the pen down, looks up at me. Defiance takes hold of her face, though honestly, with her wide blue eyes and perfect nose, high cheekbones, and knot of hair on the top of her head, the defiance hardly shows.

Who?

Me.

My hand shakes as I write. *No. Whose?*

It's just a beautiful room built for reading magazines or it used to be but it's not that anymore. Everything is changing.

I stare at the *Vanity Fair* on the table. I consider Princess Diana in a diamond crown and diamond earrings, the row of small ruffles at the collar of her gown. Her head is dropped slightly in shyness or subservience, but her eyes, like Chry's, are defiant. The mouse that roared. Some roaring mouse, she's a virgin brought in to be seeded and she complied with an heir and a spare. Her place in the castle is secure.

Danny. That night in the woods, Chry writes.

I could strangle her. I contort my face to keep it calm but it tingles with rising...fear? Fury? I try to identify a precise emotion, so I can tie it up in a package and shove it in a drawer, or better, throw it out with the trash.

Hate. For Nyro, who proves over and over he only ever wants to ruin everything he touches. And maybe for Chry. We have things to do, both of us, in this life, but she drops herself down the empty well of crazy, mad love for Dare and comes up with this. I can't blame her for Dare, I loved him before she did.

Chry stares at the page we've been passing back and forth, holding the pencil with the eraser in her mouth. *Also, Mina...* she writes, then stops, the pencil point on the paper where the next word will go.

I wait. What could be harder to tell me than this? This is my punishment for kissing Jamie Risk when he laid on top of me in the Thistle and put his tongue in my mouth, punishment for the fucking millisecond when I thought, *Yeah, I'll be your next wife. I'll go to White House balls and run charities and whatever congressman*

wives do. I'll quit my job and buy Hermès scarves like they're cups of coffee.
Yes. My punishment. Whatever's coming next is something I earned, for my momentary fucking lapse of judgment. What kind of person comes on to their daughter's best friend? He turned me out of the Risk family, a break never to be fixed. He took me in, then sent me away. Maybe it never existed for me, this circle of love and money and history and generations of traditions, like eating oysters on New Year's Eve and St. James Day. As I wait for Chry to tell me what comes after, *Also, Mina,* I make a hierarchy of hate—Nyro, Jamie Risk, Chry, in that order. The woman who left me to die in the baptismal font of the Dutch Reformed Church? Dare? The mother who raised me to sit by myself at the kitchen table, night after night after night, while she wiped the asses of everyone in town, then took me to church every Sunday to remind me to feel grateful to be rescued.

Chry cannot bring herself to write what's coming next. I don't push. I savor the last moments of not knowing.

Also, Mina. I'm sick.

?

Positive

Of what?

HIV positive.

My mind blanks in the way minds do when the worst possible thing to hear has been said. I don't look at Chry; instead, I look at Princess Diana on the cover of *Vanity Fair*, "The Mouse That Roared." I think about Dare, the Vestal Virgin—who, I will say to myself again, I fell for first, until Chry came up out of the East River and demanded him for her own. In ancient Rome, Vestal Virgins vowed thirty years of virginity while they kept the sacred fire burning; after that they retired and were allowed to live like the men, in complete freedom. The punishment for letting the fire die was a beating. The punishment for violating their oath of celibacy was to be buried alive since it was forbidden to spill their blood.

I don't write anything on the yellow legal pad.

Chry writes, *About the Queen Anne's lace, it looks almost like hemlock. Poison hemlock. It will kill you in a two-minute violent death. Extreme.*

I draw a face with two X's for eyes and straight line for a mouth. I can only joke. There's nothing else to say.

I checked out the book with pictures, to be safe.

I take a deep breath, the last best breath of my favorite place in New York City. I won't be back.

Can we go? Chry writes.

Yes. I press the pen into the page so hard the second part of the Y rips through.

29

Walking up Fifth Avenue, the jingles and rattles of bright shops with cheap clothes and blaring discounts give way to the hush of expensive merchandise in low-lit establishments. Cameras, cheap suitcases, rayon scarves, and cheap shoes become cashmere, calfskin, platinum. At Fifty-Eighth Street is a childhood dream, FAO Schwarz, a store filled with toys and delights for the next generation of haves.

At the fountain in front of the Plaza, a crowd is gathered. Hip hop booms from a box and a troop of young teens dazzle weekenders with their impossible dance moves. Across the street, horses and carriages are lined up along Central Park South. The buildings on the Upper East Side are lit up by the sinking sun as it disappears behind the buildings on Central Park West.

Chry doesn't look pregnant or sick. We walk the eighteen blocks from the library fast, me trying to keep up, neither of us speaking.

We cross over at Central Park South, not wanting to go through the park as the light fails. On the steps of the Plaza Hotel, out-of-towners are returning from a day of shopping or museums to get ready for the evening's plans. It's the in-between early part of the night, when the day's business fades, and evening's fantasies have yet to begin.

We pass the entrance to the Plaza's Oak Bar and Chry says, "Let's go here."

We hadn't talked about going anywhere and she doesn't wait to see if I follow her through the door, but I do. We sit at a table by the window in the half-deserted room. The waiter, formal and silent, takes our order. I ask for a gimlet, a good compromise between the martini this swank room calls for but I don't want, and the kamikazes of our college days. Chry orders a seven and seven, her father's drink.

The waiter delivers a dish of peanuts and pretzels along with our drinks. My cocktail arrives put together, but Chry's comes in parts: a highball glass filled with ice with a wedge of lime perched on its edge, a shot glass of Seagram's 7, and a miniature bottle of 7UP. This looks like fun, but Chry isn't interested. As the waiter turns to leave, she throws back the shot of whiskey. She doesn't look at me to see if I think this is funny. I might have. Another day. She uncaps the bottle of 7UP and drinks that in three long sips. Chry is an entertaining friend, but she's not entertaining me now.

I sip my gimlet. The rack gin and Rose's lime juice are unworthy of the grandness of this room, though something about the nicotine-stained murals of old New York suggests maybe they're just right.

Out the window, the carriage drivers lined up on Central Park are feeding their horses, getting them ready for the evening's customers. A white horse with dapples of gray across its rump shits. I've never been on a horse.

Chry signals the waiter for two more drinks, though I'm not nearly finished. When the new one arrives, I line it up next to the one I'm still working on. The waiter clears Chry's empty shot glass, mini 7UP bottle and accompanying detritus, but for some reason leaves the unused glass of ice with its lime wedge.

This goes on until there are seven glasses of ice lined up in front of Chry. I'd waved him off after number three, not because there wasn't more drinking to be done, but because I discovered that I hate gimlets.

I guessed that Chry was coming to the end when she held up her shot glass of Seagram's 7 and stared at it like maybe there was an option not to drink it. She agreed when I said we should go.

When the bill comes, she offers to split it, which strikes me as supremely unfair, but I don't argue. Chry slurs and fumbles as we prepare to leave. For all the alcohol we've consumed together over the years, I've never seen her behave like a comedy-act drunk. Maybe it's that we've never been this out of sync. Either way, nothing is funny.

It's still a long walk home and I wonder if we shouldn't take a cab, but a simple directive or question feels impossible. The horses and carriages are laughable, the movie version of New York City, and they feel like total horseshit. Yeah, horseshit.

The afternoon's golden warmth has turned on us, but the night air revives Chry and we make it to West Seventy-First Street easily enough. I stop at the steps of our brownstone. There is something I need to say before we go inside. I don't know why, but if I wait until we're in the apartment, it will be too late.

"Am I?" I ask.

"Are you what, Mina?"

"I mean, would I, be positive too?"

"How the hell am I supposed to know?" Chry bites and spits the words.

"Well?" She is shrinking me with her hands on her hips, her mouth venom.

I force myself to finish. "Nyro." When she doesn't answer, I say, "I mean, have you talked to him?"

"No, why would I?"

I open my bag, feel around for the keys, and unlock the gate. I hold it open for Chry against my will. I don't want her near me.

In the shower, I wash my hair twice. With a fresh washcloth and a new bar of soap, I scrub and scrub my legs and arms, torso, neck, and face; I let the water scald me red.

Chry sits on the sofa with her legs crossed underneath her and her headphones plugged into the fretless bass. I learn something in the silence. I've liked living with the sound of her trying to play that thing like Jaco.

I motion for her to take off the headphones. She stares at me with pursed lips but pulls the Sennheisers down around her neck.

"How do you know?"

She pulls in air, lifts her chest, and lets it drop, hugs her bass. "I went to the clinic."

I wait.

"They make you take a blood test, to be sure you're, you know, pregnant. They tested me for HIV, I guess."

"What do you mean you guess?"

"I don't know. I signed a bunch of papers. Maybe it was in there, you know, permission. I would have signed anything. Then they canceled my appointment. Said they wouldn't do it. I was a danger to the rest."

Her face is a blank. The walk and the night air and, I suppose, the subject have sobered her.

I get up to search the kitchen cupboard for Tylenol. When I find it, I run water into a coffee cup and wash down the pills. The night Chry met Dare they'd had hot cocoa from Vote for Cuomo Not the Homo mugs, and I'd had Cristal at the Oyster Bar with Jamie and Marg. This mug is white with an *I* next to a heart above an *N* and a *Y*. I Love New York.

"So, listen." Chry is her old animated self again. "We have to be careful, really check to make sure it's Queen Anne's lace and not hemlock. They look a lot alike. A lot. G.A. planted them, so I think she would have done it right. I mean she never poisoned herself over all those years."

"What are you talking about?"

"I have to do it myself. With the seeds."

"No. Go to another place, Chry. Come on, no."

"Listen, Mina, I can't wait. I can't wait another day. Do you understand?"

"No. Chry." I shake my head back and forth hard to empower the word. "NO."

"At least help me make sure it's not hemlock. Can you do that? Make sure I don't accidentally kill myself? And…" She laughs. "It's a violent painful death involving your nervous system shutting down, convulsions, spasms, eyes inside out. You don't want that for me, do you?"

"This is crazy."

"Yeah, it really fucking is." Chry gets the grocery bag from the top of the refrigerator and a clean towel and lays it on the table. One by one she pulls out the dead flowers. Each a little nest. "The hemlock doesn't make a nest like that. Also, hemlock seeds don't have those little spikes, see?"

I pick up a tiny, dried cluster and compare it to the picture in the book Chry brought back from the library and has open on the table.

When every nest has been inspected, Chry signs off on the operation, "No hemlock. I knew G.A. wouldn't let me take hemlock by mistake."

I think of my mom. Efficient, smart, hardworking. A nurse. She would never let me eat seeds. Never. She would never let anyone let me eat seeds. I think of the notes she left with my dinner. Instructional kinds of things, about habits and hygiene. I think about clean sheets tucked in tight. A book. The click of a light. The brisk goodnight. I think about her small smile when we found out that there'd be scholarship money for college. I hadn't expected that, such an impractical place to go to school. For an English degree. She was happy for me.

Chry goes back to the kitchen, takes the bottle of Absolut out of the freezer, and comes back with a tall glass.

"Jesus, Chry."

They say you have to chew them, a teaspoon, every day for a week, wash it down with water or wine, or..." She holds up the Absolut.

"How about water?"

"How about not."

I watch as she gathers a teaspoon's worth of seeds and chews them, making a face like a kid forced to eat lima beans. She chugs the glass of vodka. Looks at me and shrugs. "Family tradition."

30

Chry wakes me up, shaking me and saying my name. When my eyes adjust to the hour and the darkness, I see that her legs are soaked in blood. "No ambulance," she whispers.

We take a cab to the hospital. She'd cleaned herself up before we'd gone out to Columbus Avenue and hailed a stray middle-of-the-night cab, but when we exit, there's a smear of blood on the seat. In the ER, they see that her whole backside is soaked red, and take her in right away. I try to fill out the paperwork. "I need to speak to someone. A nurse, maybe, or the doctor." When the receptionist doesn't look up, I lean in and repeat myself. "I need to speak to a nurse."

"Wait," she says.

"It's important." I'm thinking about my mom. The thousand and one nights of staunching the blood and troubles of all those people who came through the ER door. "Please."

She shakes her head but picks up the phone.

A nurse comes. She's older, with wild gray hair pulled off her face. She looks the same as my mom when she'd leave for work—white short-sleeved dress, white stockings, and white rubber-soled shoes. She'd drop me at school, then go to straight to the hospital, not returning home until well past eight. My afternoons were solitary, but she was always home in time for me to be tucked in tight. A book. Click of the light.

"I don't know what's going on," I say. This isn't true, I've watched Chry chew the seeds and wash them down with vodka the last four nights. "But I have to tell you, she's HIV. She has HIV. Her blood..."

The nurse's face tightens, whitens, changes. "Thank you," she says. "Why don't you take a seat in the waiting room."

I take a seat in the waiting room. It's too late in the night for cooking accidents, broken bones, the kind of stitches drunks need when they fall in the gutter. The room smells like un-washed bodies, though the only other people here are a neatly dressed elderly couple. The woman clutches her abdomen and takes shallow breaths while her husband rubs her back. "Not much longer," he says.

I sit on the other side of the room to give them their privacy and take some for myself, settling in on an ochre-vinyl mini sofa. I never saw the emergency room where my mom worked. Why would I need to go? She could take care of a fever or know if an ankle was broken or just sprained. I was a careful child. The river was far below us. I was safe.

And anyway, most of my time was spent at the kitchen table doing homework, reading, wondering, writing down questions and making plans. The last being the most dangerous thing I ever did. Why leave me in a pool of holy water? One of two reasons—either to die by it or be saved. Both suggest a belief that a body of water, no matter how small, has life-taking and life-giving properties. The leaver believed one or the other. So, while Baby Boy Boogman could trace his ancestry back to the Dutch settlers and their tracts of land, maybe even to Henry Hudson himself, my ancestry is the hand that laid me down to live or die and the heart that let that hand do it. That was the wondering. The planning came in pages I always threw away. To live on top of a mountain. To meet a woman with seawater eyes and a mess of red hair so I could ask her, which was it that she wanted for me, to live or to die?

The gray-haired nurse appears. "It's a miscarriage," she says. "We gave her Demerol. She's sleeping now in her...uh...she has a private room. She can stay awhile, but we won't admit her. You should wait, she'll need you when she wakes up."

I have work in two hours, but I tell her yes, I'll wait. I lay my head down, contorting myself onto the little sofa and pulling my oversized thrift shop men's tweed coat over me like a blan-ket. I close my eyes and think about my mom, the real one who raised me. She's here with me tonight.

It wasn't until I left home that my head began offering up machine gun attacks when I tried to fall asleep. I hadn't realized that until now. For the hours I spent alone in our little Cape on a cliff over the Hudson River, nothing ever changed about the way it felt to fall asleep. My mom never missed a night. Even when I was old enough and didn't need to be tucked in tight or read to, she'd come in and click the light. Every night until the day I left.

I don't sleep. At six when I know the London shift has arrived at Merton, I find a pay phone to call in sick. Then I go back to find Chry. I bypass the woman at the reception desk and walk right through the swinging doors. At the nurse's station, I say I'm looking for Chrysanthi Risk. I follow the directions, go down a hallway and take a left, but before I turn the corner, I hear voices rising.

"I had the last one, Beth. This one's yours."

"Jesus, Patty. They don't pay us enough. Female. Miscarriage. No track marks, she's not on the needle. How's she positive?"

I turn the corner. The nurses stop talking when they see me. I tell them I'm looking for Chrysanthi Risk.

"Here," says one of them. "This is her room."

Here is a door with a red star. Chry is on the other side. I don't know how to handle these nurses who are arguing about which one has to walk through the red-starred door. I decide to do the thing my mom would do. Help. "I'm going in. Can I do something for you?" I say.

They look at each other. "She needs to get cleaned up. They say she needs a change of clothes. Do you have one?"

"No. Give me the stuff. I'll do it. Is there a set of scrubs or something?" I say as rudely as possible.

"I'll find some," says one.

She comes back with a plastic basin, towels, washcloths and hospital soap, and emerald green doctor scrubs. I take them with the hardest and coldest stare I can muster. She absorbs it without complaint. Her shoes squeak on the polished linoleum as she turns to walk away.

In the empty hallway, staring at the door, my bravado dis-integrates without an audience to fuel it. I consider laying the basin and the clothes in a neat pile and leaving. I consider the lost day of work. I consider how many hours I spent planning my exit from that little Cape on the cul de sac high over the Hudson. I consider the nights of wind and freezing rain, icy drops pinging the windowpanes, the street beyond pitch dark. At 8:30 the lights of my mom's Corolla turning into our drive-way like I knew they would. She was home, as always.

I open the door with the red star and enter the room these nurses were afraid to enter. I don't do it for Chry, but for her, Rebecca Berg. My ancestry isn't the hand that laid me down to live or die in a pool of church water. My ancestry is her headlights in the driveway every night at 8:30.

"You waited," says Chry. Her eyes, dark in her pale, drawn face hadn't registered my entrance, but they look at me now and flicker a thank you. I had readied myself for her to be blood-smeared, but she's tucked into clean white sheets underneath layers of white cotton blankets. Her white oval of a face is an egg in a nest of dark hair. "Mina," she says, noticing the bathing supplies, "the nurse, the one on night shift, cleaned up, cleaned me up."

"Mina," she says my name again, then stops, looks away. Fat tears come slowly, fall down her face and fall on the sheet below her chin.

"They gave you some scrubs to go home in," I say. "Your clothes were soaked through."

She nods but still won't look at me. I wonder if she's mad at me. "I had to," I say. "I had to tell them."

"I know. It's okay."

"Who else needs to know?"

She doesn't answer.

I think of the pregnancy test we'd laughed about, Jeff Some-one. There were others, but they were Chry's late-night tales keeping me company or pee sticks in the bathroom garbage can. I think of Nyro. "You need to tell Danny," I say. The room is windowless and nearly empty except for the bed and some industrial shelving. There's a makeshift rolling cart with the usual hospital room things—tongue depressors, bandages, pads, blood pressure cuff—but nothing on the walls, no cupboards, no curtain to pull around. This is some kind of storage closet.

"Can you do it? Will you?" she pleads. She holds out her hand to me, in it is a crumpled slip of paper.

"What?"

"Tell Nyro."

"About the pregnancy? Chry…"

"That's gone. About the other, the positive. His blood needs testing." She lifts her extended hand. "Instructions."

"What about Dare?" I don't want to ask this, but I have to and I look away as I say it.

"No. Never. We never—"

I hadn't thought so, but I needed to know. "Okay," I say. "I will."

I take the paper, then put the clothes and supplies I'd been holding on the edge of the bed, walk out of the storage closet passing for a hospital room, and back to the pay phone where I dial Nyro and Dare's apartment. Dare is at work where I should be; Nyro doesn't seem to keep regular work hours. I want him to answer while I have the nerve to do this. The night nurse, someone I've never met, a woman who refused to let Chry lie in her own blood—and my mom—is the reason I can do this.

"Danny," I say when Nyro answers. "It's Mina."

"Meeeeeee nuh."

"Danny, I have something serious to say."

"You didn't say, 'Are you sitting down?' How serious can it be if you didn't say, 'Are you sitting down?'"

"Are you sitting down?"

"I'm lying down. Still in bed. We should be good."

"It's Chry." I cannot play fun and games with him on the phone.

"I thought you said it was Meeeeee NUH."

"It's about Chry. She tested positive for HIV." My heart

thumps. It's wrong to say this over the phone but as soon as I let the words go, I know I couldn't have told him in person. There is a click and then buzz of the dial tone. I shake my purse and feel around the bottom for another quarter and call him again.

"Meeeeeee nuh," he says.

"You need to get tested. There are instructions. You need to have your doctor draw the blood, then take it yourself to the health department on First Avenue."

"Test yourself. I'm fine."

"How do you know?" I say, ignoring the implication of *test yourself*.

"O negative. I'm a hero at the American Red Cross. They won't let you give if you've got HIV, or AIDs or whatever. They call you up and tell you your blood's no good."

"You give blood?"

"Yeah, Mina, that's me, O negative, the universal donor, saving lives every chance I get. Sorry about your girl. That sucks." He hangs up again.

31

When the line for Dai Ichi Kangyo Bank rings, Todd motions for me to pick it up. Now that I'm on the desk, I do voice checks with the traders, a step up from the backroom deal checks Dare and I used to do.

"Mina?" says the voice on the other end in response to my hello.

"Yes." It's Ray but I don't dare start a conversation.

"Matt told me you're working with him now. It's Ray. DiSalvo."

"Hi, Ray." I keep my voice still. Riding the ferry all night listening to Vinnie and Chry are a thousand miles away from the stress and frenzy of the trading day. He asks me how I've been, how I like working on the desk. I look up to see Todd eyeing me. I'm too new to be chatting with the traders. For now, I'm here to check deals, that's it. I read the details to Ray, "DKB Bank sells 20 million dollars to Saitama Bank, 6 months at 8 17/32."

"Okay, Mina. We're agreed," he says and clicks off.

He doesn't whisper Sirena Fuggitiva the way he had at Windows on the World. It's a taped line. Or maybe he forgot.

Dare checks the day's deals on his desk too. I haven't seen him outside work since before the night I took Chry to the hospital. By chance or by me wanting to separate what I'm trying to accomplish from life on West Seventy-First Street, I don't know. Truth is, it was always Chry figuring out ways to be in his company. She wasn't doing that now. Her talk and stories are almost gone. The sounds in our apartment are mostly Jaco. Chry clings to her fretless bass with the records on, working to make her hands match the sound Jaco is making. We are kind to each other the way strangers can be kind.

Dare and I still sit back to back, and when we finish the deal checks, we still turn our chairs partway and eat lunch together, watch as the trainees rewrite the morning prices. Funny, how when I was doing that job, running back and forth writing the prices the traders yelled at me on the board, I never bothered to notice the views from our office windows, so high up in One World Trade. Now, most days, I take a minute to look. We are high, high, high above the water.

In the early afternoons, when the market is quiet, walking to the bathroom or the water cooler, I pass by the windows that look out on the East River, the Hudson, the whole New York Harbor, the Verrazano Narrows, and silently call, *Sirena Fuggitiva*. I ask her, *Are you the mother of the monster who crawled out of the river to deposit me in the baptismal font? Do I come from you?* It would take the daughter of the daughter of a mermaid to know that drowning and surviving are the opposite sides of the same coin.

But a girl can't get caught daydreaming out the window on the trading floor of Merton Marston Forex Inc. Attention is survival here. High up in the air, above all of New York City, you pay attention or pay the price. Still, I call her name and even if it's a passing moment, I feel sure she hears me.

Afternoons in a quiet market can be mischievous with pranks and jokes. It's a city block of boys and energy revved by deals done or deals missed. This is also the time when plans get made for dinner with the traders, or drinks, or other extra-curricular activities. Since I'm new on the desk, I'm supposed to use these hours to keep learning, ask questions, study the *Wall Street Journal* and the books the brokers recommended. I reread my options theory book to resink the esoteric concepts into my brain. Volatility, probabilities, something more random than random.

"Mina!" Matt Magee yells my name loud enough for the room to go quiet.

"Yes?" I respond quietly, hoping people will go back to their own business.

"Mina, what the fuck?" he spits it.

"I'm not. I don't—"

The room is still paying attention; any small drama is interesting when the markets are in a lull. Matt stands up. "As you were, folks. All's well here on the Japanese desk." He comes over to where I'm sitting and crouches down. "How do you know Ray DiSalvo?"

"I don't really know him."

"Well, he knows you." Unable to keep his civility, his voice drops to a hiss. "What the fuck? Why are you fucking with my account? It took me two years to get this guy where I want him. Do not fuck with my account, Mina."

"I mean, we met once."

"How's that?"

I shrug. I would never tell him that Ray DiSalvo and I rode the Staten Island Ferry all night while Chry and Vinnie played music and he told me the story of Sirena Fuggitiva. Never.

"He wants you to come to dinner. Tonight. Can you come?" His attitude changes as he grapples with needing something from me.

"Do you want me to come?"

"No. Yes. Why not? First, he tells me he can't make it to dinner, then he tells me he can, but you should come. So, listen. You come for a drink…or two…but tell him you can't stay for dinner. Okay. It's good. You can help. But it's better for business if it's just me and him in the end. Ya know?"

"Yeah, Matt, sure, I know."

Matt appraises me as we wait for Ray at the Vista Hotel Bar. He's recalibrating. I can manage the trading floor, getting a seat on a desk says as much, but now it's about entertaining the trader. "Bar food," he says, insinuating that I might be useful to him in a broker/banker meetup.

I absorb the insult. One thing about being a taunted kid, you develop skills. He's not my boss but I can't cross him either. I smile my sea-green-eyes smile, my gratitude smile. My brain says, *Fuck you.* Refusing to be humiliated—for the moment—is all I have.

Ray arrives. Our drinks with him at the bar are a very different outing than trainee shots at the Seaport or broker poker at the bar in Windows on the World. A gaggle of secretaries drinking nearby don't elicit remarks about low-hanging fruit. Matt is civilized and funny. I order scotch on the rocks as they have. Matt and Ray talk about the markets, Eurodollars, Spot Yen, the stock market, the price of gold. I stay quiet, but I am not excluded. When Ray asks me what I think about an arbitrage idea, I tell him I'm still learning. Matt nods slightly. Approval.

The check comes and I make my excuses. Ray, here at the bar of the Vista Hotel, is not the guy telling mermaid stories on the Staten Island Ferry, or the one who came up behind me and whispered in my ear when no one was looking. He's a Wall Street power guy. Well-mannered because there's nothing for him to prove. He doesn't ask why I can't stay for dinner, just says it was nice to see me and shakes my hand. "Do you have a card?" he says. I take a business card from the small deck in my purse, the first one I've given out. He takes one out of his own wallet and we exchange them, Japanese-businessman style, shaking with our right hands, passing the cards with our left and bowing slightly, the way I'd been taught.

I study his card in the cab, turn it over to see if it has his name and information in Japanese characters on the back, same as mine. It does. It also has a note. *Saturday, 11 am Alice in Wonderland Statue, Central Park (If you'd like).*

I stare at the printed Japanese characters and the handwritten note. There are three days to decide if I'd like to meet Ray DiSalvo at the Alice in Wonderland statue in Central Park.

It's Saturday morning and I'd decided, Yes. I meet Ray in front of Alice, as well as the Mad Hatter, the White Rabbit, and a patch of mushrooms. The bronze statues are shiny in places where kids like to climb—Alice's lap, the large mushroom she sits on, and two smaller ones beneath—even the hat of the Mad Hatter is shiny. They're by the sailboat pond which, empty of boats, ripples and drifts in the November gusts. I had walked here from across the park, pulling my coat in close, listening to the wind blow through the bare trees in short whooshes. Ray sees me and gives a small wave. We're civilians here, outside of the trading day and the boozing night, unknown to each other after all.

"Why here?" I say. "I mean I love it here but…I don't know."

"I had to write something quick and it's the first thing that came to my head. I didn't want it to be weird. You know, I was trying to think of something…innocent."

A little boy in a puffy blue jacket and a bright red knit hat runs ahead of a woman pushing a stroller, which holds a pink-faced baby tucked into blankets and dozing. The boy jumps onto the stone edge of the pond, walking with small skips and dips. "Corey, it's cold today," the mom calls. "Corey, be careful," she says mildly as he jumps and skips around the edge.

"No boats today," he shouts.

"No boats today," she confirms back to him.

She doesn't notice us as she passes, eyes focused on the boy.

"I guess that's how you teach them not to be afraid," I say.

"You don't want to know," says Ray with a laugh. "My brothers and I…my poor mom never knew the half of it."

"Bad stuff?"

"Not really. Things like swimming in places you're not supposed to swim. I mean, we grew up on an island, what'd she expect?"

"I can't swim." I say it as an act of friendship, a bridge of honesty, a test of my embarrassment. When I said these words to Jamie Risk, it was a plea, me begging him not to exile me from their kingdom. Remembering that moment is a fist, a bloodied lip, a black eye, like it has been all these days I haven't been able to stop remembering. Some days, I remember it as the possibility that he is in love with me. Some days, I remember it as him letting me know I'll never be as good as his daughter. Fathers can be like that, I hear. Either way, my heart turns to that same dangerous shard that will slice me open from the inside if I fail to keep myself still.

Ray shrugs. "Never too late to learn."

"I'm afraid."

"A good place to start." He motions his head toward the sailboat pond.

The little boy and his mom are gone. She'd waited to let the bobbing and jumping red hat make one full circle around. He had not fallen in.

Ray runs over to the edge and stands on it, the child but taller in sneakers, jeans, and a Columbia sweatshirt. "Now you," he shouts over to me.

"Now me what?"

"Come on." He waves his arm for me to join him.

"Can't we just sit on a mushroom like normal people?" I call to him.

Dare, Nyro, Chry, and I lay a whole afternoon in a ring of red-capped mushrooms with white spots in Chry's fairytale woods staring up at the clouds and treetops.

"Come on." Ray waves me over again. I square my shoulders and walk to him. "It's not deep, like two feet, not even."

"The wall is slanted."

"A little bit, yeah."

I take his hand and step onto the stone edge of the pond; it's wide enough for a little boy to skip and jump around on and not fall in.

"Try a few steps."

I take a few careful steps. "Some mermaid, huh?"

"Don't worry about that, that's just a story the grandmas tell."

"I like it. I've been calling to her, from, uh, work. I can see the Verrazano Bridge from our floor."

He puts his hands loosely on my waist. "A few more steps," he says. We walk partway around the pond. I understand it's not deep, but if we fell, it would be cold. There would be suffering.

"That's enough for one day," says Ray.

He asks me if I want to get something to eat and we walk to a place he knows on Third Avenue. We're ruddy-faced and windblown by the time we get to the café, but inside it's warm and smells like freshly baked bread. The waiter knows Ray and when I ask him if he comes here a lot, he tells me, yeah, he lives nearby.

"I thought you lived on Staten Island?"

"You know," he says, "growing up there, with the Manhattan skyline across the bay, it was what I wanted to do. Make my fortune here, live here." He reddens slightly, then shakes it off. "Hey," he says, reaching into the pocket of his coat, which is hanging on the back of his chair. "Want to play?" He tosses a deck of cards on the table with soft thunk.

I shrug.

"Tarocco Siciliano. Sicilian tarot cards."

"Are you going to read my fortune?"

"No. Play cards. Tarocchi. It's a game."

He takes them out of the pack. "I play with my grandmother and her friends on Saturday mornings. She lives down the block from us on Staten Island. I used to watch them play when I was little. When I was old enough, I'd sub in if someone couldn't make it. You know…I think it's how I got interested in trading, watching the grandmas in the neighborhood play this game." He sorts through the deck. "My grandmother learned to play on the way over, on the boat to America."

"They didn't send her back."

"Nope. No. No one sent her back, she made it." He smiles. "And here I am."

He shuffles through, holding up the interesting cards as he comes across them. "Sole, the sun. Luna, the moon. Stella, star…Torre, the tower. Other tarot decks—each country seems to have their own version—in the other decks the tower is in ruins, cracked and crumbling from a lightning strike. The Sicilians? No way. They'd been conquered too many times. The towers on their coastline protected them. They didn't even like the *thought* of a wrecked tower, so they changed the card, to this."

He gives me the card so I can get a closer look. It's smaller than a regular playing card. The tower is made of stone with an arched doorway at the bottom and a turret. "Looks sturdy."

"Yes, sturdy. Sicilian. Sturdy and stubborn," Ray says as I hand back the card. "Now, if they're not stubbornly protecting our island, they're sailing away from it. Vascello." He gives me the Vascello card which is a ship. "If a destroyed tower was troubling to the Sicilian sensibility, imagine how the devil card made them feel. The devil became the ship. No point in hanging around evil, better to sail away. So, no devils or wrecked towers for them, although…they let this guy stay." He holds up a card. "The Hanged Man."

"Luca Brasi sleeps with the fishes."

"Something like that. As a kid I was afraid of him. My grandmother said, 'Then behave.'"

He thumbs through the deck, Death, Time, Wheel of Fortune, Justice, Love. He pauses, "And here, Fuggitivo, the fugitive, the runaway, the fool, a trump card with no point value. *Scusa*, the ladies say when they lay him down. The fugitive has his own set of rules. He can't lead a trick, unless it's the last trick."

The waiter clears our table and we order cups of tea. There's a line of people at the door, but he lets us stay. We sit in the warm café. Spats of rain tick at the window and Ray DiSalvo teaches me to play tarocchi. "It's really a game for more people but there's a way for just two." He smiles. "There's a chance my grandmother invented it to keep me sharp for the Saturday game." When it's time to go, he gathers the deck, knocking it on the table both ways until it's packed tight then puts it back into its green box. He hands it to me. "A present."

I love the way the little box fits in my hand but I have to ask. "Is it because I look like Sirena Fuggitiva?"

"No."

"That's not why you wrote that note for me to meet you?"

"No."

"Is it disappointing I'm afraid of water, even a little pond, two feet deep?"

"No."

"Thank you," I say, "for the cards."

32

Dare never went back to eating liverwurst sandwiches, now it's turkey on dry toast. He says he's trying to lose weight, which he is. One afternoon when it was quiet, he fell asleep in his chair, his head bent to the side, mouth open. I saw before anyone else and gave him a gentle push. His eyes blinked wide and he stared at me like he didn't know where he was.

"You were sleeping."

He nodded a thank you, then shook his head in quick spurts to revive himself. A few days after that, he was out sick. When he missed a whole week of work, I called the loft on Franklin Street. The machine answered and I left a message, "Dare. Nyro. Pick up if you're there. Dare, you okay? Pick up. All right. Call me. Pick up. Pick up. Pick up." No one picked up.

I know something. I know from the way Dare's athletic build is disappearing. I know from the day he and I didn't swim at Arcadia, when we had a tug-of-war with the blanket. I know from the ragged ovals I saw on his legs, part crusted over part raw and angry looking.

When Dare is gone for the second week in a row, I call the loft again. No one picks up. I call again and again but no one ever answers the phone. I stop leaving messages and consider going to Franklin Street, but I would only buzz and buzz and no one would buzz me in. If I threw rocks up at the window, no one would look out.

I ask Chry if she's heard from Dare and she tells me no. "Chry," I say, "how are *you*?"

"Fine," she says, like *Why wouldn't I be?* She'd recovered from her self-induced miscarriage, every day she was a little less pale until she looked exactly like her old self. She started temping again, but she stopped playing the bass, the regular bass and the fretless bass, altogether. She stopped trying to find Jaco. Still, she played his records nonstop. She preferred listening to him on vinyl, but she also had cassettes, ones she bought and mixtapes. She stopped talking me to sleep altogether, so I started relying on Jaco. It was all I had. I even had my favorite. "Okónkolo y Trompa."

"It's Jaco on bass with the okónkolo and French horn," says Chry. I can get her to talk if I ask about Jaco.

"Okay, I know what a French horn is. What's okónkolo?"

"The batá is three drums, the largest is iyá, the mother; the middle, itótele, is the father; the smallest is okónkolo, the child. They're Afro-Cuban, originating with the Yorùbá in West Africa but then in Cuba, part of Santería ceremonies. Santería, the way of the saints, the drums are…sacred."

Chry will answer my questions about the music, but if I try to talk about anything else, even Dare, she waves me away. She is uncurious about where he might be. Dare, the boy who had brought her back to life on New Year's and turned her easy heart into a longing heart.

"Sandy to You said you'd be side by side. Don't you want to?"

"Don't I want to what, Mina?"

"Don't you think, I mean, don't you still love him?"

"What does that have to do with anything?" She stands and faces me. "Mina? Well?"

"I don't know."

"I didn't think so."

She puts on her coat. It's electric blue cashmere and comes down past her calves with a shawl collar.

She wraps a bright white scarf around her neck. She is beautiful in these colors with her dark hair and bright blue eyes. "I'll see you later," she says.

I hear her key in the locks, one by one, on her way out, making sure I'm safe inside. The wind rattles the French doors. Anyone could break in through the back. The garden is weeds again. I start calling, hospital by hospital, asking for Darius

Fiore. I find him. He is at Bellevue Hospital. Sixteenth floor. Tomorrow, I think, I'll go see him.

I don't tell Chry and I don't visit Dare. Not right away. I go to work, to my job. Dare isn't there, he's at Bellevue, on the sixteenth floor. I tell no one.

He's been absent three weeks, but they haven't replaced him. They won't leave his seat empty for long. A chair without a broker making money is a chair losing money. There was whispering when he first stopped coming, around the second week, and then nothing. Not the usual, *Where the fuck is so and so?* Information is power and everyone guards it. I could have asked when the chatter started, *What's up with Dare?*, but now too much time has passed. For his sake I don't say anything. Or for my sake, I don't know.

On Friday after work, I go to Bellevue Hospital. Night falls fast this time of year and it's dark when I arrive. I take the elevator to the sixteenth floor and ask the nurse at the desk for Darius Fiore. The sign behind her says, *The Only Difference Between This Place and the Titanic Is…They Had a Band!* She tells me Dare's room number and explains how to get there. She asks if I'd like a mask. Without waiting for an answer, she hands me a paper surgical mask off a pile on the desk.

"No," I say. "No." I live with Chry. No. Everything is moving too fast for me to comprehend whether I need a mask or not.

The door to Dare's room doesn't have a red star like Chry's had. It's painted completely red. All the doors on this hall are. I lean my ear to it. Silence. I knock and when no one answers I push the handle slowly so if he really doesn't want a visitor, he has time to call out. I want him to call out. I want him to yell, *No, no thanks, no visitors today,* but there's only silence.

I peek in to make sure it's the right room. It is. It's him. It's Dare.

I push it open all the way. "So, Fiore," I say, "this is where you've been hiding out." I dose the words with cheer to cover my shock. His eyes are large in his face, his arms from the sleeves of his hospital gown, thin. I shut down the cheer. I

don't know what I am, who I am, but I know what I'm not, a
liar. "Sorry, Dare," I say.

"Hi, Mina." He smiles. "I'm glad you're here."

There's a metal chair against the wall and I pull it up to the
bed.

"My first visitor, actually."

"I called. Everywhere. I didn't want to ask at work and Nyro
won't pick up the phone."

"You knew though, right? You saw when we were at Arcadia."

"I didn't want to know, so I didn't know."

He tilts his head, a slim nod.

"Your parents?" How could I be the first visitor in three
weeks?

"No." He shakes his head

"Why. Why didn't you tell them you were in the hospital?"

"I called them." He looks away, smiling slightly. His crooked
nose in profile reminds me that his dad is the one who broke
it. When he turns back to me, his eyes, so large in his shrinking
face, show pain. "It's not like I didn't expect it. I did, but then
again, I didn't."

"What do you mean?"

"They said their goodbyes."

What the fuck is wrong with people? I don't say this, but I want
to. I want to shout it. I want to say a million things but none of
them make sense.

"Don't take up poker, Mina," Dare says, acknowledging my
inability to hide my fury. "It's okay. It's not okay but it's okay as
far as you and me go."

"What about Nyro?"

He shakes his head.

"Is he?"

He shakes his head again. "He's not gay, just crazy. And I'm
the opposite."

"Dare."

"Yeah. That's how."

"And Chry. That's why."

"I never...we never. I wasn't. Girls aren't my thing. She must be so glad. Now."

It occurs to me he doesn't know about Chry. I don't tell him, though I wonder if she will. It's her prerogative but, I wonder. Chry surprises me. That's the constant. Sometimes in a good way and sometimes in a bad way. I ask him how long he'll be here, and he says he's not sure, that he has pneumonia. As if to prove this is true, he begins to cough, a horrible and painful-sounding cough. He turns his head away from me. I ask him if I can bring him some water or something. He coughs out, yeah.

I return with a tall Styrofoam cup with room temperature water and a bendy straw. When I asked for ice, the nurse said it's better for him without it. I wait for the coughing to subside, then let Dare gather himself with small sips of water.

"Want to play cards with the Sicilian tarot deck?" Dare tries to smile. "Sounds dangerous, but...what the hell."

"Nah, it's just cards." I show him the cards the way Ray had shown me, but I don't tell him that the ship used to be the devil and the tower used to be destroyed. I don't show him the hanged man.

My smart, funny friend learns the game even more quickly than I had. He doesn't flinch when the Hanged Man appears, he raises his eyebrows and says, "Just cards, not fortunes, right?"

There isn't any information about visiting hours and no one tells me to leave. When Dare's dinner arrives, I sit by while he attempts to eat it. It's almost midnight when I get up to go. Dare looks out the window as I put my coat on and when he turns back to me, his eyes are glassy. "I never thought I could feel this alone," he says. "I thought maybe my dad...I didn't think he'd come, but my mom, I don't know. I didn't think she would let me die alone."

"Dare, you are not going to die alone."

"How do you know?"

"I won't let you. I'll see you tomorrow."

"Really?"

"Yeah, Dare. Really. Who exactly do you think you made friends with?"

"Okay, I'll see you tomorrow." He lifts the edge of the blanket in an attempt to pull it up over his chest. I pause with my hand on the doorknob, drop my purse, and go over to help him. "Can you sleep?" I say as I arrange the blankets up around his shoulders, tuck them in tight. He doesn't answer. On my way out, I click the light.

In the elevator, I try to answer the question I asked him. Who exactly had he made friends with? We're both about to find out.

When I get home, Chry is there, sprawled on the couch, Pat Metheny with Jaco on bass is playing "Bright Size Life." When the song is finished, she walks over to the turntable, picks up the needle and starts it over again. This used to drive me crazy but tonight I don't mind.

"Dare is at Bellevue," I say, "on the AIDS floor. Dare has AIDS. I was there tonight and I'm going tomorrow. He doesn't have any visitors. No one. His parents already told him goodbye. That's what he said, Chry. 'They've already said their goodbyes.'"

Her mouth opens but nothing comes out. Her eyes widen. I am sorry for her in a way I have not before known how to be sorry. Chry is so herself, I forget most days she's HIV positive. Her night in the emergency room is a million years ago. It didn't happen. That's the way we've been playing it. Or I've been playing it. I look at Chry's face, seeing for the first time that she hasn't forgotten for a second. She couldn't put it out of her mind as I had been doing, the seeds and the abortion in the room with the red star. She has not forgotten she is HIV positive.

"I understand if you don't want to go," I say

"I'll think about it."

"It's okay, Chry. I get it." And I do, finally. Get it.

There are no more words tonight, there's only Jaco playing "Bright Size Life."

When the song finishes, Chry gets up again and moves the needle back to the beginning.

"What do you think?" I say as carefully as I can, as carefully as I've ever said anything in my life. "What do you think about not telling Dare. You know, about you."

"I'll think about it," she says again.

33

On Saturday morning, Chry and I go to Bellevue. If Dare's appearance shocks her, she shows no signs of it. We are all formal, new to each other in this new situation. When we run out of small talk, we sit for a while in silence, but it isn't uncomfortable, each of us in our own heads rethinking the world. Finally, Dare says, "What about those cards, Mina."

Dare and I teach Chry to play tarocchi. He had learned quickly from me the way I had learned quickly from Ray. We both have a knack for cards, the same knack that makes us good at work which is also a game of skill and chance. Chry takes a little longer to learn but she catches on. I thought Nyro would make a good fourth, but he isn't answering his phone and anyway Dare says he won't come to Bellevue.

Chry and I go back the next day, Sunday, but I leave at lunchtime. Chry stays on, keeping the cards so they can go on playing. On Monday, when I go to work, Chry goes to Bellevue.

Dare's chair is empty, but they're keeping it for him. I hear someone ask where the fuck has he been and Nick, who runs the desk, says, "He's on a short leave—death in the family or something."

Chry goes to Bellevue every day and I go when I'm able. By the middle of November, they can both beat me at tarocchi. Handily.

Dare will be allowed to leave the hospital if he can shake the pneumonia, but his cough, rumbling, and persistent, won't go away. He becomes increasingly emaciated and his eyes are rheumy and yellow. Chry doesn't notice or pretends not to notice. She never mentions his wasted face and body to me.

On the Saturday before Thanksgiving, I see Nyro in the Bellevue lobby.

"Came to get my boy," he says, like he hasn't been MIA all this time.

"Where you been, Danny?"

"You ask too many questions, Mina."

"It's just that…"

"He's coming home to my mom's out on Long Island. She has all the dying gays in for the holidays."

"What the fuck is wrong with you?"

"A lot, darling, but he is coming to Thanksgiving with me."

When we get to Dare's room, Chry is there and he is much worse. The cough seems to have subsided, but he is thinner than ever and has a lesion on the side of his face like the ones I'd seen on his legs at Arcadia.

"I'm finally presentable enough for this jackass to take me to his mom's house," he says, his voice like a shadow. He tilts his head toward Nyro with a thin smile, the joke itself is a monumental effort.

"Do you think this is the best idea?" says Chry.

"Are you a nurse or fucking something?" Nyro barks back.

"No, Danny, but neither are you." She stands up and puts herself between the bed and Nyro. She steps up close to him and hisses in his face, "He's not your fucking show and tell."

Nyro doesn't react. "There's maybe some kind of drug in the works, my mom's involved. She gives money. It's none of your business where I've been. It's none of your business, Chry, if I…" He stops and I know it's occurred to him, the thing that is so easy to forget because Chry is healthy-looking and fierce and beautiful. She, too, could use a new kind of drug. She, too, needs someone to save her life.

What it will take for Nyro to help Dare get dressed and down to his car will be excruciating and, Chry and I seem to understand, private. She is going to trust Nyro not to hurt him and I am too. This is a leap. As always.

"Hey, Dare," says Chry, as if Nyro's not in the room. "My dad is a member of the United States Congress. If this asshole does one single thing to put you in harm's way, like I don't know, stopping in the middle of a bridge or dropping you into one of the New York City waterways, I will have Congressman Risk call out the National Guard and run him down like the dog he is."

In all the time I've known her, I've never, not once, heard her pull the "my dad's a congressman" card.

"You have my word," says Nyro, and he is so solemn there's a chance he means it. Chry and I want to believe.

The tarocchi cards are on Dare's table and he asks if he can keep them for the trip. Chry says, "Yeah, Dare, sure," then turns to Nyro and says, "I hope he wipes your ass with them." Fact is, they're my cards to lend or keep but I don't mention it.

On the elevator down, Chry asks if I want to go to her mom and dad's in Atlantic Highlands for Thanksgiving. When I tell her no, she asks what I'm doing, when I shrug, she says, "Well, how about we go see G.A.?"

"Okay," I say, "yes."

"Oh, oh, Mina." She hugs me. "Mina, really?"

"Yeah, Chry. Really."

"We can take the jeep; I'll ask my dad to drive it in for us."

"No. We can take my car."

"Since when do you have a car?"

"Since an hour from now. I bought it last week and I'm on my way to pick it up." I didn't know it but my spot on the desk was a trial; I didn't know it until my boss called me into the conference room and said it would now be permanent, I would be getting my own accounts, some small Japanese banks, they didn't do much business, but he thought I could do something with them. And he gave me a small bonus of five thousand dollars, which I used for a down payment on a car, a new Chevy Blazer. It isn't a BMW, but it can climb a mountain. Of course, it doesn't make any sense, there aren't any mountains in New York City, but I was on the car lot on Twelfth Avenue and I could smell the salt from the Hudson River and I thought, *I need a car that can climb a mountain.*

Chry comes with me to the dealership and my car is waiting

out front. It's dark metallic blue with white trim. "Stay here," I say, and she obeys.

I bought the car from a friend of Ray's. I'd told him I was thinking about it the afternoon he taught me to play tarocchi. "Call this guy," he said. "I'll make sure he gives you a good deal." So that's what I did, and we drove every make and model on the lot. He knew Ray from high school, his brothers too. While we test drove all those cars, he talked about the DiSalvos, how half the family was in the fish business the other half were cops. Ray had gone a different way. Gone to Columbia, then to Wall Street to make his first million. But even though he'd moved into the city, he still played football with them out on Staten Island, in the flag league and pick-up tackle games for fun. "He still plays cards with the ladies on the block," he said, which I knew.

When I knock on the door to his glass office, Ray's friend looks up from his work and waves me in. "They delivered it last night," he says and hands me the keys.

Chry and I drive up the West Side Highway and there are so many potholes, I'm immediately glad for my little truck. I merge onto the Henry Hudson Parkway and drive up past the entrance to the George Washington Bridge. The river is to our left, alive with waves and light. When we pass the entrance to The Cloisters, Chry says we should go there someday.

"Someday." Today we're just driving. We wait in traffic at the tollbooth for the bridge across the Spuyten Duyvil, Spit of the Devil or Spite of the Devil depending.

"Where are we going anyway?" asks Chry.

"Nowhere," I say, but I realize I am going somewhere. I'm going home, just not today. I turn around at the first exit past the bridge and get back on the road heading south. When we cross over the devil's spit or spite, I hold my breath like I did the first time. The bridge is high and narrow, even more upsetting than the George Washington Bridge. How many times a day can a person encounter the devil's spite before something terrible happens?

On the Wednesday evening before Thanksgiving, they're inflating the giant balloons in Central Park for tomorrow's parade. Kermit the Frog! Underdog! Superman! I'm sorry to miss this but Chry and I need to get on the road. We pile into the Blazer and head for G.A.'s "facility." It had happened at Arcadia, the fall that fractured her hip. She never even made it home to Pittsburgh and after the accident and the surgery, she was too fragile for the trip. So, the place she's staying is near there. And even though Arcadia is closed up for the winter, the water turned off and pipes drained to keep them from freezing, that's where we'll be staying.

Except for a couple of visits from Chry's dad, G.A.'s been mostly by herself. "She cried on the phone when she described the place, the dining room, and the food especially. It's not a crap place—according to my dad—some old mansion or something. I don't care how fancy it is, I'm just glad I'm not letting her eat Thanksgiving dinner alone."

When I ask why her mom and dad don't go, she tells me their Thanksgiving in Atlantic Highlands is a "thing" with so many people they set up a heated tent behind the house. It makes his donors feel like family, being at the Risks' on Thanksgiving.

We drive all night, fueled on cups of coffee and gas station snacks, having both agreed it would be too dangerous to let either of us fall asleep. We make one last stop before arriving at Arcadia to go to the bathroom since, like everything else there, the plumbing's shut down till spring.

At the gates, Chry gets out of the truck to push them open. The stones under the wheels break the dark silence as we pull in. It's a very different place than on St. James Day. The porches are wrapped in green-and-white-striped canvas to protect them from the weather that comes off the Great Lakes and batters Arcadia with snow and cold.

Chry finds the key under a loose windowsill, its hiding place for as long as she's been alive. We leave our things in the car, no point in bringing them in, there's no water to brush our teeth and it's too freezing to think about changing out of our jeans and sweaters. Inside, it's the same smell of old wood and books as summertime, but even more so; the house is bedded down for the winter.

"We should have brought a flashlight," says Chry. We stand on the compass rose in the hall, hugging ourselves against the frigid air and the pitch dark. "There are candles and matches in the kitchen."

Our eyes adjust as we make out the doorway to the living room. The furniture is covered with white sheets so we're able to pass through without walking into anything. In the kitchen, Chry feels around in the drawers as she opens and closes them. "Watch for knives," I say.

She produces two tall pillar candles and lights them. We take one each and make our way up the back staircase. The creak on the stairs, the curve of the banister, the wide hallways, it's all as it was this summer. I'm not afraid of this house, all closed up in the dark, it's just something beautiful asleep.

"We may as well take the beds in our room," says Chry, and I am reminded again that she doesn't know I'm out of the family. *Her asshole father had made sure of it.* This is the first time I've referred to him in my mind as an asshole, which is a step toward something.

We go from room to room with our candles pulling extra quilts off beds. When I get to the room Dare stayed in, I think about how I'd seen the lesions on his leg but could not believe it was what it was. I hold the candle up to the Grateful Dead poster, the grinning skeleton in its wreath of roses. I don't understand anything. I put the candle on the dresser and pull the quilts off the beds, gather them in one arm and walk with my candle back to Chry's room.

Chry is in bed already, propped up with a pile of quilts on top of her and pulled up to her chin. She's put the candle on the dresser beside her and her face glows in the soft light. On her head is G.A.'s crown. I put my candle down too, lay the quilts I've gathered on the bed and crawl underneath.

"Mina," says Chry, and it's like old times when she knew I needed her to talk me to sleep. "G.A. wanted me to wear this for my wedding."

I nod but she's not looking at me.

"So. I'm not going to have a wedding, right."

"Chry—"

"It's not a question."

I nod again.

"I'm going to wear it now. Just for a little while," she says.

34

We wake up late, the sun bright in the windows. We pee in the dry toilet—what else can we do? Then we put the quilts all back on their proper beds, return our candles to the kitchen, and lock the house up like we'd never been there. Chry hides the key in its regular place, not so much of a secret after all.

G.A.'s facility is not the stark hospital-type place I might have expected. It's an old mansion, redone for, I guess, rich people to decline in style. We arrive at noon and the woman working the front desk tells us G.A. takes her meals in her room these days. "She's having her Thanksgiving dinner right now if you'd like to join her," she says. "And…" She pauses, then says gently, "She may not know you."

Chry shakes off the shock of these words, puts her hands on her hips, and tilts forward toward the desk clerk. I've seen her do this before, it's an elegant version of getting in someone's face. "No one eats Thanksgiving dinner at noon."

The clerk doesn't respond to Chry's snipe; she just says, "She's upstairs in room 202."

"Thank you," Chry responds, composing herself. "Yes. My father told me."

We find room 202, but when we open the door, G.A.'s asleep. There's a rolling table with her dinner on it over her. Chry swivels the table away. She sits on the bed and takes G.A.'s hand. She holds it to her lips and kisses it gently. G.A.'s eyes open. "Oh my, I dozed off," she says and then, "Chrysanthi, darling, how lovely to see you."

"Mina's here too."

"Well, that's wonderful."

"We came to wish you a happy Thanksgiving." Chry shoots a look at the turkey and mashed potatoes on the table, gravy hardening on top. "Do you want me to get your dinner warmed up?"

"Oh no, darling. That's fine. I don't have a taste for it." She seems to know us and not know us.

Chry is still holding her hand. "I love you, G.A.," she says, quiet and vehement.

"Don't worry about that." Her hand still in Chry's makes a motion toward the food. "No Thanksgiving dinner could ever compare to oysters on St. James Day, and we've had so many of those, haven't we?"

Chry nods.

"So many," G.A. says, then adds with a precision and clarity that has been missing since we arrived, "Mina, darling, will you give me a few minutes alone with my granddaughter?"

I go out to the parking lot and sit in the idling truck with the heat blasting.

When Chry comes out, she asks if she can drive. I don't argue. Seeing her grandmother so feeble, who so recently had gotten Arcadia into shape after a disaster, a force of nature outdoing any tornado, has exhausted me. It seems to have had the opposite effect on Chry. Either way, we are both famished.

She drives us across the empty landscape, at one point passing the entrance to Arcadia, all the way to the Breeze Inn. The little pub sits on a curve of Lake Avenue, the one main road into town. The wind comes off the lake hard. A sign, *Breeze Inn*, handpainted in swoopy letters and with a puffed-cheeked breeze-blowing cloud, flaps and creaks. There's a lit-up neon green and white Rolling Rock sign in the window. The summer screens on the outside door are replaced with storm windows. Chry pulls it open and it flies out of her hand, banging against the peeling clapboard. She grabs it, holds tight, and pushes the heavy main door open. I follow her inside making sure both doors are closed behind us. This is Cass's place; she'd told us about it on St. James Day, how it's cozy in the winter, and it is. Though it's empty, except for Cass herself. She's sitting on a stool at the end of the bar with a pen, a pile of papers, and a calculator.

She turns around to see who's come in, and her expression is at first blank, then baffled. I can't think why Chry would bring us here except there's no place else to find something to eat. We shouldn't be here, though. We should have kept going.

Cass stares at us. "Hi, girls."

"Hi. Um, are you open?" says Chry.

"It's Thanksgiving."

Silence. "Does that mean yes or no?"

"I don't have turkey or anything. No."

"Oh," says Chry. I half turn, take the handle of the door, but I stop when Chry doesn't move.

Cass drops her shoulders. "I could make you a couple of burgers, throw some fries in," she says.

"Cass. That would be…thank you…we're starving."

"Sit here." She points at the row of barstools.

We each perch on a stool tentatively. Cass hops off hers, goes to the other side of the bar, and puts a square napkin in front of us both. She pulls two pint glasses up from underneath the bar and fills them with ice. She puts them on top of the napkins with the fluid motion of someone who's done it many, many times before. She takes the soda gun, aims it at Chry's glass, and lifts her eyebrows.

"Coke."

"Coke," I say, after she's filled Chry's glass and aimed her gun at mine.

She presses a button and shoots the bubbly brown liquid in, returns the gun to its holster and walks to the kitchen, banging the swinging door in her wake.

"Why are we here?" I whisper, trying to keep the urgency out of my voice.

"I really wanted her fries. They're my favorite. I'm just really hungry."

Chry is so healthy, so unchanged, I forget she must wonder what's ahead for her and this burns me with shame. Who in her life will be the person she's been to Dare these past months? Her mom, so rarely home. Her dad, so…

Cass comes back through the swinging door wafting delicious smells and sizzling sounds.

"Why did you come?" she says.

"I don't know, Cass…your fries. And…I guess we have things to talk about."

Cass shakes her head very slightly. Something takes a hold of her and she grabs Chry's wrist, not hard, but not gently either. "Why did you take my dress?"

A buzzer goes off in the kitchen and she drops Chry's wrist and goes back through the swinging door. She returns with two oval plates with cheeseburgers and piles of fries and bangs them on the bar in front of us. "Careful the plates are hot," she says, and walks back into the kitchen. The steaming burgers and the hot fragrant fries look and smell delicious. We eat everything on our plates, like well-behaved little girls, then drink down the sweet bubbly Coke.

The food is so good, we forget about Cass, at least I do, but she has not forgotten about us. She comes out when we're finished and clears our dishes. She takes our silverware and napkins with our plates and stashes them in a bin under the bar. She collects our glasses, throwing the ice into the sink with a violent thrust, then places them in the bin with the dirty plates. Her wrist and hands are ropy and strong, empty of bracelets or rings.

"Do you have a pay phone?" I ask.

She nods. "Out back."

I take out a five-dollar bill and ask for change. She opens the register and counts out quarters then puts five small piles in front of me. I gather them up and tell Chry I'll be right back.

Shaking from the raw November air, I attempt to put the quarters in the slot. I was in such a hurry to use the pay phone I hadn't bothered to put on my coat. I'm not surprised when I hear the recording of my mom's voice on her answering machine. She always works on Thanksgiving; they pay time and a half. "Hi, Mom. Happy Thanksgiving. I miss you. I love you. And, Mom, I'll be there tomorrow. Chry too."

Back inside, Chry is alone, still at the bar. Seeing I'm there, Cass comes back out of the kitchen. She walks over to the window, switches off the Rolling Rock sign and locks the door. "Let's go upstairs," she says. "We can talk there, in my apartment. Bring your coats."

We follow her into the kitchen and out the back, past the pay phone, and up a rickety set of steps single file, Cass, Chry, me. There's a small covered porch at the top and on the door to her apartment there's a fabric wreath with fall-themed appliques—an acorn, a yellow leaf, a scarecrow. Cass puts her shoulder to the door when it sticks and pushes it open. "Come in," she says, flipping on the light.

It's just one main space, a living room with a table and a kitchen against the opposite wall, but it's pretty, with high ceilings and huge old windows, like at Arcadia. The drowned boy is everywhere. I recognize his picture from the paper and by the way Chry draws a sharp breath, I see that she does too. There are the typical school pictures, group shots of teams at different ages in all kinds of uniforms—baseball, soccer, hockey; there's a black-and-white hockey action shot, blown up and a little grainy; there's one of him in a Boy Scout uniform holding a trophy. There's a shelf with a stereo and a record collection. Another shelf has more photos, these in frames, one of a man and a girl with wide smiles, standing on a dock, the girl holding up a fish as big as she is. Another shelf has rocks in a variety of shapes and sizes—a big purple amethyst, crystals, and quartz in pale colors.

Cass points for us to sit on a faded turquoise sofa. We obey, holding our coats on our laps. The sofa fabric is rough, and the color is from another time, but there aren't any raw patches or threadbare seams.

Cass sits in a chair opposite and begins speaking with an authority brought on by being in her own home. At Arcadia, she'd deferred to Chry's family; in the restaurant, she'd been direct but deferential to the business. Here, surrounded by her rocks and photos and record albums, she is forceful. "The storm, the tornado, were you here for that?" She doesn't wait for an answer. "I rent storage space in a friend's barn, up over on Sullivan Hill. Well…I used to, till that twister took it out. My stuff…I got some of it but most of it was gone.

"It was your dress," says Chry factually, but I can tell she is thrown by this realization.

"Yeah, it was my dress…no…it was my mom's." Cass gets up and takes a picture off the shelf to shows us.

We nod. I feel sick. It's a woman in the dress, her mother, yes, a version of her. The groom is the man in the fish picture.

"It was hers and then it was mine. I never wore it. That's okay, I was going to, but I didn't. I never wore it, but it is still mine and I want it back. But you ruined it," she looks at Chry, "didn't you?"

I make circular motions with my flat palm on the rough fabric.

"I'm sorry," Chry whispers.

"Is the compass rose box yours? The compass rose box with the poem?" I say. Chry turns her head partway toward me. She doesn't know I opened the box the night of St. James Day and found the *Wand'ring* poem with those two words scrawled on the back. She was in the fairy garden fucking Nyro my maybe boyfriend.

"Do you have that too?" says Cass slowly.

"Yes," I say, "it's at Arcadia."

Chry faces me full on, her confusion and rising anger focused on me not Cass or the situation.

Cass understands she's been forgotten for the moment. She shakes her head, first a little, then big wide exasperated back and forths. "You people," she says.

She walks over to the sink and runs water from the tap into a glass tumbler. She comes back and stands over us, deciding, I think, whether to drink it or throw it.

"I'm sorry," Chry says again, her attention returning to Cass, her voice still a whisper.

Cass drinks the water, then walks to the shelf with the rocks, puts down the glass and picks up a smooth, flat rose-colored stone and holds it in her palm. If it would help her to throw it, I'd let her, but she does something worse. She turns her back to us. She holds the stone to her forehead and stands there, holding the stone on her head with both hands, breathing deep long breaths and letting them out slowly. We should go. But I want to know something.

"And the paper…with the poem?" I ask.

She turns around with the stone between her palms.

"It says *Marry me*. On the back." I say this for Chry's benefit; Cass no doubt knows what's written on the back of the poem.

Cass walks over to the large black-and-white photo of the boy playing hockey. It's from behind so you see the name on the jersey, GREENVALE. He's got his stick way over his shoulder, winding up to let one fly.

"He made that shot," says Cass and stops, her shoulders sag slightly as she looks at the picture, but only for a moment. She straightens and goes on. "So that year, the year you two were born…" She does not mean Chry and me, she means Chry and the boy making a goal in the photograph. "Jamie made a choice. Well—" She snorts a sarcastic laugh. "He made two choices. The first was to leave your mother—" She says this to Chry matter of factly, making it clear she doesn't care if it burns. "And the second was to stay. Somewhere in between those choices, your grandmother got involved. She paid me to go away. She gave me a large sum of money and I took it and bought this place, the restaurant. I took it and raised my child with it. And before you say a thing, before you pass judgement on me or anything about me, know this: You don't know anything."

Chry stares hard at Cass. "I have a brother."

"Had."

On Chry's face is an expression I've never seen before, an expression of loss like a thousand sinking ships.

"Why did you come here?" says Cass, repeating the question she'd asked earlier.

"My grandmother sent me."

35

We drive all the way to my mom's, stopping only for gas and coffee and junk food. Chry has never been there. I'd always been too embarrassed to show her the tiny Cape where I grew up, perched on the edge of the Hudson River. Now I couldn't wait for her to feel the locked-down order and safety of my mom's little house. We arrive in the middle of the night as we had at Arcadia, but this time we bring our things in from the car. Chry slides into the clean sheets and fresh blankets tucked tight on my bed, exhausted. I click out the light and settle myself on the sofa which has been made up for me.

In the morning, my mom is gone, already working another extra shift for the nurses who want to travel for the long weekend. "We'll stay another night," I tell Chry. She hadn't argued when I had made these plans without consulting her and she doesn't argue now. She sits at the kitchen table in the seat I'd sat in for so many nights of homework and eats a hot bowl of oatmeal from the crockpot left for us, slathered in butter, cream, and brown sugar.

"I have to run an errand this morning. Do you mind hanging here on your own for a little while?"

"I'm so tired, Mina. I'm going back to bed." She leaves her bowl in the sink and walks to the bedroom. I run warm water in it, so the oatmeal doesn't glue itself to the sides.

Before I leave, I check on her. "Shades up or down?"

"Up, the sun feels good. I haven't been able to get warm since we left Arcadia."

I nod and tell her I'll see her later. Then I drive my truck to the Dutch Reformed Church. I've been by this place a thousand times but never inside. Even though I spent the first hours of my life in the baptismal font here, my mother did not count that as a proper baptism. She accomplished that at Our Lady of Sorrows where I spent all my Sundays until I got on the Hudson Valley train line and left for college.

The church is open and empty. It's a simple space—stucco walls with dark beams and pews. The windows are arched cathedral-style but with plain glass. The font where I was found is on the altar, up on the right side. There is no sign of any person, any saint, or any God. I close my eyes. Monte Carlo. That I lived is something more random than random. That Dare is going to die, the same. And Chry? And then there's the boy in the black-and-white photo, the one who'd *made that shot.* Cass's son. Chry's *brother.* We were in the parking lot, getting into the truck when Cass came out onto her upstairs porch and yelled into the bleak November afternoon, "He went to Cornell." She glared at us with her hands on her hips. "He was hockey first team all-Ivy. Twice." Then, she slammed the door so hard, the festive fall wreath bounced off and fell to the ground.

I was never good at sports, but I did get a scholarship to college. It got me halfway down the Hudson River, and I got myself the rest of the way down. Far, far, far away from Baby Boy Boogman and the Ford dealership he'd be inheriting. I hope he is driving by this very instant, noticing my dark metallic blue and white Chevrolet. You're not supposed to want for spiteful things in church but that's more fact than spite. The devil's spite, I suppose. What can I do? I hold my breath against it, but it doesn't work.

I sit on the step to the altar, lean back on my elbows, and look out on the simple space. There are only twenty rows of pews or so. Was the person who left me here a member or did someone drive through town, drop me, and keep going? Was it someone with seawater green eyes and hair the color of an old copper cooking pot? Was she the daughter of the daughter of a woman who refused to be sent home? The woman who jumped into The Narrows between Brooklyn and Staten Island? Am I the granddaughter of Sirena Fuggitiva, the Fugitive Mermaid? How sad she would be to learn I can't swim. I lie back and close my eyes. *God, please tell me who I am.* It's not a prayer, just a simple question. I spread my arms wide. *Answer me, God; answer me, God; answer me, God…*

I'm awakened by the sound of a throat clearing. Standing over me is a woman in a sky-blue pintuck shirt dress, with a white cardigan over her shoulders buttoned at the throat, loafers, and short white hair in a neat bob. The smile lines and laughing crow's feet on her face suggest she's had many friends. She crouches down. "You're Becky Berg's daughter," she says softly.

"I'm s-s-s-s-sorry. I came in for a minute. I didn't mean to fall asleep."

"It's all right. I've been expecting you."

"Expecting me? For how long?

"A while now."

Her small windowless office is floor-to-ceiling books and papers and there are three side-by-side gray metal filing cabinets. She gestures to a chair across from her desk. "Can you scooch through there?" she says, referring to the books stacked up all around it. "Let me bring you some water." She leaves and returns with a small paper cone filled with water. I drink the few sips the cone has to offer and wait. The name plaque on her desk, partially buried in papers, reads *Susan Botolph.* She sits down opposite me. "I've been the church secretary since, well, since before you were born." She smiles. "I found you, Mina." She doesn't add a smile to these words, knowing, I guess, that the news might be hard for me to hear.

A lifetime of tears fall down my face in quiet streams. I try to make them stop, hang my head so she won't see, but they come and come. She hands me a tissue and waits.

"I was so backlogged." She opens her arms with her palms up to acknowledge the piles of papers on every spare surface and to suggest the circumstances haven't changed in twenty-two years. "The New Year's Day games were on." She leans forward conspiratorially. "I don't care for football so I decided to sneak out to get caught up." She leans back. "Start the year on the right foot. I came in through the sanctuary…and there you were. I heard you before I saw you, I don't know how, you were barely making a noise, but I heard you, then, of course, I found you."

I am more composed than the tears suggest, which I can't stop from falling. They continue to come; the tissue she's given me is a wet shred. She hands me another one and waits.

"Was I—" I say finally. "Was I almost drowned?"

"No," she says, with a gentle head shake. "No. The font is round, deep and curved. You saw it. You were tucked in tight, the water barely covering your legs; you couldn't have drowned."

"But I would have died if you hadn't come, right?"

"But I did come. I came and called for help, and help came—a firetruck and an ambulance and a police car. They took you to the hospital and there was your mother, waiting to receive you. So, you see?" She tilts her head forward and lifts her eyebrows, her gesture asking me if I understand.

"Yes. I see." And I do. I see everything. I see my mother, Rebecca Berg, taking me, wrapped in a thin emergency blanket, from the arms of the fireman who took me from the arms of this very Susan Botolph. Under the thin blanket, I'm wrapped in a white cardigan, like the one she has on now; she'd un-buttoned it at the throat, taken it from around her shoulders, and used it to swaddle me. The fireman saw my red hair and wondered if it was a red-haired girl who'd left me, not to die, but to be saved by him, or was it the EMT who thought this, or maybe the police officer who took me from this Susan Bot-olph's arms. It was the police officer, Tony—not Tony DiSalvo, another brown-eyed man descended from Sicilians and named for the patron saint of missing persons—who took me in his arms. He saw my eyes and hair and knew I was the daughter of the daughter of Sirena Fuggitiva. He knew it was an honor to rescue me and that fortune would follow him for the rest of his life. I see. I see. I see.

Susan Botolph says, "I have something for you. I've been saving it." She gets up from her desk and goes to the middle filing cabinet. She crouches down like she had when she was helping me up off the altar, pulls open a drawer, and leafs through it. She returns with a folder. She puts her elbows on top of the desk, with the folder underneath them, and clasps her hands. "It's hard to know sometimes, what the exact right thing to do is. This was on the altar when I found you, right in the center where you were just now sleeping. Maybe I should have given it to Becky, I don't know. I always hoped you'd come to find it. In the end, I thought it should be your decision. I hope I've done right by you. I pray to God I've done right by you."

I get up from the chair and sidle my way through the piles of books and papers. She stands up and lets me hug her. I hold tight, my tears falling on her shoulder, hers falling on mine. "One more thing." We are still embracing, her chin on my wet shoulder, her mouth near enough to my ear to whisper, "When the emergency crew arrived, I told them your name was Mina— to blend in, to protect you. I hope that was okay."

Back in the truck, I put the folder down on the passenger seat and stare at it while I wait for the heat to come on. I don't open it in the parking lot of the Dutch Reformed Church, instead I drive to a place I know that overlooks the Hudson River. The Hudson River isn't a river, it's an estuary, part salt, part fresh, with tides as rhythmic as the ocean. The water moves down to the New York City Harbor and out to sea through The Narrows but also the other way, back through The Narrows and the Harbor all the way to here.

In the folder, is a makeshift birth certificate, drawn on a torn, flimsy piece of white cardboard. *Jacomina, born 12:04 on January 1, 1963.* Jacomina. Wait until I tell Chry.

I return home later than I'd planned and the house smells delicious—not burgers and fries delicious but Thanksgiving delicious. We are celebrating the holiday, like we always do, on the day after, just me and my mom, and now Chry. I stand in the doorway to the kitchen where Becky Berg is peeling potatoes. She puts down her peeler, wipes her hands on her apron, and moves her black wavy bangs out of her eyes with the back of her wrist. "Mina," she says, words brimming with joy. "I'm so glad you're here." She is a head shorter than I am, but her arms are strong around me. "I have *missed* you," she says.

"Me too, Mom."

"Your friend has been sleeping all day."

"It's been a long trip."

She asks me if everything is okay. When I tell her I'm not sure, she hugs me again. "Let her sleep. She'll wake up when she's ready."

I help my mom finish preparing the dinner and we set up the dining room for the meal. The table is small, it only seats four. My mom lays down pads to protect the wood surface, then puts a tablecloth over it, gold with cross-stitched fall leaves at the edges. There are two tall silver candlesticks, holding new cream-colored candles. I get flatware from the kitchen drawer and lay that out. We don't have a set of silver, just our everyday stuff. Chry walks in as I'm putting a wine and water goblet at each place. She stares, still waking up from her day-long sleep. Rubbing her eyes with the end of her fists like a child, she says, "So pretty."

After the meal, the pie and whipped cream, after we clear the table and wash the pans and dishes, my mom takes off her apron and hangs it on the hook on the inside of the cellar door and comes to sit in the living room where Chry and I are already sprawled. "I'm so glad you were able to join us," she says to Chry.

Chry looks down. Nods. Something in my mom's words gives her pause. Maybe we're both wondering why I never brought her here.

36

Chry fills a Bonwit Teller shopping bag with cassette tapes and tells me about Dare. He's in the hospital again. It's a large white bag with a partly scattered bouquet of purple and blue flowers printed on it. Surely something her mother had dropped at the apartment, filled with clothes she wanted Chry to wear to the job interviews she would never go on. Chry lifts it up to make sure it can hold the weight of her tape collection. They're all in there, Jaco and all kinds of everything else too. She unplugs the boom box, gathers the cord, and puts it near the bag. "Will you drive me?"

It's a pain to own a car in the city. There's a complicated set of parking rules, tickets, and towing, but so far I don't mind. I'm happy to have a chance to tell her yes. "They were at Nyro's mother's house," Chry says as I ease the Blazer away from the curb. "Out on Long Island."

It's late on Sunday, we've only been back on Seventy-First Street a few hours and I have work tomorrow. Part of me thought, since Dare had been released from Bellevue, he might be well enough to come back to Merton.

"He passed out or something. Nyro drove him back into the city last night." She grinds her teeth and frowns. Nyro's not exactly the person you want to be counting on in an emergency. She pushes the button for the electric window forward, lets it come down halfway, then toggles it back to raise the window.

I'm still getting used to driving in the city. I focus on the cars and traffic lights. It begins to drizzle, throwing the streets into a reflective sheen. When we get to Bellevue, I pull up in front and double park with my flashers on.

Chry jumps out and gathers the shopping bag and boom box from the back seat, but before she darts off, she knocks on the passenger side window for me to roll it down. When I do, she blows me a kiss. "Thanks, Mina. Thank you for the ride and for coming with me to Arcadia and inviting me to your Thanksgiving."

"You're welcome," I say. "And hey, Chry?"

"Yeah?"

"I've been wondering for a while now."

"Yeah?"

"Why did you let Nyro drop you in the East River?"

"I told you. I wanted Dare to notice me."

It doesn't occur to me until after I pull away that it's very late and Chry won't be coming home tonight. I always understood visiting hours to be a strict thing but on the sixteenth floor at Bellevue, any visitor willing to come was welcome, no matter what the time.

At work the next morning, Dare's chair is still empty, but the following day there's someone sitting in it. When the markets go quiet, I ask Nick if I can speak to him in the conference room. He nods and we go in and sit at the table where Dare ate all those liverwurst sandwiches. I ask Nick if he's kicked Dare off the desk. He tells me he called last night from the hospital to say he won't be coming back. "Did you fire him? His insurance—"

"I gave him a leave of absence, so he's still covered." He crosses his arms, leans back, and tilts his head. "You know, Mina, not everyone's an asshole."

"I know," I say. "I know that, Nick."

Chry doesn't return home. She calls me from Bellevue to say they brought her a chair that pulls out into a bed to sleep on, that she'll be staying with Dare from now on. I tell her I have a busy week, but I'll come on Friday.

That Friday, when I arrive at Dare's room, he is gone. There's only Chry, lying in his bed, weeping. She knows I'm here, but she doesn't speak to me or acknowledge my presence. I stand and wait. I go to the nurse's station and ask for water and she tells me it will be a minute. I stand and wait. The nurse brings me a tall Styrofoam cup with a bendy straw, like another nurse

had given me the day I first came to visit. She says they are
having trouble finding someone to take the body. Most all the
funeral homes are afraid.

I walk back to Dare's room. The body. The body. I will never
think of Dare this way. The body. I put the Styrofoam cup on
the table where I'd taught Dare to play cards with the Sicilian
tarot deck. The same kind of table G.A. had at her fancy mansion old age home. It was terrible, what they tried to pass off
as Thanksgiving Dinner. I don't see the cards anywhere. I hope
Chry and Dare had a chance to play some hands before he died.
I hope Nyro didn't take them.

Chry's boom box is set up on the windowsill with cassette
tapes strewn around it like the flowers on the Bonwit Teller bag.
It's worse for the wear, still full of tapes but ripped down one
side, smudged and tattered. I fish around in the pile and come
up with one of Chry's mixtapes labeled *Okonkole Y Trompa*.
The child drum and the French horn. The boom box has two
cassette decks. The left one is empty, so I put the tape in and
press play. The song comes on, but Chry doesn't lift her head.

I look out over the East River, Brooklyn, Queens, beyond
Queens, Long Island, I suppose, past Long Island, the New
York-New Jersey Bight, the Atlantic Ocean, Sicily, all the way
around the world to the Hudson River, the Manhattan skyline,
West Seventy-First Street where I live, One World Trade Center
where I work.

I never gave money to the woman in the bathroom.

Now, here, with Chry weeping and Dare dead and no one
to take his body, I wonder how I could have forgotten, all this
time, to go back and give the lady that works in the bathroom
at Windows on the World her money.

There's a tape in the second compartment. I press the button to eject it. Maxell 120 minutes. In the same handwriting as
the *Okonkole y Trompa*—Chry's—it says, *The Nights and Days of
Chry and Dare*. "Okonkole y Trompa" still plays, the peripatetic
beat of the child drum, the French horn, Jaco on bass. When
the song is finished it plays again, then again, then again. Over

and over. I watch the world, all the way around until I'm back to here again.

I put the *Nights and Days* tape in my bag. I don't know what happens next, but it strikes me as the one tape in the pile that is irreplaceable.

Then, I know what to do. I find the card from Anthony DiSalvo, the one he gave me in Washington Square Park, the afternoon Chry auditioned to play with Vinnie, Vincent, Vin on the Staten Island Ferry. I find a pay phone and call him with quarters left from Cass making me change for a five, and when he answers I don't say I have a body, I say I have a friend with nowhere to go. They want to send him to Potter's Field. Help, I say. He tells me there's a place on West Fourteenth Street that will take my friend. He will call. He will come.

And that's what happens, like my birth day, there is a parade. A death day parade with a fireman, a cop, and an EMT. They take Dare to the only place in Manhattan that will receive him.

I tell Chry that I am taking care of the arrangements, then I gather her up and take her down to the police car where Tony helps us into the back seat. She lays her head on my lap and cries again. In the rearview mirror, I see the brown eyes of Tony DiSalvo. He's looking back at us to make sure we're okay. But before any of this I happens, I'd gone to the nurses' station and told Our Lady of the Styrofoam Cups that I was leaving the boom box and the tapes. Contrary to the sign there would be music, like on the *Titanic*.

37

Chry calls Dare's parents in Vestal, New York. They answer only once, the first time.

It's his mother. "Hello," she says.

"Hello," Chry says, eager to have a chance to speak to Dare's mom, to move things forward; surely now that he is gone, his parents will be bereft. "My name is Chrysanthi Risk. I'm a good friend of your son, Darius. He's gone…"

Silence.

"He's, uh, he died and—"

Click. Dial tone.

We are in our apartment. Tony had brought us home in the police car after we delivered Dare to the place on West Fourteenth Street. Before we got out of the car, he told us what to do next. There needs to be a place of internment or he will be taken to Hart Island and thrown in a grave with the others who've died from AIDS. "I've never been there but the way they do it, it ain't right," he said. "People are afraid. You don't know what I've seen, grown men, big guys, cops, terrified of the bodies, living, near-dead, dead."

"Are you afraid?" I asked.

"No. You can't get it like that. Some of these guys either don't know it or don't believe it. Why'd I become a cop, to be afraid of the sick? Anyway, who else is there to help?"

Night falls earlier than ever. I sit at the table in our apartment, the darkness just outside the doors, while Chry calls and calls and calls Dare's parents in Vestal, New York. She hangs up the phone with a bang each time it rings through and the machine answers. She holds out the receiver for me to hear a woman's voice say brightly, *You've reached the Fiores, Bob and Marla. Leave a message.* When it becomes clear they are not going to answer the telephone ever again, she leaves a message:

"Your son is at the funeral home. Waiting on instructions about the service and where he should be buried." Certain this will compel his mother to get on the line, she waits for her to pick up. When the machine beeps off, Chry slams the receiver down, her face red. She picks it up again and dials to leave one more message. "Listen, Marla, your son is dead, and his friends need to know what to do with his body." She waits, but before the beep cuts her off, she adds, "You motherfucking piece of shit."

Chry slams the receiver down for the last time and throws the phone as hard as she can. It reaches the end of its cord in midair and hits the floor with a crash. "Goddammit!" Chry screams and then furious tears and sobs come in waves. The phone, off its hook, makes a low buzzing tone which changes to ear-banging beeping. I pick it up off the floor, put the receiver back, and return it to its place on the dresser.

Our apartment, once cozy with lamplight and music and wind-swayed weeds and wildflowers through rattling French doors, is now a cacophony of grief, terror, and rage. Jaco's harmonics are gone and we are left with the sound of the world crashing down.

Chry dials her mom and dad, then takes the phone into the bedroom, the cord just barely reaching. The call goes on for a long time and though I try not to listen, I can't help hearing some of it. Chry's voice is quiet and pleading, rising, begging, falling, sobbing.

Number theory teaches me that Random multiplied by Random equals Monte Carlo. Grief times Grief equals something like that, something more than the mind can hold.

Chry bangs the bedroom door open. Her face is contorted with anger and her eyes are puffed slits. She is gaunt, drawn thin in a way that's new. "I asked my parents if we could bury Dare in our church cemetery. It's up on the cliff, not far from our house in Atlantic Highlands. My mom—I—have family buried there from the Revolutionary War. The goddamn Revolutionary War, Mina." She says the goddamn Revolutionary

War part quietly, with no voice left to shout, no tears left to cry.

"What's the problem?"

"My mom says it's too much to ask. She says no one really knows how safe these corpses are." She stops. "That's the word she used 'corpse.' She said that some people wouldn't understand, the church people and…you know…my dad's constituents. It could affect the election."

"Chry, I—do they know. About you?"

She shakes her head no. "Fuck them."

I walk over to the sofa and put my arms around her, pull her in close and stroke her hair. "Oh. Oh. Oh," I say.

"You have to tell them," she says. "I can't."

"Chry—I—" She doesn't know that I am never going to speak to her asshole father again and, by association, her mother.

"You have to. You have to tell them to let Dare be buried there and to leave a space next to him for me."

"When?" I say, not making a fuss about Chry's mention of her own grave designation. I know things I didn't use to.

"Now. We're out of time."

She dials the number and I take the phone into the bedroom just as Chry had. Luck comes and goes for me more random than random, but I get a piece of it when Jamie picks up instead of Marg. I lower my voice to keep Chry from hearing, but also to sound menacing. Sexy and menacing. Hard to admit but I wanted him to remember me, at least for this moment, as the girl he wanted to fuck on his sailboat. His daughter's friend who could not swim. She was a girl who thought he might be her family. I call him Jamie. "Jamie," I say. "It's Mina Berg."

He doesn't answer but I can hear him breathing. Finally, he says hello. I ask him if we're on a private line and he says we are. I say his name again, "Jamie." I wait for him to think about things, then I tell him that if he does me this one favor, and, Jesus, it's a favor for his daughter anyway but as far as this conversation is concerned, we'll call it a favor for me. "Jamie," I say, "you need to make a place in your churchyard for our friend Dare. There's no place for him to go except Hart Island, and I have on good information that Hart Island is a terrible place for a burial. Jamie, think mass graves. Can you picture it?"

Silence.

"So, no. I'll be honest, I'm striking a bit of a bargain here." I lower my voice further, to a course whisper. "Do me this favor and you won't hear from me again. Don't do me this favor and I will haunt you to your fucking dying day." He makes a noise like he's going to speak but I cut him off. "And one more thing, and this is hard. It's hard for me to say, and it's going to be hard for you to hear but when I say it, you just fucking do it. Do you understand? We're not going to have a good cry together. I'm going to fucking say it, and you're going to fucking hear it, and then I'm going to hang up the phone. I'll let you wait a half hour or so and then I want this phone to ring with you telling your daughter that everything will be taken care of. Jamie, and here comes the difficult thing. You need to find two places in your Revolutionary War cemetery, one for Dare and one, eventually, for Chry. She has it. She's positive. HIV." I hang up the phone, think about how Chry's coming death is news, even to me, but feeling her body gaunt against mine and seeing the small red oval on the back of her ear moments before I dialed, I know it's true.

Even though he'd humiliated me, and I'd suffered in the silence of not being able to tell Chry, I take no pleasure telling Chry's dad he'll be burying his daughter before this time next year.

WINTER

38

Chry moved out. I came home from work and the apartment was empty of nearly every trace of her. That night she calls me from New Jersey to say her parents had come to get her. I'm not surprised. I'd told Jamie Risk we'd never speak again, but when Chry developed a cough that rasped and rattled like Dare's, I called them. I didn't want her spending her last days behind a red door at Bellevue. It was her mom who answered. I said Chry was in trouble and what about a full-time nurse or something at their house. If this was a betrayal of Chry...well, I hope it wasn't...they'd been calling and leaving messages since the night I told Jamie Risk he would be needing two graves.

Dare is buried in their Revolutionary War cemetery with a place next to him for Chry. They'd held the burial without me there, or Nyro for that matter. I don't know how Nyro felt about it, but I had to think long and hard about forgiving Chry. She told me it was just her and her parents at the burial, which infuriated me. But I knew Chry and I had only peace to make, anything else was a waste. I made a vow to pay my respects to Darius Fiore my own way, in my own time.

Chry says her parents have set up a bed downstairs in the room that looks out over the water and she'll be there for the foreseeable future. I thank her for leaving the turntable and some of her records. "You're gonna need them," she says.

I don't want to bring up the matter of whether I'll be allowed to stay in the family apartment on this first phone call, but I'm worried. I don't have any place else to go. I suppose Nyro has a spare room, but that, no doubt, is out of the question. Chry saves me the trouble of groveling and tells me straight out that I'm invited to stay on at West Seventy-First Street indefinitely, and her dad will even pay her share of the rent. I tell her yes to the apartment and no to her half of the rent. "I'm doing really well. I can afford it," I say, which is true.

Over the next several weeks we talk every night even if it's just for a minute or two. She asks me how I'm sleeping without her stories, if the records are helping.

"I took your advice and called a psychiatrist," I say, and I had. I called the day after she moved out. Her absence was terrifying. Chry's turntable and the remnants of her record collection weren't enough. Even the nights she'd slept at Bellevue, she'd felt close by. But the night I'd come home to her complete abandonment, things changed. She was in New Jersey, in the home of Jamie and Marg Risk, where I could never go again. I couldn't lay my head on the pillow for fear of the gunshots and explosions that may or may not happen as I attempted to pass through the doorway between awake and asleep.

"So, get this," I say cheerfully. I am always cheerful on these phone conversations, whether I want to be or not. I imagine her mother with her denial and fluttering arms and her father with his constituents and secrets being unbearable for her. "It's an actual thing. I have a thing. It's called Exploding Head Syndrome."

"Well, if you're gonna have a thing, at least it has a spectacular name, not like…" She trails off.

"It's nothing, though, just a kind of brain quirk, some misfiring neurons. Point is, I can stop being afraid."

"Lucky you." She says it more factually than sarcastically.

"I guess so."

"You didn't need my stories all those nights, after all."

"I did. And I still do. Your stories were—are—one of the best things to ever happen to me."

"Not my playing?"

"That too."

"I never did it."

"Never did what?"

"Played the bass like Jaco."

"Well, Chry," I say, "you made a lot of music trying."

"I guess so."

Before we hang up, I say, "I almost forgot, Vinnie called."

"Vinnie, Vincent, Vin?"

"Yeah." I smile, thinking of them playing all night on the Staten Island Ferry. "He wants you to call him." I give her the number and say goodbye. I didn't ask why he was calling, and he didn't ask why Chry was in New Jersey. I've come to realize when it comes to Chry and Dare and all of it, the less said the better. I had gone to the doctor and had my blood drawn. He gave me the red vials in a brown paper bag and I walked them over to First Avenue like I'd instructed Nyro to do the day I told him Chry was HIV positive. Two weeks later, I got the call. I was negative. While I waited, I wondered, Who would I tell if I were positive? How would it go? How long would I have to live? So, when Vinnie asked how Chry was doing, I didn't say anything about it. Instead, I said fine and told him he could reach her at her parents' house in New Jersey.

The next night when I talk to Chry, she says, "News."

News can go either way. I hold my breath.

"Vinnie asked if I wanted to play with him on the ferry. I told him I wasn't doing too well and then he told me a rumor. Jaco is going to be at the Lone Star Café *this Saturday night.* An afterhours gig, around two a.m. *Supposedly.* It's like a secret thing. *Supposedly.* Hold on." Chry muffles the phone but I can hear her coughing. Dare's coughing. I have not seen her since her parents moved her home and have been picturing her the same as always—dark blue eyes that spark, glossy dark hair, pink health in her cheeks—but now I wonder, no, I'm sure, that she is becoming a living ghost, her failing body keeping her soul on this earth with increasing effort.

"Chry. Chry. Are you okay?" I say, though I can still hear the muffled sounds of her coughing.

"Yeah," she says, her voice a torn scrap of paper. "I have to go."

"I'll come get you, okay? It's the day after tomorrow. Try to sleep until then. I'll drive over around eight, and we'll just head out...like the night we saw South Side Johnny. Like then."

"Ha," says Chry in her torn voice. "That seems so long ago." She's right, the night we caught South Side Johnny at The Stone

Pony was a million years ago, the night Sandy to You told her future, another lifetime.

"Look for me this Saturday. We'll do this, even if I have to break you out of there." A rush of excitement and happiness comes over me, something I have not felt in a long time.

On Saturday, I take my Blazer down the west side of Manhattan, along the Hudson River to the Brooklyn Battery tunnel. I go under the East River to Brooklyn. The tunnel is hard, but I make it through with a new philosophy. Instead of holding my breath, I try breathing. I take the highway to the Verrazano-Narrows Bridge. The bridge is high above The Narrows, more frightening than the tunnel. I try to breathe but it comes in gasps; I am suspended. The more I gasp for air, the less I can gather into my lungs. Then it comes to me—Adriana's song—and I begin to sing, *Brilla brilla una stellina*…but that's all I can remember so I sing the second line in my mom's version…*How I wonder what you are…* I sing the mixed rhyme over and over until I am at the very top of the bridge. When I reach the center, above the place where Audenzia jumped away from a life of exile in her home country and toward her new life in America, I roll down the window and let the cold air rush in, smelling of salt and fumes, whipping my hair across my face. "Sirena Fuggitiva! Fugitive Mermaid!" I shout it to the sea and sky.

Down and over the bridge, I travel the Staten Island Expressway across the island. Somewhere along that way, I close the car window and stop shouting. And then it's just cars and lights and a single-word. *Help. Help. Help.* I don't even know what kind of help I'm looking for. Not to be afraid to see Chry? Her withering body, her soul preparing to depart, like I'd seen with Dare?

I want magic. I want a fugitive mermaid to grant me a wish. I want to go with my friend to see Jaco Pastorius. I want her dream to come true. I want death to be far away.

Another bridge. The Goethals over the Arthur Kill, the river that separates Staten Island from New Jersey. Then the turnpike to the Garden State Parkway. Another bridge, this one over the Raritan River. So many bridges and tunnels. So much water. As I travel the last stretch to Chry's house, I change the word from

Help to *Please.* I beg and beg and beg—*Please let her be well enough for me to take her; please let her mom or the nurse be home; please don't let it be Jamie Risk*—but my pleases go unheeded. When I ring the doorbell, her father answers. I stare at him, tight-mouthed. I don't say a word, not even hello.

He doesn't say hello either, just, "She's been waiting for you." He doesn't gesture me in, but steps aside for me to pass. I walk to the back of the house, to the big room off the kitchen. The furniture is pushed away and there's a hospital bed in the center, facing out for the view of the Bay, Sandy Hook, the New York/New Jersey Bight. The same view as the Fourth of July, the night she swiped a bottle of champagne, and we drank it on the porch, and then she swiped another one and we drove to Asbury Park.

From her eyes, wide and yellow in her drawn face, comes a barely perceptible crinkle of a hello. Sirena Fuggitiva has answered the prayer I didn't know I was praying, that my face and voice would not register shock. My shock and my sorrow stay bundled tight as I take off my coat and sit in the chair next to her bed.

"Ready?" she says, her voice a torn whisper. Her laugh is a cough which goes on for several minutes. I worry her dad will hear her and come in, but he doesn't. "I didn't think you'd come otherwise," she says finally.

This rips at my tight sorrow bundle, but I keep it closed. "Chry, I was…I was always going to come."

She nods. "It's just…you haven't…"

"I—I—I'm sorry." I take her hand and hold it loosely, so light and frail, so unlike the one I watched practicing and reaching for Jaco's harmonics. We stay like that, me holding her hand, both of us looking out over The Bight.

Around ten o'clock her father appears. Chry is asleep, her breathing like sandpaper. "I don't think she'll wake up again tonight," he says.

I kiss Chry's hand, the one I've been holding these past hours, put on my coat and leave. He doesn't call after me.

39

I leave Chry's house high up above the New York/New Jersey Bight and go home the way I came. I cross over the Verrazano-Narrows Bridge and call out to the fugitive mermaid, though quietly this time and with the window closed against the freezing night. I don't say *help* or *please,* just call her name. I don't want anything more than to make it home before the sorrow she'd helped me keep wrapped up so tight unravels.

I park on West Seventy-First Street and unlock the gate under the stairs where Nyro had tried to kiss me. I open the locks to our apartment, push the door open, and turn on the light. Roaches scatter and disappear under the baseboards. No signs of Chry except for her albums and stereo, same as it's been since the day I came home from work and found her gone. It's a good thing, the way her parents are taking care of her, so unlike Dare's, who had disowned him in the end, maybe even before that. His dad had broken his nose with a Kiwanis Award paperweight. I don't know. If I had a gun, I'd drive to their house and shoot them both in the face, see how they like it. I wouldn't. They're not worth the effort it would take to splatter their blood. A mother and a son. A father and a son. A father and a daughter. A mother and a daughter. All of it a betrayal.

And then it's gone, the thin rope keeping the pieces of me in one place lets go. The tears come, all of them. More than I ever knew I had. I lie on the sofa and shake and cry. I make a straitjacket with my arms, hold myself tight to keep from flying into a million pieces. An hour passes, or a minute. A layer of grief peels away, but underneath, a raw-edged fury. I stand up, looking for someone to hurt, something to break. There's a sugar bowl on the table. Chry brought it or it was here from her uncle. It's a delicate thing, white china with blue flowers. I grab it and throw it against the wall. It shatters, spraying sugar around the room. Something for the roaches to enjoy the minute I turn my back. Who cares? Everything good is gone, Chry and her bass and her boom box, her pile of mixtapes, her gorgeous wardrobe, bought by a misguided mother, a mother who wanted a girl who was trying to play the bass like Jaco Pastorius, to put on a business suit and waste away in some nine to five. Nothing is left but the crap furniture that was here in the first place and a garden gone to seeds and weeds. All that's left is me, me and my Hermès scarf, the thing I came to New York to get. I had done it. Made enough money to spend one hundred dollars on a silk scarf. I wish I could say it doesn't matter but at this moment it matters more than anything. I have nothing else.

Jaco's albums are the next thing left to break. I pick up the pile, feel its heft, deciding whether it will be more satisfying to drop them all at once or pull the records out individually and throw them at the wall the way I'd done with the sugar bowl. I don't break them, but I leave them out on the table in case I want to later.

I go to the closet and pull out the square orange box that holds my Hermès scarf. I take the gorgeous silk square out, unfold it, and lay it on the table. It had taken me forever to choose this design. Green, blue, and purple jewel tones with flowers in a graphic pattern. Scheherazade, it was called, for the storyteller from *A Thousand and One Nights*. I chose it because it reminded me of Nyro, the night we were snowed in on Franklin Street. He said I looked like the jeweller's wife in the Chagall painting on his wall, from one of Scheherazade's stories. I find a pair of scissors in the kitchen junk drawer. Back at the table I attack the scarf, slicing it in half with ragged chops, then quarters then random slices and snips until it's in more pieces than the sugar bowl. I can feel each cut and slash, pointed and sharp and destroying. The floor is littered with tiny scraps. Maybe the roaches will take them for their nests or wherever they go when the light comes on. What fancy roaches I will have, bedded down in French silk.

I call the number I'd written on a scrap of paper for Chry.

Vinnie. I hadn't asked Chry if Jaco was going to be playing at the Lone Star Café tonight after hours, or if she made it up to get me to come see her. I would have come. I was planning to come. Or maybe she really thought she was well enough for me to take her. No one answers the phone, and I don't leave a message.

I don't want to smash the records, Chry's last best gift to me, and there's nothing else to do. The Lone Star Café is near the bottom of Fifth Avenue, in the teens somewhere. I know because there's a giant iguana on the roof. It's a windy night, cold as shit, and not just with the windows open on the Verrazano Bridge. I put on boots and a long, thick fisherman's sweater. I wrap my old wool scarf around my neck, the one that's long and warm and kept my nose from getting frostbitten by the winds off the Hudson River. Over that I put my big tweed thrift shop coat and set out to walk the sixty some blocks to the Lone Star Café.

Down Central Park West, across Central Park South, then down Fifth Avenue. I pass the big library where Chry had written, *I'm pregnant. I'm sick.* I'm on rewind, everything is happening in reverse. Chry had tried to see Jaco, not only in Washington Square Park, but at the clubs she'd hear he might be playing. Hard as she tried, she never caught a show. Down, down, downtown, I walk, reliving everything, the day we saw Vinnie playing in the park, that same day Chry said it was wrong after all to search for Jaco off his luck. The farther I get, the more I know even if there was no Jaco to hear tonight, Chry would want me to try.

It's past one when I get to the building with the iguana on the roof. The city is cold and quiet, but there's a small crowd outside the club. I cross over Fifth Avenue and join it. Everyone has heard the same rumor. It's in the air. *Jaco, Jaco, Jaco.*

I stand close in with the strangers, for warmth and company.

I never told Chry. I kept meaning to tell her, but I never did. I never told her my name is Jacomina. I'd been waiting for the perfect moment. I wanted to blow her mind. I'm Jaco. I've been here by your side the whole time. I vow to call her in the morning.

There's movement. They are letting people in. Collecting money and stamping hands. The crowd tightens with a collective excitement that the show must really be happening. As I push in with the rest, there's a hand on my arm. "Mina."

It's Vinnie and behind him, Ray. They're both smiling and excited to see me and when we get situated inside, we say our hellos. They ask where Chry is and I tell them she has AIDS, she's too sick to leave home. I say it in a way I've never spoken about it before, in the plain truth. I don't know if Tony ever told them about Dare, how he helped the day he died. I don't know if when I say my roommate has AIDS, they'll want to get away from me. I decide that people fall into two categories, fearful or fearless. I would like to be in the second group.

Vinnie still has his hand on my arm, but he doesn't take it away. Instead, he pulls me in tight and hugs me even as we are moving with the crowd. "I'm so sorry," he says. He lets me go and Ray comes right up next to me, looking so different in his Timberland boots and ski coat. He puts his arm around me and kisses the top of my head, tells me he's sorry too. Tells me he's been meaning to call, but anyway we can talk about that later, him meaning to call.

Inside, there's a set-up for the band on the main floor not far from the entrance. It's tight, even smaller than The Stone Pony. We find a place to stand near the bar, which is not more than a few feet from where they'll be playing. Ray hands me and Vinnie a beer. We wait.

They come out, four musicians, and one of them is Jaco Pastorius. Vinnie catches his breath, then whoops; the crowd, jammed together tighter even than when we'd been outside, yells and cheers. Jaco is wearing white pants and a white shirt. He has long hair down to the middle of his back. It's him. Same eyes and mouth as on the album cover. *Chry.* She is sleeping. *Chry, I'm going to send Jaco to your dream.* That's my plan. It's a good one. It's as obvious and real as any plan I've ever had.

There's a guy on the trumpet, a guy playing guitar, a keyboardist, and then of course, Jaco on bass. They play a mix, songs I've heard Jaco play and songs I haven't. They play "Dolphin Dance," "I Shot the Sheriff," and "The Christmas Song."

Jaco doesn't look at us. He's somewhere else, sending notes from another plane. He leans into his bass and throws his head back and forth, his long hair flying. Farther and farther he travels away, bringing us with him.

Chry is here. It's so clear to me. The most mysterious and obvious thing in the world. She's standing behind me. I can feel it. We are crowded in so tight; I can't turn around. I so recently left her, propped up in a hospital bed, looking out over the New York/New Jersey Bight from yellow eyes and a face of bones with a soul barely clinging to its body, but she's here.

Out of the corner of my eye, I see dark hair on the shoulder of an electric blue coat. I twist my neck and head enough so she can hear what I have to say, "I'm Jaco!" I laugh. "Chry, my name is Jacomina. I've been here the whole time." She doesn't answer but I feel her delight and surprise. "We made it, Chry," I whisper.

I stop talking after that because Jaco is playing and if Chry is well enough to make it to the show, she'll be well enough to come back to West Seventy-First Street and tell me again how Jaco reinvented the bass. We heard it with our own eyes. So, I stop trying to talk to Chry, knowing we'll talk later. I spend the rest of the night at the Lone Star Café receiving the messages Jaco is sending, note by note.

40

The telephone rings but I don't answer. A man's voice leaves a message, but I don't listen. I need a roach motel.

It's the day after the night I saw Jaco, the Sunday before Christmas. Vinnie and Ray had brought me home in a cab after the show. They waited, the cab idling, while I retrieved my keys and opened the gate. When I got inside, Chry wasn't here. I'd looked for her after the show. When I couldn't find her, I thought maybe she'd made it out ahead of me, but she wasn't here. I lay on the sofa in my coat and boots waiting for her to come, she didn't but sleep did.

Awake now, the sun is streaming through lacy patterns of ice on the windowpanes, but the apartment is so cold I can see my breath.

I turn on the shower and let it run until the bathroom is clouded with steam, then I stand under the hot needles, feeling the warmth and pain. I had seen Jaco Pastorius. I had seen him grab hold of his bandmates with every note. There had been murmurs before he came out that he was slipping, the show might disappoint, but it did not disappoint. But what do I know? Maybe I don't know a lot about music or jazz or harmonics or the bass, but I do know what happens when someone unlocks a door and shows you the other side. Jaco, with his gold knife cutting chicory at midnight on St. James Day. I had been in the room while he performed feats of magic and so had Chry.

The hot water pounds my head, neck, and shoulders. I turn toward it and let it hurt my face and chest. I have no exit plan for this shower. What would it take to stay here forever? My own life would be the price. I consider paying it. I don't think of luck like most people. Number theory tells you it's mathematics, the possible and impossible.

How would I do it, die here under hot needles of water and steam? There's a razor by the sink. Another thing missed in the sweep to remove Chry from West Seventy-First Street. It's a gold straight edge like the one she told me about the night she split her lip on Nyro's mirror, the night she swapped blood with Dare. His razor, it must be. I reach around the curtain through the fog and steam and take it in my hand, feel its heft, press the latch to open the blade. I could use it to let all the blood out of my body. It would run and run, mix with the water, circle the drain and wash away. Wrists would work—I've heard it's a good place to start. There I'd be, unwasted, so unlike Chry and Dare, blood gone, soul gone. Soul gone through the door that Jaco opened. I know why Chry hadn't come here after the show last night.

The water runs while I think about gold knives and opening doors and then I remember the Hudson River flows in both directions; I don't have to depart this world for the next. I turn off the water and step out of the tub, swaddled in the warmth of the steamy room. Jaco opened the door and left it open; Sirena Fuggitiva opened the door and left it open. Chry waited at the open door long enough to say goodbye.

Warm and dressed, the blinking light on the answering machine reminds me there'd been a call, a phone call and a message. *It's Jamie Risk. I called to tell you, Chry died last night. It was right after you left. We are planning a ser*— I shut it off, hit erase. I don't need to hear her name in his mouth. I knew. I knew.

I go out to Columbus Avenue in search of roach motels. Christmas is coming. The apartment is littered with the tiny shreds of my Hermès scarf. The roaches haven't scuttered them back to their lairs as I'd hoped.

They're selling trees on the corner and the shop windows glitter and wink with holiday cheer. The kids in their colorful stocking caps and mittens are pink-faced with cold and anticipation. They hold their mothers' hands and skip along by their sides instead of running full tilt to the corner making the mothers shriek, "Stop!" like they do the rest of the year.

I buy the motels. I'll be home for Christmas, home on West

Seventy-First Street, such as it is. My mom is working like she does every year, Thanksgiving, Christmas, and New Year's Day and thank God for that because where would I be otherwise. And thank God because someone needs to be at the door to receive them, the half dead with their injuries and accidents.

41

C hristmas Day and the roaches are snug in their motels. I turn on the light and there's no scattering, only light. There's a present for me on the table. My mom had sent me a card last week with five new twenty-dollar bills, a hundred dollars, so unlike her. There was a note on the envelope that said, *Do Not Open Until December 25th*, but I had opened it, having lost my appetite to be surprised. The card had a religious scene, Mary with her ultramarine blue dress and veil holding the baby Jesus with his gold foil halo. The printed message inside was something about this being the season of miracles and below that written in my mom's familiar handwriting it said, *Merry Christmas, my daughter, my miracle, I love you. Mom.*

I had used the money to buy Chry a present, which I'd planned to bring her sometime soon. It was a cashmere sweater the same color as Mary's dress. Whether I'd done it intentionally or not, I don't know. It's a beautiful shade of blue, ultramarine, made from the lapis lazuli the Italian painters of the Renaissance had shipped to Italy from Afghanistan. It was too expensive, too precious, to be used for anything except Mary's garments.

I make coffee and the aroma fills the apartment with a feeling of satisfaction. From the refrigerator I take a naval orange and dig my thumb into the thick peel, pulling it back until it's completely removed. I hold the fruit in my palm, inhaling its essence while I pull off strands of pith. Finally, I dig both thumbs down into the middle and pull the bright, juicy segments apart. I eat them one by one, feeling the sweetness in my mouth as I bite down. Did a girl ride her bike through an orange grove in California the morning of an earthquake the way Adriana rode her bike through the lemon grove on the hill above Messina? She and Audenzia coming to the United States with nothing but a blue wedding dress and a bag of blood oranges, the ones that only grow in the ashes of Mt. Etna. *Tarocco!* the Sicilian farmer had exclaimed when he sliced it in half and saw what was inside, part garnet red, part pale yellow. Tarocco after Tarocco Siciliano, the cards he used to play his nightly games of tarocchi. Cards from the open door between here and there, the sun, the moon, the stars, the hanged man, the fugitive. Or did he say *Tarocco!* for the word the Arabs brought to Sicily, *turuquín,* wayfarer, the fugitive, the fool, the one with the wisdom that comes from losing everything. Or another meaning. *Tarocco* from the word *sirocco,* the winds that blow hot and strong from the African desert, winds they call blood rain from the way they mix with Sicily's red coastal sand, winds, they say, that can turn a man's mind to madness.

Ray told me these stories the afternoon we met at the Alice in Wonderland statue, the day we sat in the café and he taught me to play his grandmother's card game. He gave the deck to me and I gave it to Chry who gave it to Dare who, I think, gave it to Nyro. I want it back. I want my cards back.

I call Nyro, expecting to get his answering machine, but he picks up with a civilized, "Hello."

When I say it's me, he doesn't say Meeee Nuhhhh like he used to do. He says, "Merry Christmas." I tell him Merry Christmas but stop short of demanding my cards back. It seems wrong to ask for something on Christmas morning, the one time of the year you're supposed to be offering something.

When I don't say anything more, he says. "Do you want to come over? For dinner?"

A drunken, drug-infused Christmas is the last thing I want, but I surprise myself and say yes.

I take a shower. Quickly. I don't contemplate the razor or draining the blood from my body. I have a present to open, Christmas dinner—whatever that looks like—to have. I put on a pair of black wool slacks and black boots but before I finish getting dressed, I sit down to open my present. It's an ultramarine blue cashmere sweater. I take it from under the tissue and hold it to my face. "Thank you, Chry," I say. "I love it."

I take a cab to Franklin Street and give the driver a twenty for a tip, tell him Merry Christmas. Nyro buzzes me up and when the elevator door opens, the delicious smells overwhelm me. He kisses me and smiles when I close my eyes and breathe in the fragrance of his cooking. "My dad always made sauce on Christmas Day. Someone had to keep it going. My mom's not even Italian."

"Is she coming?" The thought of meeting Nyro's mom fills me with uncertainty. I'd seen her picture on "Page Six" and elsewhere. She was a skeleton about town, always at charity affairs in designer dresses. I don't want to spend Christmas with her.

"No. She's out on Long Island. I didn't invite her, said I had plans. And…I do." The way he says it indicates no one is more surprised by this than he. I sit at his kitchen counter and watch him uncork a bottle of red wine and put it to the side to breathe. He lifts the lid of his sauce pot and the essence of the ingredients, singularly and combined, waft over me. Tomatoes, garlic, onions, basil, tear at my defenses, reducing me almost to a swoon. He pulls out another pot, fills it with water, and puts it on the stove to boil. Then he pours himself a fistful of salt and throws it in.

He's wearing a blue shirt and jeans and his wild head of curls are cut close in a way I haven't seen before. I hop off the stool and walk to the other side of the room. On the wall is the huge mirror he and Dare had taken down to make a lake. My reflection is a splintered form of Chry, the outline she left when she fell into it. "Her lip bled that night," I say, loud enough so Nyro can hear me across the room. "And Dare's neck." Nyro looks up from his cooking and I walk over and lean across the counter. "You don't die from just kissing," I say for myself as well as him.

"That's right." Nyro holds the wooden spoon above the pot, then freezes in midair. There are splatters of red sauce on his shirt. His mouth is open in surprise, his eyes are hurt.

"I'm sorry, I thought you knew."

He shakes his head no.

"I mean I told you she was positive, what did you think was going to happen?" I say it gently. I feel the fact of it. Part of me hadn't thought it was possible either.

Nyro stares at the spoon in his hand, as if he's not sure why he's holding it. He puts it into the pot, stirring circles in the sauce, and pulls it out with a meatball which he holds up to show me. "I made these too. I made everything," he says quietly.

I set the table with things I find in the cupboard. Beautiful things. Cut-crystal wine and water glasses, translucent china, and heavy Tiffany silverware and candlesticks. I find tapers for the candlesticks and matches to light them. Lastly, I put the bottle of wine on the table. When everything is ready, Nyro brings over two heaping plates of rigatoni with sauce and meatballs, then sits down and pours wine in each of our glasses and we toast Merry Christmas. The fractured mirror version of Chry hangs on the wall over Nyro's shoulder the way the ghost of her had hung over my shoulder the night I saw Jaco. But that night I could see her hair against her electric blue coat, I could hear her attempts to play harmonics, trying to match Jaco, and I don't feel any of that here. I feel sorry for Nyro. The only thing he has left of Chry is a broken mirror.

When dinner is over, I ask Nyro if he wants to play cards—my cards. "Do you have them?"

He does. He gets up and returns with the small deck.

"We never played. He was too sick. I had to take him back to the hospital before he had a chance to show me the game." He takes the cards out of the box. "Teach me?" he says and hands them over.

"I'm too tired."

He takes a drink of wine and sighs. "Me too, Mina." Then he brightens and says, "You could tell my fortune."

"They're just for playing."

"Try."

I pick the cards up and drop them over and over into my hand, shuffling rhythmically. We are comfortable here in the candlelight, me shuffling cards to some faraway beat, Nyro staring off, waiting for me to tell him the future.

"I'll skip over the coins and cudgels, swords, kings, queens, and knaves. Just the trump cards, one through twenty, plus Miseria and Fuggitivo, the no-point trumps."

Nyro shrugs and throws out his arms palms up.

I lay the trump cards down in a line as they come up through the pile, discarding the others.

Star. A man on his horse reaching up to hold the circle around a blue star.

Moon. A man sleeping under a tree with a woman over him making a *can you believe this?* gesture.

Death. A skeleton on his horse holding a sickle; beneath him, two heads on the ground, the king and the priest.

Sun. One man is beating another with a cudgel, above him a cloud, above that, the sun.

"I'll do it," says Nyro, meaning the fortune. "We were all having fun riding around under the stars. Then one day we went to Arcadia and laid down under the trees, paying no attention to the possible consequences. Death comes for the government and the church, neither care to help. Now this one, this guy getting ready to beat on his friend here. I think this one means there's nothing new under the sun. All right, that's our story so far. One more, Mina."

"Let's stop here. Let's not know."

"C'mon, c'mon, c'mon." He makes a *hurry up* gesture with his hand.

Number 11. The hanged man. We see him from behind, dangling from a tree by a rope tied around his neck, his hands tied behind his back.

I lay it down.

Nyro stares at the Hanged Man. "Mina, that's no good."

Tears come but I hold on. They brim my eyes until one falls out, and I wipe it away with the back of my hand.

"No, no, no, no," says Nyro, "this isn't you or me. This is my dad. A year ago, today. He was going to prison...a year ago to-morrow. He was going to jail for associating with some crooked people. I mean, construction in New York City? There's no other way, you have to pay them. Christmas Day, he jumps off the George Washington Bridge.

"And a week later you hang Chry down into the East River."

"Yeah, that's weird. I'll have to mention it to my shrink. Anyway, it wasn't by her neck."

I lean back in my chair, gather my hair up and twist it on the top of my head, let it fall.

"One more," says Nyro.

I'm too tired to argue so I take cards off the deck until I come to another trump card.

Fuggitivo. He's wearing a jester hat and cap, holding a ball and blowing a trumpet, a fool.

"The fool is the wise man," I say. "He knows this life is a wild card and there's nothing you can do about it so you might as well just get on with things. Fool for the world, fugitive from it."

"Are we running away together?" he asks.

"No, Danny. It's just cards."

42

The morning of New Year's Eve I receive two phone calls. The first is from Jamie Risk inviting me to their gala at the Oyster Bar in Grand Central Station, same as last year.

"Thank you," I say, "but I have plans." I don't have plans. He remains on the line without speaking. I don't want to hang up on him, but I don't want to say anything more either. The weeds in the garden are iced over. They sparkle in the sun and tinkle with the small wind gusts that are coming through. The radiators hiss and pop, countering between cacophony and music. In another lifetime they took a backseat to Chry's bass. Or Jaco's. I'm so entranced by the sights and sounds of this little room and a half, I forget I'm holding the phone with Chry's dad on the other end. Time moves slow and fast. It's either five minutes or five hours before he speaks.

"We're sorry you weren't at the service."

"Me too."

Silence. He should say it. He should tell me he's sorry for doing a shitty thing. He should apologize for turning me out from the family. Making me other. Less. I wait.

Silence.

"Goodbye," I say. "I loved her. She was perfect." I say it for Chry. Not for him. Then I hang up the phone and begin the rest of my goodbyes. They are all to this apartment on West Seventy-First Street where I lived with Crysanthi Risk. I move out next weekend.

The second call is from Ray DiSalvo. "Happy New Year," he says. He asks me what my plans are, and I tell him I don't have any, just an errand.

"How about after your errand?"

"No plans."

"Vinnie's playing on the ferry. Do you want to come? Not all night or anything." He laughs. "Maybe just over and back."

We decide to meet at the ferry terminal for the nine o'clock boat. I put on a pair of jeans and the present from my mom to me to Chry to me, the blue cashmere sweater. I wrap my neck in my old wool scarf and put on my big tweed coat. Scraps of Hermès silk dance along the floor as I move around the apartment, getting myself dressed and ready. Outside, underneath the stairs, I bang the iron gate shut and give it a shake to make sure it's locked, then walk over to Broadway to the Seventy-Second Street subway station to catch a downtown train.

The car is crammed full of New Year's revelers with paper crowns and noisemakers and fifths of whiskey in their coat pockets.

I take hold of an empty strap as the car rocks and sways on the downtown track. I rock and sway in unison with it and with the revelers, all of us in a mutual dance. Sitting below me is a young mother holding a baby to her chest. She's oblivious to the party and the party is oblivious to her. Her hand is on the back of the small child's head in a white cotton cap. She pulls the blue blanket wrapping her baby in more tightly and lays her cheek gently on his head. Next to her, a guy pulls out a gold-spangled noisemaker. Once I had a birthday party with the same noisemakers but in pink and blue. They make a loud bleat and a paper tube unscrolls like a reptile's tongue. The guy next to the woman with the baby breathes in hard and holds it to his lips in preparation for a loud Happy New Year bleat. Before he can let go, I touch the top of his forehead, the only part of him I can reach, and give him a little push. My touch shocks him.

"*Hey,*" he says, and his face contorts with anger. I point to the mother and her baby and put my finger to my lips. His mouth makes a surprised O. He whispers, "Sorry," then leans back in his seat, his body in sync with the train's thrum.

When the doors open at WTC Cortland, I push through the crowd and step off onto the platform, my regular work-day stop. I take the stairs up to the escalator that goes to the big lobby of One World Trade. From there, I take the express elevator, bypassing 106 floors straight to 107, Windows on the World. The Tower. That card didn't come up in Nyro and my fortune telling session, yet here I am. The Tower in the Sicilian deck is different from every other tarot deck, it's not struck by lightning and crumbling, cracked, and falling. It's sturdy and unbroken, like the towers they built to protect Sicily against centuries of intruders. Up, up, up, I go to the top of this tower, my tower, my city, my home. After over a year working at Merton Marston Forex Inc., I've seen the views in every direction and in every atmospheric condition. I've seen the buildings and bridges and rivers, the Statue of Liberty, Ellis Island, all of it, in daylight and starlight, but tonight I am only looking for one view. I go to the bar on the south side and stare out across the harbor to the Verrazano Narrows where I know she is listening for my call. I couldn't whisper it to the wall outside the Oyster Bar in Grand Central Station, I tell her, but this is better, I think. *Sirena Fuggitiva, Sirena Fuggitiva.* I say her name and that's enough. Saying her name means I know her story is true. I thank her for the good tidings I can already feel coming my way. Then I go to the ladies' room, the same one where I cried the night Dare stood up for me, the night Ray whispered Sirena Fuggitiva into my ear, the night I forgot to leave a tip for the woman who gave me a towel to dry my eyes, twice. She is here, organizing her combs and soaps and bottles of perfume. It's early and her basket is empty. I wash my hands in the sink. When I'm finished, she hands me a towel and I dry my hands on the warm, clean terry fabric. I put it in the discard bin when I'm through and take out my bundle of twenties and put them in her basket. "Here's to luck in the New Year," I say, though I don't really believe in luck. I believe in the randomly associated possibility of luck.

She nods.

Ray is waiting for me at the pizza stand in front of the ferry terminal. "Slice?" he says when he sees me and orders two when I nod yes. He folds mine in half with the paper plate around it, hands it to me and folds his the same way. We board the ferry and climb the stairs to the top floor with our pizza slices cooling in their paper plate blankets. We sit near Vinnie to hear him play, on the side of the Statue of Liberty. Her new torch is up, though she's still surrounded by scaffolding. *Soon*, I think.

On the trip back we sit on the side facing the Verrazano Bridge. We go out on the deck into the cold night, sliding the heavy door in its track and letting it roll back with a thud. The N-Y-R-O crane is where it had been the day Chry and I traveled to Staten Island to look at basses. As the bridge comes into full sight, Ray goes quiet. I know he's asking Sirena Fuggitiva for everything good in the new year. I look away to give him his privacy, look up at the orange life preservers in the ceiling, blackened by the back and forth trips in the oily salt air. They won't save me. Nothing will save me if this big boat breaks in half and sinks into the Harbor. Ray's eyes are closed. A believer. I remind myself of the wish I've already made to Sirena Fuggitiva. I wish to be the boy in the red hat, skipping and jumping along the wall around the sailboat pond in Central Park, so close to the water with no fear of falling.

Out beyond the bridge are the cliffs of Atlantic Highlands where Chry and Dare lie side by side in a Revolutionary War graveyard. I haven't been there yet, but I plan to go. Maybe this summer when I know everyone else will be away. I'll bring Chry's tape, the one from the hospital, and listen to it for the first time. Maybe on St. James Day. Yes, on St. James Day, I'll go to the graves of Chry and Dare, and then I'll eat oysters and drink from the cup of suffering.

The Twin Towers loom large over our heads as the ferry closes in on Manhattan. Ray and I go through the big door, slide, clunk, slide, clunk. Inside, Vinnie is singing "Holiday" not peppy and bright like Madonna but low and cool. Ray goes over and kisses him on the cheek. Vinnie tips up his chin and smiles but doesn't miss a beat.

We take a cab up the FDR Drive, along the east side of Manhattan, the rivers and bridges on our right, the buildings towering up on our left, so different a view than from up on the

107th floor of One World Trade. "Almost my birthday," I say. I'd forgotten that this will be the first year I know for sure that I was the first baby born in 1963.

"Almost happy birthday!" says Ray. "I have something for you." He picks up my hand and turns it over, kissing my palm. "At my apartment."

"Is it something to eat?

He smiles. "It is."

Ray's apartment has a wall of windows with a view of the East River and Queens. There's not much furniture but what's here is elegant and modern, like he's taking his time to not clutter it up with a bunch of junk. I sit down at the empty table looking out at the city and try to fill my head with nothing. It's a few minutes from midnight's open door. Ray comes to the table with forks, knives, napkins, and plates. He puts one down in front of me. "Insalata Tarocco," he says. "Blood oranges, fennel, olive oil, salt, and pepper."

I lean into the food, so beautiful, and inhale the sweet smell of blood oranges and the licorice tang of fennel.

"It's private, this dish. You don't see it in restaurants. It's special for having at home." Ray looks up from the blood orange salad he's describing, pauses, then says, "From love."

In front of me is a meal that cannot be found in any restaurant, it's made only at home and only from love. I taste the exquisite beauty of the tarot blood orange, the Tarocco, named for the decks of cards that hold everything known and unknown, or named for the *turuquîn*, the wayfarer, or named for the sirocco, the hot winds that come bearing madness. I eat the pale yellow and garnet tarot blood oranges grown from the ashes of Mt. Etna. I taste the rugged everchanging landscape, I taste danger and reasons to flee, I taste a sun-soaked island and a cerulean wedding dress, I taste destruction and resurrection. I taste love.

ACKNOWLEDGEMENTS

Sincere thanks to:

Chris Scalzo, constant, never once, not ever, a shade of doubt. Robert Scalzo and Lucy Scalzo, strong-willed, strong-minded, fun, funny, smart, loving, surprising, keepers of the faith. I love you all.

Sisters, Clare Girton, first and last reader, a place at her table for all of us, always, and Pam Weiss for enthusiasm and support in sharing my work. Our parents, Frank Marino and Carroll Marino, for showing us what it means to live a generous life. Rest easy, Dad.

Susan Shreve, for your friendship, kindness, and singular brand of practical magic, for welcoming me into your studio and for that golden September week on MV where the end to this novel came into sight.

Margaret Hutton, Alexandra Zapruder, Molly McCloskey, Mary Kay Zuravleff, you keep me out of the muck of writer despair each and every day and each in your own way.

Tracey Madigan, for your gentle ear, and humor, and for reinventing the meaning of the word pass.

Jodi Moraru, for all that. All that.

Fran Brennan and Katherine Martin, you fierce, lovely souls, thank you for your friendship.

Leslie Miller, for your sharp eye, steady editing, and enthusiasm for this story. And for draft number seven.

Madison Smartt Bell, your graceful intelligence, humor, and generosity elevated everything.

Jaynie Royal, for your vision, not only for this work but for a new way of bringing books into the world.

Early readers, Clare Girton, Susan Shreve, Carol Shiner Wilson, Hunter Bennett, Margaret Hutton, Alexandra Zapruder, Mary Kay Zuravleff, Michael Raibman, Seth Rosenthal, Bill

Clifford, Gracene Sirianno, Kim Stephens, Maria Petaros, Tony Mazza, Kate Mazza, Michael Ognibene, Mark Finkelpearl, Rue Zitner, Max Finkelpearl, Talia Zitner, Jodi Moraru, Dean Girdis, Molly McCloskey, Melissa Ostrom, Wayne Johnson, Rachel Volpone, and Maria Rodale, and Melissa Scholes Young, your enthusiasm and kind words were steady vessels on the raging sea of publishing angst.

Thanks again to Hunter Bennett and The Nevada Avenue Outdoor Free Bookshop for publishing my real-life essay about the time I saw Jaco play.

Tom Hubble, who spent a very long time talking with me about the particulars of Thistle sailboats. And apologies . . . I didn't know things were going to turn out as they did.

Anthony Madrid, who not knowing me at all, responded to an email I sent while in the throes of identifying what I even meant by invoking Arcadia and after reading his spectacular Paris Review essay, "Et in Arcadia Ego," —*in other words, Arcadia, which is not home, which is largely fantasy, which can never be adequate, which does not relieve us of our sorrow one little dot and even instead almost seems to make things worse*—

Prof. Roberto Sottile, Dipartimento di Scienze Umanistiche dell'Università di Palermo, who so graciously helped me with questions about the Sicilian dialect.

Celia Byrne, neighbor epidemiologist, thank you for sharing your thoughts and pointing me in the right direction.

Erik Kvalsvik, who rescued me from the existential freefall of the author photo. Like having Picasso paint your living room.

Mark Knopfler, who generously granted his permission to include his song lyrics mid-stream when I wasn't sure if I would sink or swim. And many thanks to Paul Crockford and Sherry Elbe for their help.

Jaco Pastorius, for opening the door.